Make an appoin...
Reyn Marten S...
Outrageous, flirtatious, a...
Mohawk, Reyn tracks twi...
knots, and never, ev... leaves loose ends.

Be sure to read
THE BRUSH-OFF
First in the Hair-Raising Mystery series by
LAURA BRADLEY

"Sassy hairstylist Reyn Sawyer makes a hilarious debut in this zany mystery. . . . The dialogue is snappy and the characters are likable. Fans of cozies, screwball comedies and Sarah Strohmeyer's Bubbles Yablonsky mystery series will savor this."

—*Publishers Weekly*

"With a clever plot, high style, and razor-sharp wit, Laura Bradley makes a grand [mystery] debut with *The Brush-Off*. This is one you'll definitely want to keep on your reading shelf . . . perm-anently."

—Maddy Hunter, Agatha Award–nominated author of *Pasta Imperfect*

"Charming, funny, and exciting. . . . Laura Bradley has a refreshing writing style that uses humor to diffuse some tension. As much as she tries to deny it, the heroine is very interested in the sexy detective, making *The Brush-Off* of interest to fans of romantic mysteries."

—AllReaders.com

Sprayed Stiff is also available as an eBook

Also by Laura Bradley

The Brush-Off

Published by Pocket Books

SPRAYED STIFF

LAURA BRADLEY

POCKET BOOKS
New York   London   Toronto   Sydney

An *Original* Publication of POCKET BOOKS

POCKET BOOKS, a division of Simon & Schuster, Inc.
1230 Avenue of the Americas, New York, NY 10020

ISBN: 0-7434-7112-1

First Pocket Books printing May 2005

10 9 8 7 6 5 4 3 2 1

Cover art by Ben Perini

Manufactured in the United States of America

For information regarding special discounts for bulk purchases,
please contact Simon & Schuster Special Sales at 1-800-456-6798
or business@simonandschuster.com

For

my incredible husband

and

my incomparable children

and

my indefatigable mother (a.k.a. taxi driver)

who keep home and family together
during my long (mental) absences
while Reyn and I play all day . . .

I love you

There is some soul of goodness in things evil,
Would men observingly distill it out.

—William Shakespeare

one

I GOT ON MY KNEES, held my breath, and extended my fingers.

It was sleek and firm, but it sprang slightly at my touch. I kept my eyes closed and continued my exploration.

Suddenly, the surface gave way. My fingers sank through, diving into a wet, gooey pit.

"Ugh," I groaned, and squeezed my eyes more tightly shut as I extracted my hand.

"Gnarly nuns and timid terriers, Reyn. What *are* you doing?"

I really didn't want to look at what was hanging off my fingers, and I really didn't need to open my eyes to see who was standing over me. Instead, I eased to my feet, trusted that my guest would stay out of the way, and did the blind-man's grope to the sink. I cranked the handle up and slid my hand under the stream of water.

"Ow, damn!" My eyes flew open and took in the kaleidoscope of neon that was my best friend, Trudy, as

I danced around the kitchen shaking my seared hand in the air. I'd forgotten that, just minutes before, I'd cranked the water as hot as it could go, which felt like somewhere around eighteen million degrees. That's what I got for being forgetful.

"I hate to repeat myself," Trudy said as she handed me a dish towel, "but I will anyway. What the hell are you doing, Reyn?"

"I'm cleaning out my refrigerator."

"Dun, dun-dun-dun," Trudy sang out a dirge. "Dun, dun-dun-dun."

"Very funny."

"From the looks of what was hanging off your fingers a second ago, it's not too funny. What *was* that, anyway?"

I peeked into the half-open hydrator. "Rotten eggplant. If I left it a little longer, maybe it could ooze out of there on its own." I looked a little more closely at the gray-green fuzz near the semblance of a stem.

"I'm not going to ask why you are cleaning your refrigerator. Obviously, it's needed to be cleaned almost since you bought it. However, I will ask, why are you cleaning it now?"

"It's one of my if-I-live-through-this resolutions to myself."

"Wouldn't those be made *after* you survived the refrigerator cleaning?"

I glared. "I made three resolutions to myself while that maniac was trying to erase me."

"That was a long time ago, Reyn. You're just now getting around to it?" Trudy pointed out with irritating accuracy. Why couldn't I have a best friend who thought I was brave and brilliant, who never pointed out my faults

and always praised my virtues? Because I'd never buy
that load of crap, that's why. Trudy was shaking her
head. "What about the other two resolutions?"

"Well," I began as I replaced the dish towel on its
peg, "one of them I can't do yet—or, hopefully, ever."

"Why not?" Trude cocked her hip and put a fist on it.
Her rayon minidress looked like something straight out
of *That '70s Show* (or, of course, the actual '70s) with its
psychedelic wiggly bull's-eye business and the clash of
electric green, traffic-cone orange, and spastic yellow.
Its hem hit three inches below the crotch of her Victo-
ria's Secret undies (I didn't have to look, she just didn't
own anything else). People would be thrown into peals
of laughter had I worn anything like this. The same people were paralyzed by awestruck ogling when Trudy
wore it. Her legs were that good. Even better now, after
a summer out in the sun. The thing is, summer in San
Antonio lasts until November, so she'd still be tan for
Christmas. Now, me, I never tan. I just get freckles.

"I can't do it because the resolution is that I will hide
all the knives and other sharp, potentially homicidal objects in my house the next time I go poking around in a
murdered friend's life."

Trudy rolled her eyes. "You're right. What are the
odds of that ever happening again? I mean, how many
people have friends who are murdered—and then, of
course, even if that did happen again, by some bizarre
twist of fate, you've learned your lesson on not messing
around with murder investigations because you nearly
got killed. Right?"

Uh-oh. I really wasn't sorry for what I'd done about
Ricardo Montoya's murder, even though my best friend

and the man who occupied my dreams at night thought I was sorry. But I wasn't letting on to them about my lack of remorse. "Right. Sure. I'll never conduct my own murder investigation again. No sirree. So the odds are way too low, even to consider resolution number two," I agreed, moving past the eggplant and on to the jars along the refrigerator door.

"And the third if-I-live-through-this resolution?" Trudy asked, not effectively distracted by the pungent odor of apricot jelly that had fermented nearly to wine. I closed the jar and pitched it into the garbage can I had dragged into the middle of the kitchen. Its twenty-gallon capacity was already half full.

"It's a little vague."

"Vague?"

"I was under a lot of stress at the time, remember? I was being pursued by a duct-tape–wielding killer with an affinity for sharp objects."

"You made this resolution before or after you were victim of the sharp object?"

"Before. But I already had been attacked by the duct tape. It tore the first six layers of skin off my face."

"Uh-huh, the excuse you used to keep Scythe at arm's length for a month." She let that hang in the air for a minute. I wasn't going to bite. Talking about the hunky police detective gave me a headache. And hot flashes. I was too young to be having those. He was a helluva good kisser, that's all I knew, even after months of pussy-footing around our sexual attraction and "the deal." Frankly, it was enough hassle to make a woman go gay. But Trudy didn't need to know even that much. Especially since this "deal" was really something she and

Scythe had come up with, and I was more than a little hazy on the details.

She raised her eyebrows, reached for a container of tofu, and checked the expiration date. "And the resolution?" she insisted.

I lowered my head and muttered, "To get organized."

Trudy's giggle always starts like the peep of a newborn chick and gets louder and louder, until it reminds me of a Ritalin-deprived three-year-old playing the violin. I saw tears in the corners of her eyes. It really pissed me off.

"What prompted you to make this particular resolution?"

"Besides imminent death?"

"Besides that."

"I couldn't find my extra set of truck keys for a getaway."

"Okay." Trudy rubbed her hands together. "So, you found them and got all your keys set up in an organized manner."

"Umm." I considered reapproaching the eggplant and toed the hydrator open further.

"You didn't find your extra set of truck keys, did you?" The self-righteous way she said it made me think the nuns at Trudy's grammar school had rubbed off on her a little too much.

"Not yet."

Ever optimistic, Trudy smiled, a little too brightly. "Instead, then, you tackled the job from a different direction. Taking on your closets, maybe."

"You think I should start there?"

"You haven't started at all?" Her shoulders slumped

in disappointment. The too-bright went out of her smile. Her neon was suddenly the only thing lighting up the room.

"I wanted to do the refrigerator first, considering it involved perishables." Bravely, I swiped up the oozing eggplant and slam-dunked it into the plastic pail.

"It involved perishables, *months and months later.*" Trude threw her hands into the air and sashayed to the kitchen door. Shaking her head in disgust, she let herself out and slammed the door. My Labrador retriever trio, mother and two daughters, looked at me in question. They'd been observing the scene quietly since Trude walked in. I think they were on their best behavior in hopes of me slipping them a molding slice of Brie or something worse. You know dogs. Remember where they like to sniff.

"I'm definitely looking for an ass-kissing friend," I told Beaujolais, Chardonnay, and Cabernet. "Starting tomorrow."

I returned to my grim work in the refrigerator, and, aside from taking the time to eat two pieces of turtle cheesecake before they went bad, I kept at it for a couple of hours, until I was interrupted by the ringing of the telephone. Since I'm so supremely organized, I ran around, knocking into things, listening for the direction of the ring. I found the phone between the cushions of the couch in the den (duh, the first place everyone looks!), and also found the truck keys, but not before the call went to the answering machine. I hated the sound of my own voice, so I hummed through my greeting, then listened to the reedy-voiced caller: "Reyn, this is Lexa . . . Alexandra Barrister. I am so sorry . . . so sorry to bother you so late, and at home, too. I promise, I tried the salon. No answer."

For the first time, I glanced at the clock. It was eleven-nineteen. But I'm a night person, so I was just coming alive, which is why I kept listening.

"If you could call me back . . . at any hour, really. I have an emergency. It involves Mother. I mean, Wilma."

I picked up before I could really register how rattled Lexa—one of the most eccentric clients to cross my threshold—must be to call her mother "Mother."

"Hello?"

"Reyn? Oh, Reyn! I was beginning to think I was going to have to manage it alone."

"What's *it*? What's the emergency?" *Managing* made me think of large sums of money or large objects that needed to be moved, like cows and big-ass great-aunts. With my luck, it involved the latter.

"It's Mother. Wilma. It's her hair." The silence stretched out for nearly a minute.

Wilma Barrister was one scary woman, and I didn't like the way this conversation was going. Somewhere between fifty and sixty, Wilma could be described as "handsome"—you know, one of those horse-faced, hard-eyed ladies who rose above the "plain" moniker by the grace of expensive cosmetics, designer clothing, and a commanding presence. Her thick silver hair was her best feature, its simple turned-under, chin-length style emulated by the high-society senior set. She was on this month's cover of *San Antonio Women,* along with an article detailing her extensive philanthropic work. My only personal encounter with the charity maven had been about three years ago, just after Lexa had become a client. Lexa asked me to cut her long, fine black hair with its split-end hippie style into a short, punky, spike look. With her fine bone structure and perfect alabaster complexion, it truly did suit her, and when I told her so, Lexa had responded that she didn't really care how it looked as long as it drove her mother crazy.

Well, it had. Wilma hated her precious daughter's punkified do, or, more likely, hated the fact that her daughter had gone directly against her orders to finally "grow up" and get a country-club cut. Wilma Barrister arrived at my salon loaded for bear—accusing me of "stealing" one of 'Om's clients (ha! I only wish I could steal the clients of that overpriced Dallas hairdresser of the rich and famous). When she saw that I considered her criticism a compliment, she changed her tack—up-braiding me for having "experimented" on "misguided Alexandra," who never would have chosen such a hideous hairstyle had it not been for me. She intended to turn me in to the ethics division of my professional association. When I pointed out that I was a hairstylist and not a psychiatrist, and that the National Association of Hairdressers didn't exactly have a powerful ethics division, she said she'd report me to the Better Business Bureau. I told her I thought Lexa would explain to the BBB that she'd been given the service she requested. Wilma told me we'd see about that. She did report me, the BBB did talk to Lexa, who did stand up for me, and that was that, except for the extra wrinkle I earned between my eyes from frowning for three straight days. It took me a year of visits from Lexa to realize how much she had enjoyed putting her mother through the

wringer. By then I liked the young woman too much to
be mad about the wrinkle.

"O-kay," I responded evenly as the silence on the
phone threatened to become permanent.

"Okay, meaning you'll come over to the house?" Lexa
asked, a little desperately.

"No. Okay, meaning I'm listening. If your mom is
having a bad hair day, why doesn't she call Om? I'm sure
he'd be happy to talk her through this. He's such a big
deal, I'm sure he has some sort of stylist outreach—in-
city hairdressers who have the authority to work on his
long-distance clients for emergencies."

Instead of answering, Lexa hummed Outcast's latest
hit. When Lexa hummed, it meant she was stressed-out
to the max. This usually happened when one of her outrageous stunts failed to irritate Wilma the Hun. Lexa
lived to bother Wilma. She'd moved back home after
graduating Dartmouth with a philosophy degree to
make that her full-time occupation. So, if Wilma was
having a bad hair day, why was Lexa scrambling for a so-
lution instead of celebrating?

Before I could ask this aloud, Lexa said flatly, "She
can't call 'Om."

"Why? He owes her, after all the publicity she's given
him in the media. Her hair is the most talked-about
style in South Texas, and she never fails to ensure his
name gets in print along with hers."

"Reyn, you don't understand. You are the only one I
trust to fix this." Now she was humming Smashing
Pumpkins. Hard to do. Worse to listen to. "Mother . . ."
That word again. ". . . Wilma has been sprayed . . . stiff."

Great. Sounded painful. For me, and for Wilma. But

the humming was getting to me. I was such a pushover.
I sighed. "What happened, Lex? She do some touch-up
and go overboard on the hairspray?"

"I don't know what happened. I just know you'll
know what to do about it. You are the most capable, reasonable person I know."

Yikes. That in itself was scary. I had seen the kind of
multipierced, personal hygiene–challenged people Lexa
tended to hang with, and I daresay she was right.

"What's going on at this hour, anyway? Your mother
have a late-night soiree planned—another one of her famous midnight buffets at the Argyle Club, maybe?
Some kind of moonlight campaign fund-raiser?" I was
dying to talk myself out of this. If I found out the house
known as Horror on the Hill was about to be inundated
by a bunch of soused Republicans in Versace, I was not
going. No way, nohow.

"Please, Reyn. It's nothing like that. It's for the photographers that are sure to come."

Maybe Wilma had been named Mother of the Year
in an after-dark vote of homemakers. Lexa wasn't giving
it up, whatever the big news was. I tried one last-ditch
effort to get out of what was sure to be torture. "Remember, your mother doesn't like me."

Silence stretched on again for a minute. Maybe Lexa
had covered the receiver and was telling Wilma exactly
whom she was recruiting. Goody, that would get me off
the hook. Suddenly, a big sniff snorted in my ear. Alarm
bells rang in my head. I'd seen Lexa vexed, depressed,
and exhilarated, but never had I seen her shed a tear. As
she cleared her throat, her voice sounded strangely high,
but certain. "Her opinion won't be an issue. I promise."

Holding the receiver to my ear, I wandered back over to the refrigerator and reviewed what remained to be cleaned out—some plastic bags filled with coagulating mystery fruits, Tupperware containers of multicolored leftovers. Wilma might not be so bad after all. Maybe the old bat mellowed after midnight. And, even if she didn't, at least I'd be making some money. I'd never made a house call before. How much extra could I charge? Hmm. Maybe that hairstyle simulation computer program I'd been coveting would be within reach after tonight.

"I'll be there in about ten minutes, Lexa, just tell your mom to sit tight."

Little did I know, Wilma was already doing just that.

two

THE BARRISTER ESTATE was in Terrell Hills, a two-square-mile incorporated city within the city limits of San Antonio, and five miles from Monte Vista, the historical area where I lived and worked. I'd gotten my two-story Spanish Colonial home for a song and recruited my brothers and sisters to help me renovate. Three years later, I still needed to finish those renovations—at least the part where I had my salon, Transformations: More Than Meets the Eye, was done—but I'd learned the hard way that in a hundred-year-old house, maintenance never ended, repairs were never finished, and the checkbook was always open. Owning a historic house was worse than having a drug habit. On this midweek midnight, quiet streets met me as I eased my three-quarter-ton pickup away from home along Hildebrand Avenue, crossing the highway and heading straight into Poshtown.

I slid across Broadway, which ran from downtown to the first urban loop that encircled the city, to heavily treed New Braunfels Avenue and wondered how so much of San Antonio's old money had ended up here in the 78209 zip code. The acreage estates, their pretentious homes hidden behind motorized wrought-iron gates and limestone walls, were so imposing one could easily imagine cattle baron heirs raising their perfectly well bred, private-schooled, towheaded children behind them, but many of the homes were ordinary, with only a rare picket fence to contain the ankle-biters. Though extremely well kept, with three-hundred-dollar brass planters in the front yards and gleaming new Yukons in the driveways, these homes were still cousins of ones that could be found across the railroad tracks in lower-middle-class neighborhoods—some retro-fifties asbestos-sided, some one-bedroom clapboards small enough to be considered cottages, albeit cottages that sold for a quarter million dollars and up.

I turned onto the Barristers' street and began looking for house numbers. The confining perfection of the neighborhood gave me more insight into the enigma that was my client. I could imagine how a rebel could feed off the suffocation of money and expectation here. I'd often wondered why Lexa hadn't taken her degree (what was one supposed to do with a philosophy degree anyway, except answer the tough questions in the crossword?) and gone to grad school instead of choosing to slip back under the thumb of her domineering mother. Of course, she often wiggled out from under that thumb. Had done so since she was a baby, to the point that it was more than a habit, it was a profession. She'd told me she hadn't gone to law school because her father had told her he expected her to either get a law degree or marry one. " 'Our name is Barrister, after all, Alexandra,' " she'd mimicked Percy's pompous tone for me. " 'It's predestined that you become part of the bar one way or another.' "

I knew that, financially, she did not have to live at home as many twentysomethings do as they make their starts in life. At twenty-one, she'd gotten a trust fund that would cover the expenses of a modest lifestyle. Wouldn't we all like the luxury of one of those? But Lexa didn't use it to buy freedom. Why? At some point, while contemplating the revolving door that is my receptionist desk, I'd offered Lexa the job of answering phones and setting up appointments. Her eyes had lit up with a combination of hope and fear, and in that fear I saw a little of my answer. Drifting down her street, I understood some of the rest. What happens when what you're pushing against stops pushing back? You fall. And the reverse would be true. Maybe Lexa was afraid she would leave her mother with an empty life if she ever stopped pushing back.

Or maybe she was afraid of falling herself.

I mostly blamed Wilma for fostering this codependence in a sensitive, free-spirited child who was clearly not suited for what she was trying to make her. But, by the same token, Lexa surely was old enough now to get over it. And to tell her mother so, in words instead of actions.

I knew she'd been tempted to break free that once by my offer, so I'd dropped a few more lures—passing along news of available jobs I heard about from clients—but Lexa never bit, so I gave up and just supported her small rebellions, like the time she wanted chunky lime highlights in her hair. Just thinking about dinner in the Barrister manse that night was enough to make me smile for a week. Now I was headed to the manse in question to do something that likely wouldn't make me smile unless, of course, I suddenly took leave of my senses and gave Wilma a buzz cut.

I flipped on my blinker and turned my seven-year-old truck into the driveway—or, rather, the six-foot stretch of cobblestones outside the wrought iron gate that led to the driveway. I pressed the button on the intercom and waited.

"Oh," I heard Lexa's soprano moan, "I wish you hadn't done that."

"Done what?"

"Rang the intercom. Did you use your finger?"

"Yes," I answered carefully, looking at the offending digit. "Was I supposed to use my nose?"

"No, no. I had planned to open the gate when I saw you turn in. I was watching for you from the downstairs drawing room, but, um, then, ah, I had to check on Mo—Wilma."

What was going on? Was she afraid the buzzer would disturb a party in progress? Why was she checking on Wilma the Hun? I stared beyond the closed gate. The three-story dark and rather imposing Tudor seemed quiet, with only a few lights on within the second story. I was getting weird vibes on top of an already queer twist in my gut. Of course, an impending close encounter with Wilma Barrister probably gave that combo to everyone who knew her. "How about opening it now?"

"Opening what?"

"The gate," I said, my patience wearing thin. I might

have snapped at her if her behavior hadn't been so out of character. Lexa was a lot of things, but spacey wasn't one of them. What was going on?

"Oh, the gate. I'll be at the back door; drive around the right side of the house."

The servants' entrance? I cranked the truck back into drive and eased forward as the gate slowly swung open.

"Wait, Reyn!"

I slammed on the brakes. "What?" I yelled back toward the little metal box.

"You didn't notice anyone following you?"

Following me? Why would someone want to follow me—to do an exposé on two-timing your hairdresser at midnight? Surely the media couldn't be that hard up. "No, Lex, I wasn't followed."

"Okay, come on, then."

Had the girl finally cracked? There was no doubt she had enough personal pressures to throw her over the edge into insanity. I slid my foot off the brake and glided down the cobblestone driveway toward the Barrister castle, looking at the dark, heavy stone and thick, blocky columns. Yuck. I could envision medieval warlords inside, splattered with the brains of their enemies as they gnawed on celebratory mutton legs. Evoking that kind of imagery would have made sense if this were really a seven-hundred-year-old structure in Scotland. But this was the middle of a South Texas neighborhood, and the house was probably built within the last fifty years to intimidate no one but the neighbors. Really sick. Lexa said she'd never lived anywhere else. What kind of people would choose to raise kids here? Gargoyles perched on corners of the gables; bloodthirsty-looking, six-foot-tall lions guarding the front steps. I knew I was going to have nightmares, and I was thirty-one. I tried not to imagine little five-year-old, artistic Lexa catching a ball in the yard and looking up into one of those pointy-toothed faces. I was amazed it had taken her this long to go loopy, having to sleep here night in and night out.

The house—castle, mausoleum, whatever you wanted to call it—certainly made a statement. To me, it screamed, "Run for your life!"

I'm going to learn to listen to my intuition one day. It just wasn't going to be this day.

"Psst!"

I'd gone around the back of the house as instructed and saw Lexa's slim, pale arm beckoning me from a doorway. I parked the truck next to Lexa's battered old orange Pinto and got out. I considered locking the doors, then scoffed at myself. Although the three-car garage about forty yards from the house could hide the Barristers' cars, no others were evident on the premises. No party was happening, that was for sure, not unless they'd been bused in.

"Psst! Reyn, hurry, please!"

"I'm coming," I assured her as I slammed the truck door shut and stepped around a fifteen-pound (five of them hair) gray and white cat who'd slid out the door and was now winding around my ankles in an overly friendly manner that made me instantly suspicious. I like cats, but I've got to say, they *are* a little sneaky. They are the only animals on earth with an ulterior motive.

"Guinevere," Lexa called. "Leave Reyn alone."

Guinevere? Now I knew her ulterior motive—she

wanted to find a new home where she would be named
Fluffy or Mouser or something much less fatuous. With
my new best friend between my legs, I walked to the
door like a cowboy after a ten-day cattle drive. Lexa
grabbed my forearm and drew me into a kitchen lit only
by a couple of night-lights. Guinevere came, too, and
I nearly tripped and fell over her as I made my way into
a chef's paradise. The kitchen had not one, not two, but
three islands—one with a built-in cutting board, one
with an eight-burner stove, and one that was plain countertop, albeit two-hundred-dollar-a-foot Texas pink
granite countertop—probably where Wilma let the
servants eat. Perfectly polished copper pots that had
never graced a burner hung from racks. Four ovens
banked the back wall. The gleam of a chrome Sub-Zero
refrigerator/freezer could be seen at the end of the cavernous room. This was a kitchen for the Four Seasons,
not the private home of a family of three, one of whom
was skinny enough to be on the verge of anorexia. I
reached up to the wall to flip a light switch, but Lexa
caught my hand. Okay. Maybe they were into energy con-
servation—in a ten-thousand-square-foot mansion. *Right*.

"Where is everybody?" I asked. This kind of space required reinforcements. No three people could keep this
much kitchen clean.

"The help?" Lexa asked. I held my hands out, palms
up, hoping she would volunteer the whereabouts of
everyone she could think of. I didn't want to catch Mr.
"Predestined for the Bar" Barrister in his skivvies in
the hall. Lexa's eyes shifted to the closed doors that
led, presumably, to the rest of the house. "The staff?"
She paused, distracted, then her eyes cleared. "Micah

does the yard; he leaves at dark. Cindy is our house manager . . ."

"House manager"? Was that the current politically correct term for "maid"?

Lexa must not have noticed my eye roll. ". . . she goes to her sister's for dinner every Wednesday night. Mr. and Mrs. Carricales, the butler and cook, live in. But it's their night off. They usually go watch their grandkids at flamenco class, get some enchiladas at Blanco Café, then play bingo down on West before heading home."

Suddenly she gasped and grabbed my forearm again, dragging me through the French doors, then through a dining room with an ornate mahogany table for at least two dozen (I lost count at twenty-five) to the stairway in the foyer. "We have to hurry, before they all descend. The vultures."

"They who? The Carricaleses?" I was confused. From her warm tone in talking about their evening with their grandchildren, I could've sworn she was fond of them.

"Oh, I guess I should worry about them, too," she mused, running a hand through her cropped hair.

Too? I stopped her on the fourth stair. "Where are your parents, Lexa?"

"Father is at some lawyer get-sloshed dinner-and-what-all. Moth—Wilma . . . is . . ."

I waited—rather patiently, I thought—as she tugged on my arm. Finally, I had to prompt her. "Wilma is . . . where?"

Lexa's eyes snapped back to reality. "In the study."

"To get her hair done? Why?"

Lexa looked at me like I was nuts for asking the question. "Reyn, go in there and you won't have to ask why."

That wonderfully useless sixth sense I have about danger warned me to no avail. My gray ostrich Tony Lamas lost their purchase on the oriental rug running up the stairs as Lexa, showing amazing strength for such a rail-thin little thing, pulled me forward with her.

Okay, maybe it was none of my business. Maybe Wilma was entertaining the other two members of a ménage à trois while hubby was away. Maybe she was hosting vampire bridge. Guinevere tiptoed up the stairs past us, ran down the hall, and vanished through a door that was cracked open. It emitted just enough light into the upstairs hall so we could see where we were going.

Just barely.

I wondered why Lexa liked knocking around in the dark. Maybe she couldn't bear to see all the ostentation surrounding her. Feeling a pang of empathy for her, I reached for the light switch at the top of the stairs. Lexa grabbed my hand away. "Please. I don't want anyone to know we're up here."

"I thought you said no one else was here."

"Who knows? After what's happened tonight—" She paused, darted a look left and right, then dropped her voice to a whisper. "What I mean is, someone else was here. With Wilma. Before I got home."

Okay. Maybe it was an affair, after all. Maybe Lexa thought she'd surprised her mother's *sancho,* and he was hiding in a closet. Wild sex had mussed Mum's hair and I had to fix it before Percy the Perfect arrived home. She was of the Donna Reed generation after all, like my mother, who couldn't do more than surface-comb her own hair between visits to the salon. Wild sex was one thing (my mother certainly had a corner on that one, but that's another story), wielding a curling iron was another. I had to see this. I took off down the hall toward the study with Lexa scrambling to catch up with me.

I pushed the door open and wondered immediately why Wilma would let the fuzzball of a cat up in the middle of her Yves Saint Laurent gown. It just seemed so out of character. Guinevere was hunkered down in Wilma's royal blue lap, getting her fur all over the taffeta, licking her mistress's heavily bejeweled fingers. My mouth opened to scream before my brain registered that the cat wasn't licking Wilma's fingers, she was *chewing* Wilma's fingers, and the cat hair wasn't the worst thing to happen to Wilma's gown that night.

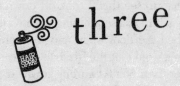 # three

"WILMA, REYN'S HERE. Your hair is just moments from being its perfect self again," Lexa cajoled.

I jumped and sent a Ming vase, along with the ceramic pedestal it sat on, crashing against the wall. Lexa, who'd eased up next to me, didn't flinch. Uh-oh. Bad sign.

Instead, she smiled beatifically at Wilma, whose luxurious silver hair was brushed straight out from her head and sprayed absolutely stiff. To complete the look, she was wearing full clown-face makeup. The cat was still chewing. Ick.

Lexa hadn't seemed to notice Guinevere. It might be a while, since she apparently hadn't noticed her mother was dead either. I took a tentative step forward and tried to shoo the cat away. She stared at me and licked her lips. I wished I had a barf bag, which made me think of Police Lieutenant Jackson Scythe, which made me realize I was in big trouble, and I hadn't even done anything yet.

Wait, I was within the Terrell Hills city limits. Yahoo. That meant we'd be calling its tiny police department, not the SAPD. Scythe would never know I'd been here. Boy, what a relief. I'd just have strangers to answer to, and that I could handle. No laser blue eyes and no half-hitched rusty blond eyebrow to contend with. I was home free.

Well, except for the body in front of me and the crackpot next to me.

"That's right, Wilma," Lexa called out. "No worries."

Understatement of the year. The only thing Wilma was worrying about right now was choosing which cloud to lounge on in heaven, or choosing which hot poker on which to perch in hell. I glanced over at her slightly un-hinged daughter. Wilma had to be blamed for loosening those nuts.

Even though the hole in her chest was pretty defini-tive and her eyes were open in an unblinking look of perpetual surprise, I thought it might be good form to check for a pulse. I swallowed bile and strode forward, put a finger to her cold wrist, then used the opportunity to backhand the cat onto the worn (read, "expensive an-tique") Tabriz rug. She growled at me, swished her tail, and sashayed off like it was *her* idea to find something better to do than gnaw on her dead mistress's fingertips. To be fair to the feline, perhaps she had been abused by Wilma, and this was her revenge. Like a rubbernecker with no self-control, I glanced at Wilma's fingers even though I knew I shouldn't. *Eee-uw.* The mortician would have to employ some creative hand positioning if the family wanted an open casket.

Wilma had been secured to the Duncan Phyfe

straight-back chair with clear packing tape before she'd been shot. The hole went through the tape and the taffeta before going through Wilma. Blood wasn't still flowing from the wound, so she'd been dead awhile. That was the extent of my postmortem expertise. I'd seen only one other dead person before and not this close. Besides, the police had already been there and that somehow made seeing that body easier. And I'd had the comfort of a barf bag. I glanced at Wilma's gnawed-on pinkie again and turned away. That sight made me want to hurl more than the bullet hole. Go figure.

I spun around to put some distance between me and the departed to see Lexa holding up a Fendi makeup case.

"What are you doing, Lex?" I asked after a pause during which I warned myself to be patient.

She zipped it open and pulled out a bottle of Erno Laszlo foundation. "I thought I could redo her makeup while you repair her hair."

I sucked in a cleansing breath. I blew it out. "Lexa, we need to call the police."

She shook her head and dove back into the makeup bag for a sponge. "Come on, Reyn, we have to fix her. For the cameras."

I put a hand on her arm and gentled my voice. "Lex, your mom is, uh . . ." I searched for a way to relate to her odd mental state. ". . . deceased."

Shaking off my hand, Lexa looked at me, raised her eyebrows, and widened her eyes. "I am aware of that, Reyn. That's why I called *you.*"

Oh, *good.* That was good, wasn't it? But it was also

disturbing—that she was cognizant enough to realize Mum had moved to another reality but not cognizant enough to know that she needed to notify the authorities first instead of her hairdresser.

Maybe I should focus on the friend angle. Sure, that's why she'd called me—to provide moral support for the call to the cops. She probably told me more things while sitting in my chair than she'd ever admitted to her bizarre band of buddies, an interchangeable group that had in common the ability to irritate Wilma. None of them hung around long. Hadn't Lexa said I was the only one she could trust to come tonight? Yes, that must be it. I could hold her hand. Maybe I'd even dial. Anything to get the cops there and me outta there. I looked around for a phone. "Okay, let's go ahead and call nine-one-one."

Lexa produced a round boar's-bristle brush from somewhere and smacked it into my hand, bristles first. *Ow.*

"Not until you fix her hair." Wilma's hair hadn't been the only thing fortified with steel. Lexa's voice was suddenly hard.

"Lex . . ." I paused, grabbing the brush handle with my left hand, extracting the bristles from my right palm. Skinny little Lexa had quite an arm on her. Who was to say that refusing to fix Mum's hair wouldn't shove her over the edge into complete insanity? What if she arm-wrestled me into doing the style? Hmm. The cops would put me behind bars for interfering with a murder investigation. Upon further contemplation, I decided I'd rather face a crazy Lexa than a pissed-off policeman.

"We can fix her hair after the police are finished with

their business. You want to find out who did this, right?
Wait, have you checked the house?" I found it suddenly
hard to swallow as I walked to the door and peeked
down the darkened hallway. I whispered, "The killer
could still be here."

Lexa didn't answer, so I turned around and saw her
standing behind the oversize mahogany desk, pointing
what looked suspiciously like a pistol in my general direction. "You will redo Mo—Wilma's hair, and *then* we
will call the police."

Uh-oh. What was that I was saying about facing a
crazy Lexa? It had been a figure of speech, that's all. I
eyeballed the gun, a two-shot derringer. Maybe we
wouldn't have to look for the killer after all. I wondered
if the thing was loaded. With one bullet left, perhaps?
The knot in my throat clotted my words together.
"Lexa"—I jangled the knot around with a clearing
sound—"what are you doing?"

She glanced down at the derringer and looked embarrassed. "I have to make sure Mother . . ." She paused
and shook her head in frustration. For a moment I
thought she would cry. "I mean Wilma. I have to make
sure Wilma is not seen in this condition by anyone. You
know how much appearance meant to her. It's the least
I can do for her now."

"Lexa . . ." My chest tightened, and I forced out the
rest of the words: "Did you and your mother have an argument? Was it an accident? Did she force you to protect yourself?" And then force you to make her look like
an extra on the set of *Star Trek: the Next Generation at
the Barnum and Bailey Circus*?

Lexa recoiled and blinked twice. Her face flushed

with anger, which I was actually glad to see. This was a normal emotion. "No. No! You think that I . . ." She waved the gun toward her mom, and I ducked for Wilma. I'm empathetic that way. "Don't be ridiculous, Reyn. I couldn't hurt Wilma."

And Lexa didn't think every time she pierced another hole in her nose that it didn't hurt the Queen of the Junior League? I didn't need to go there as I watched her blink rapidly at the tears forming in her eyes. Her shoulders slumped as she heard her own words and realized the hurt she and her mother had traded back and forth over the years.

Suddenly she collapsed into the deep burgundy leather chair behind her, and the gun clattered onto the desktop. She buried her face in her hands and began sobbing, her soprano ragged through her tears. "I know photographers arrive with the police. Their photos are displayed in the trial, sometimes leaked to the media. If she knew anyone would see her looking this hideous, Wilma would die a thousand deaths. . . ."

"But she already *has* died, Lexa. I don't imagine she'll care now." I eyeballed the gun, estimating the distance between it and my hand. Lexa was sounding more reasonable by the minute, but her eyes didn't look quite right.

"I know I didn't appreciate it, but she worked her whole life to become a famous social standard, a well-known philanthropist. Every charitable act she performed, every miracle she managed, every hairstyle that was emulated by the masses, will fade in comparison to this picture of a . . . farce. A laughingstock."

Lexa was right, of course. But, frankly, I'd rather

have laughter than the shivers of horror that any memory of Wilma as dictatorial philanthropist might elicit. I decided it was probably not a good time to bring up that factoid. I could see Lexa was about to break. Her whole body was shaking now. Tears made rivers down her cheeks.

"And if I allow that to happen to Mother, she will be unable to rest in peace." Sob.

Hmm, I hadn't thought of that. Although I still thought she'd be a more likely candidate for the stiff hot poker than the fluffy cloud option, I tried to humor Lexa. "I understand."

"And if she can't rest in peace, then she will undoubtedly haunt me. Day after day. I can just hear her: 'Why did you let this sully my memory forever, you stupid ingrate?'" Lexa let out a long, wracking sob. Ingrate? She called her own daughter a stupid ingrate? I looked back at Wilma, eyes wide in her full clown face, hair sprayed out like a wicked halo. To avoid being haunted by this image would be a powerful motivator, maybe more powerful than the sudden bout of guilt to which I was attributing Lexa's bizarre actions.

She had a point about the whole preserving-her-memory-so-as-not-to-be-haunted thing.

I had to get her back in action, back in control, or the cops would be carting her off to the funny farm before they got Wilma to the morgue. I was just considering my options when she snatched the derringer back up and pointed it at me again.

She looked up, her eyelashes glittering tears. Her finger stayed on the trigger. "Say you'll help me."

"Say you're not really going to shoot me if I don't." I

know it wasn't the smart thing to say, but my mouth operates on its own most of the time.

"Try me," Lexa threatened.

"You know, I was feeling so sorry for you that I was ready to agree to help you without the gun."

"Really?"

"But now, somehow, I don't feel so sorry for you anymore."

"So it's a good thing I have the gun, huh?"

Smart aleck. She was feeling better. "I'll help you. But only if you drop the gun." She relaxed her fingers and let go, and I hoped to holy hell she had the safety on. It skidded across the desk, and I dove for it, scooping it up and shoving it into my back pocket. I'd worry about where it came from and what to do with it later.

Had this been Lexa's intention all along, to recruit me as a red herring for investigators to throw them off her scent? Well, if she was going to be that sneaky, it wouldn't do much good to have pulled out a gun when she couldn't coerce me. No, I really didn't think she'd done anything other than be misguided. But, thanks to Wilma, she'd been that way her whole life.

"I'll wipe off her makeup," Lexa said as she jumped up on her thin legs and looked like she was pulling her psyche together.

I hated to rock it a little, but I had to. "Lex, we can't change her makeup. These makeup artists are very distinctive—the techniques they use are like signatures. That could be the only evidence that convicts the killer. Or, better yet, the techs may get lucky and find a fingerprint in there, or whatever was used could be so unique that it might lead right to the one who did this."

Blowing out a broken breath, Lexa considered it. She sniffed and nodded. "But the hair, you'll fix that?"

"Yes," I said in a determined, doomsday tone. "Go get me a rattail comb. But try not to mess up potential evidence by touching anything."

With a quick nod, Lexa ran out of the room. I was surprised to hear the door slam behind me, followed by the ominous sound of a lock tumbler falling. Her voice rang through the thick mahogany: "I'm going to lock you in there, Reyn, just to make sure you really mean to help. When you are finished with her hair, I'll let you out."

Well, swell.

"What about the comb?"

"Do without it."

I remembered the derringer. Aha! "What if I decide to shoot my way out?"

"Then I hope you brought a gun with you, because mine isn't loaded."

Double damn, did I ever feel stupid.

"How will you know I'm finished?" I stuck my tongue out at the door.

"We have security cameras."

"Good, then you can see when I flip you off," I said churlishly. Then a lightbulb went off. "Hey, the cameras will have filmed Wilma's murder!"

"No. I wish. They run in real time without a tape. Wilma installed them when Kermit and I were kids so she'd know what we were doing all the time. "

"That's sick," I told the clown-faced corpse in Yves Saint Laurent in front of me. "Talk about not letting your children learn independence."

"Get busy, so we can call the cops," Lexa advised helpfully through the door. I heard the floorboards creak as she walked down the hall.

Emitting a huge sigh, I looked around for an easy escape—but the study had no desktop computer, no telephone. I saw a flash of white and my heart jumped into my throat. I yipped. In answer, a feline face peered around the corner of the massive desk.

Guinevere.

This just kept getting better and better. Locked in a room with a clownish corpse and a creepy cat. At least I had somebody to talk to. Besides a body.

"Hey, Guiny, what's wrong with your dumb master anyway? Hasn't he heard of e-mail?" With my bad luck, Lexa's father was probably one of those old-fashioned guys who let their "secretaries" do all their high-tech work. Humph. Just because I thought my luck might be changing, I tried the doorknob. It was indeed locked.

Guinevere wound her way around my ankles. I looked down to find she was licking her little kitty lips. Oops, time to get moving before she thought I was dead, too.

I inched forward, just close enough to touch Wilma with the brush, my arm fully extended. The stand-up hair didn't budge. What the heck had been put on it to make it so stiff? Could it be that new gel the kids were using to spike their hair? I hadn't tried any, since most of my customers were the over-thirty crowd, but it sure looked like it made concrete out of hair strands. Still, it would be more like dried goop than whatever was in Wilma's hair. Her gray bob looked like it had been shellacked. With a blowtorch. I took another step

forward and sniffed. I recognized it in an instant—
Main Mane by Hair's Breadth. It had a distinctive
horehound scent that couldn't be missed. This was the
triple-super-extra-hold variety, no doubt. I was impressed. And to think the beauty supply distributor
had told me when he visited my shop just last week
that Main Mane worked better than any hairspray on
the market, and I hadn't believed him. Maybe he'd
killed Wilma and sprayed her hair just to prove his
point. Silly, I know, but I had to admit the state her
hair was currently in would make a great advertise-
ment if it weren't so morbid. Something wet and rough
tickled my elbow.

"Ack!" Guinevere had jumped back into Wilma's lap
and was tasting me. I ran to the window.

What was I going to do? I knew that messing with
her hair was going to get me in a mess of trouble. But
each second I hesitated was one second further from
the murder, one second longer for the killer to get away.
I wondered which would be a bigger sin in the crime-
fighter's bible. Not that it really mattered beyond my
ability to rationalize my screwup, because as I glanced
out the window down to the lawn, I realized the second
story in a mansion is more like the sixth floor of a high-
rise and way too far to jump.

It was a good thing the window wasn't open, because
when an orchestra blasted out a dramatic phrase at
about ten thousand decibels I jumped straight into the
glass. I would have a goose egg above my right eyebrow.
Good, maybe I could claim a concussion made me do it.

"What's that?" I shouted. Had Guinevere become
musical? Nope, she'd leaped off Wilma and was stalking

toward me with her tail swishing in that pissed-off way cats have.

"This is Beethoven's Fifth Symphony, first move-ment," came Lexa's disembodied voice from a speaker in the ceiling camouflaged within a flying bust of Ben-jamin Franklin.

"Turn it off! Guinevere doesn't like it." I shooed at the cat, hoping to change her course. She was not initimidated, and kept padding toward me.

My answer from Lexa was a rise in the decibel level. Goody.

"Lexa!"

No answer. Of course. Furious, I scanned the room for the control of the intercom. Knowing what a control freak Wilma was, I figured it was probably in the room with the security camera screens. Would her husband, Percy, have stood for this, though? Music not of his own choosing in his private domain? Sitting down in Percy's leather throne, I searched the desk, remembering at the last minute to grab a piece of paper to shield any finger-prints. His middle desk drawer was depressingly tidy— pens organized by color, then size. The rest of the draw-ers held file after file of dry legal documents. A cat paw appeared on top of the left row of files, and Guinevere slithered up on top. I scooted to the right and paused at a metal drawer divider, struck with an idea. Prying it loose, I marched over to the door and tried to wedge the divider between the door and the jamb, not caring if Lexa saw me. After all, I had the unloaded gun.

The divider was too thick. I let it drop to the carpet. It missed Guinevere by inches. Too bad. She meowed at me in warning.

I looked at the cabinet that flanked the window. It was a unique design, with open segments for books interrupted by small cabinet doors every foot or so. Maybe the intercom was hidden behind one of the doors. Maybe he stored a laptop I could plug into a handy-dandy modem and use to summon the authorities. I reached for a pencil and, carefully holding it between my index finger and thumb around the metal band, popped open the first cabinet door. It held a collection of porno tapes along the lines of *Debbie Does Dallas*. I sighed. Did all men have to be so predictable? I was moving to the next cabinet when my subconscious warned me I hadn't had a Guinevere encounter in the expected amount of time. Where was she?

I spun and found her on Wilma again, having a snack. "Shoo!" I waved my arms. She flicked me a look, and promptly ignored all my flapping. I stamped my foot toward her. She chewed harder. I grabbed one of the videotapes and flung it at her. It smacked the cat on the shoulder, sending her back under the desk with an angry growl. I would certainly pay for that later, but now it was way past time for me to get lucky. I popped open the next cabinet door. Jackpot! There was a collection of cameras. Most were so sophisticated that it would take a point-and-shoot woman like me years to learn to use them, but one camera was a simple 35mm auto-focus. Thank goodness. I felt my shoulders relax a degree and tried to act like I was still looking for the intercom. If I could take pictures of Wilma's hair and face now, I wouldn't feel so bad about messing around with the crime scene.

But what about Big Sister watching me? Hmm. I

spun my body toward the window and cocked my head like I was listening to something. I ran to the window, looked out, and let my hand fly to my mouth in mock shock. "Lexa, I think someone is at the front gate."

This was a gamble, I knew. The security camera surveillance area was a mystery to me. It could have a full-blown view of the front gate for all I knew. But I was betting it didn't.

I swallowed hard for the camera and looked out with bug eyes. "Oh, no! I hope it's not the police!"

I paused a beat, imagining her jumping up and rushing out of the room. Then I stuck the brush handle in the waistband of my jeans and got to work. I slid the Canon Sure Shot off the shelf, aimed, and clicked off about three photos of Wilma from different angles. Then I put it back and used the pencil to close the cabinet door. All in about twenty seconds or less. I'd tell the police about it on the sly. Lexa could hate me later when the photos came out at the trial. My whole goal now was to keep her semisane until the cops got there.

Rushing back to my post at the window, I held my breath as the music continued uninterrupted. Lexa hadn't blasted in and confiscated the camera. I guessed I was in the clear.

"They drove off. I guess someone with the wrong house," I mused for her benefit. I shook my head and returned to Wilma, toying with her hair. "Lexa, I have an important question," I addressed the intercom. "Does Wilma normally use Main Mane triple-super-extra-hold hairspray?"

"Heavens, no." Lexa's out-of-breath tone told me she hadn't caught my subterfuge. She'd been running to a window to check for the cops. "She's never purchased anything but 'Om's personal label. Now, get to work."

So the killer packed a can of designer hairspray along with a gun. He/she wasn't cheap. A sixteen-ounce can of the stuff cost around thirty dollars, which was why I chose not to stock it at Transformations. I was so practical and so honest that I'd have a hard time selling a can of Main Mane when customers could get the same results at a tenth of the price. Of course, now that I'd seen the results were better than promised, I'd have to say I was wrong about that one.

This was not the first time I'd be wrong over the next few days.

 four

THERE ARE ADVANTAGES to having a dead customer. Especially when that customer is Wilma Barrister. I remembered our last encounter and how she'd hammered on me mercilessly and then, when she couldn't find anything more about me to pick on, began criticizing her daughter for everything she could think of. I could see how she'd become such a successful fund-raiser: People gave her money just to get her to leave them the hell alone.

As I flicked at the tips of her stiff hair with the boar's bristles, I had to admit she was still going to be a pain in the ass, but a silent one this time.

Who would've had the balls to silence Wilma with such dramatic flair? Perfect Percy, fed up with her control over his music? Or had Lexa killed her to escape her emotional prison? While I couldn't blame Lexa if she really did off her Mommy Dearest, I didn't think she had. The police would, though. Lexa would be their number-two suspect right behind her father, leaving

Lexa's brother at number three for geographical reasons
(he lived in Houston). Cops loved to write bloodshed off
as a domestic squabble. It was so much easier for everyone but the family. And while the statistics were on their
side, sometimes they didn't even try to see through the
numbers. A small police force like Terrell Hills' likely
didn't see a murder but every decade. It didn't bode
well for Lexa.

I took a deep breath and leaned in closer to the
body. I hadn't noticed the tape around her neck before
because the high neck of her gown had been artfully
arranged to cover it. This sicko had gone to a lot of
trouble to present Wilma just so. It was the ultimate in
premeditation. Someone had hated Wilma with a purple passion. The tape held what looked to me like a
curtain rod running up her spine and the back of her
head, which the sprayed-stiff hair had been arranged to
cover as well. This was good news for me, because it
was going to keep her head from lolling from side to
side as I muscled the strands into a semblance of order.

I looked Wilma in the eye. "It's now or never." I
swiped at her hair with the brush and nearly pulled my
arm out of the socket. The brush stuck. I wrapped my
other hand around my wrist. The brush didn't budge. I
released the handle. The bristles held as if glued there.
I reversed my grip and pulled harder. The first move-
ment of the symphony moved into a crescendo. I felt
something give. *Squ-wench.* Her head wiggled. *Squ-
unch.* Either I was pulling Wilma's head off her shoulders or the tape was giving way. Uh-oh. Either way, I
was screwed. Damn. I stopped pulling and studied the
situation. Hair covered the brush completely around its

circumference. It was hopelessly tangled in a dead woman's hair with my fingerprints all over it, sticking out of her head like an absurd flag. I wanted to sink to the six-figure carpet and cry. Instead, I closed my eyes to think, rubbing my temples and humming with the bizarre Beethoven chaperone.

The first movement repeated.

I think the music was making fun of me.

Air ruffled the tips of my hair.

Wilma? Had she come back to life?

I cracked open one eye. Not Wilma.

Guinevere was perched on Wilma's shoulder, batting at the brush.

Great, at least she was trying to help.

Deciding the brush was out of commission—unless Guiny managed a miracle—I returned to the desk for emergency supplies. I was determined to pick the lock on the door. The pens would be too thick. I straightened out a pair of paper clips. Hey, didn't people in the movies use these to pick locks? I rushed over to the door and slid one of the clips into the lock. I wiggled and listened. I didn't know what I was listening for, but maybe I had some untapped lock-picking instinct that would tell me when I heard it.

"Give it up, Reyn, and get to work," Big Sister commanded from the Franklin head. "The tumblers are pickproof. Father made sure of that. He deals in all sorts of high-profile cases he can't have anyone knowing about."

Hmm, was that right? Should've paid more attention when I perused his files. Perhaps I could've blackmailed someone for an early retirement.

Sighing heavily, I returned to my customer, armed with the clip-picks. It seemed to take forever, easing one strand of hair at a time out of its chemical jail and knocking Guinevere off Wilma's lap, only to have her leap back up a few minutes later. A couple of times my head started to swim from the hairspray fumes. Finally, I had the do tamed down to what looked like a manically teased beehive. It wasn't Wilma's normal perfect bob, but, hey, I wasn't a magician.

I'd left the brush for last. The cat and I hadn't had much luck unsticking it, but at least now it was hidden behind her head, its handle resting against her back. Just as I began to wedge the paper clips between the bristles and the hair, Guinevere ran and hid. I heard the door open behind me. I stopped my head from bobbing to the dramatic swell of the wood instruments, surprised that my captor would release me before the job was done.

"Good timing. I'm just about finished, Lexa."

I heard a big sigh. "You're finished, all right."

I recognized that dry voice, and it wasn't Lexa's. It belonged to San Antonio Police Lieutenant Jackson Scythe, homicide detective. Maybe I'd gotten so high off the Main Mane fumes and the repeating Symphony no. 5 that I was hallucinating. Maybe I'd been dreaming about him so much that all men's voices were starting to sound like his. Maybe it was just Mr. Barrister behind me, and I could easily explain away my hands all over his dead wife's hair.

But when I turned my head and dropped my hands to my sides, I saw I was right the first time. Boy, sometimes I hate it when I'm right.

"What are *you* doing here?" I demanded. It's best to stay on the offensive around this guy.

Issuing another of his famous long-suffering sighs, Scythe shook his rusty blond head as the door opened wider and three other cops filtered in around him, the two younger dudes wearing Terrell Hills Police Department uniforms. The older guy I pegged as the tiny hamlet's police chief. Scythe was wearing a slightly wrinkled long-sleeved button-down denim shirt and what looked like yesterday's Wranglers. He appeared to have been summoned straight out of bed. That made me wonder whom he'd been in bed with and what they'd been doing—

"Cut the tunes," he hollered, and magically the music stopped.

Now, why the hell hadn't I thought of that?

Scythe strode toward me. "I can't believe you. You have the gall to demand what *I'm* doing here when you're alone in a room with a dead woman who looks like she's going to a Shriners' circus prom."

"Well . . ." I jammed my hands on my hips. "Are you going to answer my question?"

I noticed in my peripheral vision that the cops were watching us instead of looking around for clues. But, in all fairness, I imagine this was the most entertainment the 2.4-square-mile town had had in years. The murder, that is, not me and Scythe.

Scythe's laser blues burned a hole through my admittedly less powerful gaze. But I'm more stubborn than he is, so I held the searing look. He hitched that damned left eyebrow. "No," he said finally. "Why I'm here is none of your business. You just ought to be thanking your lucky stars that I *am* here."

Oh, sure. I'm thrilled to death. I glanced at my erstwhile customer. *Oops—sorry, Wilma.*

The police chief, cleared his throat. "Lieutenant Scythe is on loan to us from the SAPD. We are very fortunate to have him for a month to help refine our investigative techniques."

Scythe cut a look at the chief, then turned to the rest of us and smiled with no humor. "And isn't it nice of Miss Sawyer to have provided us with something to investigate?"

"Hey, I didn't have anything to do with this."

"Right," Scythe answered in that hard tone that brooked no argument. "Which is why we found you dancing to a concerto—"

"It's a Beethoven symphony. Number five, actually," I corrected pompously. I wouldn't have known it either if Lexa hadn't told me, but I had to try to hold the higher ground.

"—bent over a woman with a hole in her chest, and with a gun tucked in your waistband."

My hand went automatically to my waistband. The uniforms' hands flew to their gun butts. Scythe shook his head, so instead I dropped my hands to my sides, twisted my torso, and nodded to the offending item. "This isn't my gun."

"That's smart," the youngest of the group chirped in a weedy tenor. His nameplate said HARLAND. "You should never kill someone with your own gun. Too obvious, too easy to trace."

Uh-oh. I think Harland had been watching too much cop TV.

"It's not loaded. You can check," I offered.

"O' course it's not loaded. One bullet's all it takes and it's in the vic," the other uniform put in bullishly.

Scythe's eyes looked like they were about to roll to the ceiling before he stopped them by shutting his eyelids for a beat. Maybe this assignment was trying his patience. Probably a lot more so now, considering I was involved.

That thought cheered me up a bit, until I saw him fiddling with his handcuffs. Double uh-oh. Now, I'd had some dreams involving Scythe and handcuffs, but I didn't think that's what he had in mind just then.

"Look, let me tell you what happened. Lexa—" I nodded toward Wilma. "—that's the dead woman's daughter, she's a client and a friend of mine. She called me to come help fix her mom's hair. I didn't know Wilma was dead. When I got here and saw what had happened, I tried to convince her to call the police, but then she pulled out this gun and threatened me if I didn't fix Wilma's hair. I got her to drop the gun and talked her out of trying to change the makeup. She was really bent on doing that, but I thought it would make you guys' job harder."

"Gee, thanks," the king of the dry wit muttered.

"Well, then Lexa grabbed the gun again. Then I talked her into giving it to me. Then she locked me in here and told me I couldn't leave until I styled her mother's hair." I paused, seeing the wheels turning in Scythe's head and knowing this wasn't making Lexa sound very good, so I added, "I know she didn't mean to threaten me, not really. She was just desperate."

"Committing murder does that to a person," Scythe pointed out.

"No, she didn't do it," I put in sharply. "You see, she feels guilty about being such a thorn in her mother's side for all those years. . . ."

I looked at a phalanx of blank male faces, none of them getting the whole female emotional blackmail deal. Not even kind of. "Once I combed out Wilma's hair, Lexa was going to call nine-one-one." I paused, suddenly struck by a terrible thought. Who'd called the police, anyway? Had Lexa tried to set me up? Locking me in the room with the corpse with the blaring Beethoven so I wouldn't hear the sirens when the law arrived? Boy, was I a sucker.

"Well, unless she drove down to the Pack 'n Pay down on Broadway to place an anonymous call from a pay phone, she wasn't the one who blew the whistle."

Was Lexa working in tandem? Or maybe the killer had called? But why wait so long to do it, and from not all that far away? None of this was making any sense. Looking at the cops, I saw it made even less sense to them. That was bad news for me, since I was standing in front of them. I probably made a lot more sense as the killer than anybody else did.

"Are you going to relinquish your weapon or are we going to have to draw on you?" Scythe asked.

The two uniformed officers tensed, put their hands on their gun butts again, and looked way too excited by that prospect.

"Down, boys," I said, raising my arms slowly into the air. Scythe laser-beamed me. I glared at him. "Come and get the damned thing. I didn't want it to begin with, I just didn't want any more killing going on around here. How was I to know it wasn't loaded? Of course, it might be; I never checked what Lexa told me after she locked me in."

Scythe ambled forward and slid the gun out of my waistband, a bit more slowly than necessary, with a little more contact with the small of my back than necessary. I stifled a shiver. Behind me, he smiled. Don't ask me how I know that; call it women's intuition. Plus, I had a clue.

"What's so funny, Lieutenant Scythe?" Harland asked.

"You are, Harland," the chief snapped before turning to address me. "Miss Barrister is being held so we can interview her once we secure the scene."

"Yeah," snarled the surly muscle-bound guy about my age with MANNING on his name tag. Dirty Harry lived. He leaned toward me and I nearly fainted from his rancid breath. "So don't plan on trying to get your stories straight ahead of time. We're going to keep you separated. We're going to get the truth, or else."

"With fingernail torture no doubt," I muttered as I dropped my hands to my sides. Or they could simply hold me down and make Manning breathe on me and I'd give.

"Watch your mouth." Scythe's breath ruffled the hair at the shell of my ear. "Or I'll get duct tape to go with these." Cold steel clicked around my left wrist. He pulled it down, behind my back.

"Where did you get this rash on your palm?"

The boar's bristles had left an angry red mark. "What happened was—I was—"

"Stop," he said from behind me. "I changed my mind. I'm sure this is something I don't want to know. It probably involves something illegal."

"Do you always think the worst of me?"

"It helps me keep my perspective for when things with you get even worse later, which they inevitably do."

"Very funny."

He dragged me toward the wall to a torturous-looking Louis XIII chair identical to the one Wilma was in, put a hand on my shoulder to ease me into the seat, and drew my right hand behind the back. A cold steel click around my other wrist told me my guard was an antique. The fan-back shape of the chair ensured I couldn't get loose unless my arms suddenly achieved the flexibility of Gumby.

"Damn," I muttered as I struggled halfheartedly. "I should've spent more time practicing those contortionist moves."

Scythe leaned into me to check the fit of the left handcuff. "Been practicing, have you?" he said under his breath. "Maybe it's time for me to collect on our deal?"

Blood flooded my face as my mind's eye flooded with one too many visual images. I took a deep breath and smelled that sharp mesquite scent of Scythe's. I squirmed. Oops. That didn't help.

After a few seconds, the smoke in his dry-ice eyes blew out. "But I guess we'll have to wait until *after* you get out of jail."

Was he serious or just trying to scare me? Damn him. I watched him walk away, unable to risk a peek at the way his Wranglers snugged across his fine heinie with each stride. He sure knew how to play me to keep me off balance. I fumed. It was a helluva a lot safer to be mad at him. I reminded myself to stay that way.

❊   ❊   ❊

The evidence techs arrived. On orders from Scythe, Friendly Officer Manning nearly turned me on my head to drag me and my chair out into the second-floor landing between the study and the stairs. The handcuffs were chafing my wrists, but I'd be damned if I'd give him the satisfaction of knowing that. I could hear Lexa sobbing somewhere downstairs, and even though I was facing the possibility that she'd set me up, I felt my heart tug for her grief.

I wondered whether Manning knew he had halitosis. Probably. His type would do it on purpose just to prove he didn't give a hoot about being considerate of the rest of society. I held my breath as he double-checked that I wasn't going to make a break for it once he left. After sucking in some snot, he blew out a cough. I considered filing a complaint for harassment based on his raunchy breath. It reminded me of the rotten Brie in my half-clean refrigerator.

"Whoa, would you look at this," one of the techs called from inside the study.

Manning dropped his interest in me and rushed through the half-open door. Over the railing I could see Harland, who'd presumably been sweeping the downstairs in a clue-finding mission, glance at the open door, obviously tempted. He resisted. But when another of the techs hollered, "Sweet Jesus!" Harland couldn't help himself and hauled ass upstairs, past me, and into the study. There was a cacophonic conversation coming from the room, and I was so curious to know what they'd found that I bounced myself off the floor to inch closer to the door.

I was about to bounce myself all the way down the hall when the Carricaleses walked into the foyer from the kitchen, heads together, whispering and glancing around nervously. You'd think that the cops would've stationed someone outside the door to intercept anyone coming in, but this was Terrell Hills, more than likely understaffed to handle the murder investigation of one of the county's major citizens. Maria Carricales looked up and saw me. I'd met Maria once, when she'd driven Lexa to her hair appointment when Lex's Pinto was in the shop. She grabbed the arm of the man I assumed was her husband and they raced up the stairs.

"Miss Sawyer! What are you doing here?" She pulled at my arm and the whole chair rocked. She exclaimed to her husband over the handcuffs, "José, look what has been done to this *pobrecita!*" Then, she tipped my chin up with her index finger. "Who did this to you?"

"The police. They're holding me for questioning."

"*La policía?* What are they doing here?"

"Didn't you see their cars out front?"

She and her husband shared a look, shaking their heads. "No," José said. "We have to park in the alleyway behind the house and come in the back gate. Señora requires that. We don't ever see the front of the house."

"Why were you so nervous, then?" Had I imagined it?

They shared another look; then Maria spoke. "The gate was unlocked and standing wide open. We are certain we shut and locked it when we left for dinner and the movies earlier. I know we did. But we know we will be blamed if Señora finds out."

Her husband nodded. "We hoped to see Lexa first, to know if we need to be careful around Señora, if she knows."

"Don't worry about the Señora," I said. "She's dead."

They both gasped. Maria crossed herself. José swore under his breath. "A heart attack?" he finally asked.

"Yeah, brought on by a bullet to the chest."

Eyes to the ceiling, they said some Hail Marys and crossed themselves in unison. Then they shared another one of those looks. It made me wonder how much they could communicate without talking and if all couples who'd been married for decades managed this unspoken language. "You didn't do it?" José asked.

"Of course not," I snorted.

They nodded to each other like that was a given. *"Dios mío,* she must have found out about her. Then he got angry and shot her."

Who's "her" and who's "him"?

"Or maybe she found out about her running around with him again, even though she told her not to, and she shot her because she got angry?"

Is this the same "her" and the same "him"? I knew the shot "her" was Wilma. But the other "hers" and "hims" were different this time, I thought. I opened my mouth, but Maria spoke again before I could get the words out.

"I bet it was *them.*" Maria crossed herself again and whispered something in Spanish.

José nodded. "They came for him and shot her instead."

"Who's *them?*" I blurted out.

They looked at me and then at each other. And, you

know, they would have told me, I just know it, except Jackson Scythe, the man with the worst timing in the world, poked his head out the door. The man must have radar for messing up my life.

"Don't even think about answering her," he said to the Carricaleses. "She's under arrest."

five

"UNDER ARREST?" Maria, José, and I all exclaimed simultaneously.

José patted my arm. Maria took a step away from me, hand over her heart. "Did *she* kill Señora?"

"That is still under investigation, ma'am," Manning blurted out officiously, coming out of the study from behind Scythe.

"This little girl couldn't have managed anything like that." José smiled at me apologetically as Manning ushered them down the hall.

"I don't know." Scythe raised both eyebrows. "Reyn is extremely capable."

Wouldn't you know, the first compliment I ever get out loud from him, and it makes me look like a murderess. I glared at him, which, come to think of it, probably made me look *more* like a murderess. Oh, well, I was already in handcuffs. How much worse could this get?

I was about to find out.

Manning, rubbing his shaved pate, probably to build

his tough-guy mojo, took the Carricaleses into a room four doors down. Scythe leaned into me. I could tell he was mad, but I wasn't sure at whom. "You've left me no choice, Reyn. If you'd stuck your nose in a murder in San Antonio city limits, I could've pulled some strings and gotten you some leeway, but I am the example here. If I'm going to teach them how to do things right, you're going to have to go to jail."

I opened my mouth and the squeal-squeak that came out was akin to what a mouse sounds like when it's stepped on. "Jail?"

"I have to book you on nothing less than interfering with a murder investigation, or maybe even accessory to murder, depending on what you tell us in the interview."

"What do you mean, what I tell you? I have nothing to hide. I plan on being honest."

"Plan on being smart. Street-smart, for once." He paused, and his eyes softened as he patted the top of my head. "Not book-smart." Wow, another compliment. "Or hairstyle-smart," he added with a visual review of my hair. So much for compliments.

He turned away, heading down the stairs. As he reached the bottom step, Percy Barrister, in a thousand-dollar British pin-striped suit that was a size too small, walked in the front door. His unibrow inchwormed over his forehead. He was less attractive than I remembered from the one time I'd seen him, along the lines of an overgrown troll, with wiry red-gray hair that stuck out at odd angles from his melon-shaped head. "It's the middle of the night. What the hell is going on?"

He slammed the door, and the ensuing whoosh of air sent the overpowering scent of garlic toward me. I wrinkled my nose and saw the intrepid police detective take a step back.

Scythe, being brave, held out his hand. "I'm Lieutenant Jackson Scythe, SAPD."

The older man ignored his offer to shake hands, elbowing past him to the stairs. "What are you doing in my home, pray tell?"

"Just a moment, Mr. Barrister." Scythe put a quelling hand on his arm. Percy looked at it like it carried the plague. "There's been a murder."

"My daughter?!" Percy dropped his briefcase.

"Do you have any reason to think someone might want to murder your daughter?"

I thought it was cruel of Scythe to let Percy think Lexa had bit the big one, but then I realized he was trying to extract as much information as he could while the man was mentally off balance. I saw now why empathy probably wasn't taught at the police academy. It didn't win any points in a murder investigation.

"It's that boy. I just knew he was a bad influence and—" Oops. Percy caught himself. His mouth snapped shut. He was an attorney, after all.

Scythe knew he was too late, but asked anyway, "What boy is that, Mr. Barrister? Would that be your son?"

"Of course not. Kermit lives in Houston. He's a respected businessman, and I have nothing more to say until my representation arrives." Wow, he'd gone from grief-stricken to self-preserving in five-point-four seconds.

"That's too bad because we're losing precious time in finding who did this to your wife."

I had to hand it to Scythe, he was pretty darn wily. Slipping the real victim in at the end threw Percy off balance again. For a few seconds his face registered shock, then relief. Relief that his daughter wasn't dead, or relief that Wilma the Hun wouldn't be ruling his kingdom anymore?

I thought I saw guilt flash across his face before it went carefully blank. Then he reached down to retrieve his briefcase. "Where is she?"

"With the crime scene techs. Once they are finished, the medical examiner has cleared her, and you've been interviewed, then perhaps you can see her."

"Oh, I don't want to see her."

Scythe cocked his head in question and Percy added hurriedly, "At least not until she's, uh, 'cleaned' up. I have a weak stomach."

"I see," Schythe answered cagily.

"Where is my daughter?"

"Your daughter is being interviewed right now. She found your wife."

"Oh, dear Alexandra," Percy sighed, and I saw honest regret in the hang of his head. "I must go to her. She's . . . environmentally impressionistic."

Huh? Was this a new kind of art? Or some new tag conjured by a therapist?

Scythe didn't miss a beat. "She's an adult and holding up fine. You know you can't see her until you are interviewed. If you want to speed that up some, I'll sit down with you right now."

Percy met Scythe's challenging stare. "I'll wait for my representation. May I place the call now?"

Scythe nodded once and watched Percy pull his cell

phone out of his briefcase and dial. It was the briefest of
conversations, with the lawyer on the other end asking
little besides Percy's location. I guess when you repre-
sent criminals for a living, you get used to 2 AM cryptic
phone calls.

Percy looked up and saw me for the first time. He
rang off and turned to Scythe. "You didn't tell me you'd
caught the perpetrator."

"Who said we have?"

"Who is that?"

"A material witness." Gee, thanks. Vote of confidence
from Scythe.

"Why is she handcuffed, then?"

"To keep her out of trouble," Scythe answered. The
way he did a double take up at me made me think he
was considering keeping me in handcuffs twenty-
four/seven.

"Forget it," I shouted down.

Scythe's eyebrows rose in surprise that I'd read his
mind.

The police chief I had yet to meet formally exited the
study, silently took in the arrival of the husband, and
paused beside me. "Are you doing okay?"

I liked this guy. In his early fifties, he had a tan face
that was lined like he smiled a lot, and his gray eyes
were bright but kind. Not razor-sharp like Scythe's. The
way he hard-parted his medium-brown hair two inches
off to the right reminded me of my dad. A straight
arrow. I nodded. He stuck out his hand. "Ralph Ferguson. I'm the chief of police here in this little town."

Well, he was modest, even if most Terrell Hills residents weren't. On a cop's salary, he probably couldn't

afford to live here, anyway. I smiled back at him, looking apologetically at his outstretched hand. "Nice to meet you."

He realized belatedly I couldn't shake and rubbed his hands on his khakis. "I'm sorry, Miss Sawyer, about the cuffs."

"I understand."

"I'm not sure I do. You don't look all that dangerous to me," he admitted in a quiet voice. "But I've given Scythe my word he'll have free rein in my department to teach my greenhorns how to handle investigations. So if this is the way he wants to do it, I can't get in his way."

"It'll work out," I said to reassure him. *It'll work out in jail when I'm either beaten and left for dead, the ladies of the night recruit me, or the resident gang leader takes me as her girlfriend.*

"Lieutenant," Ferguson called to Scythe, "are you ready to interview Miss Sawyer yet?"

"Okay." Scythe ran his hand through his hair, harried. It made it look worse. I'd noticed his bad haircut earlier and it pained me to study it. But, hey, it was my business. "Can you wait with Mr. Barrister for his attorney while I get Harland started on the interview with her?"

"Works for me," Ferguson said. He descended the stairs and led a reluctant Percy into the kitchen.

Scythe trudged up the stairs, heaving the world's biggest sigh. Hell, I wasn't that bad. Just when I thought he was about to spring me from my cuffs so I could walk to the room where I would be interviewed, Scythe leaned down and picked up the entire chair. For an instant it made me feel small, light, and feminine, a lie if there ever was one. After all, I'd eaten about four billion calories' worth of cheesecake just a couple of hours ago. I'd probably already gained fifteen pounds. I hoped he was getting a hernia, or at least a hemorrhoid or two, carrying me down the hall. I knew he was playing a head game. He was the macho he-man and I was the helpless female, shackled and at his mercy.

Good, let him think that. It put me at an advantage.

"Hey, what's got everyone all excited in there?" I nodded toward the study as we passed.

"Leave it alone, Reyn. It's none of your business."

"I'm handcuffed to a chair. Of course it's my business."

"Not anymore, it's not. It's police business. It was police business from the beginning."

"I know that."

"That's your problem. You know you shouldn't go poking around somewhere, and yet you still do it. It would be better if you were simply stupid or ignorant or stumbled into things by accident. But no, you're smart, yet you willfully implicate yourself and put yourself at risk. Just like the deal with Montoya. Why didn't you let us find the murderer instead of rousting out the rattlesnake yourself? You were nearly killed and caused us a whole lot of trouble we wouldn't have had otherwise."

"You guys might not have found the murderer otherwise."

He kicked open the last door on the left and used his shoulder to flip on the light of a grim guest bedroom trimmed in black and burgundy. The wood in the bedroom suite carried the combined weight of an elephant. Scythe dropped the chair on the dank Kashan rug right next to a suit of armor that startled me so, I hit my head on the chair back.

"Plus"—I refused to be intimidated—"you're talking about one of my good friends. What was I supposed to do, just go to the funeral and let fate take its course?"

His look told me that was exactly what I was supposed to do.

"How good a friend is this Alexandra?" Scythe asked tightly. He was making a big effort to control his temper. The guy had a powerful charisma, and when it combined with anger, he was combustible. It wouldn't take much more than the wrong word to set him off. I was the teeniest bit scared, considering I seemed to pick the wrong word without even trying.

I swallowed hard. "Not that good. She's a client. I feel sorry for her. I wish she'd start a life of her own."

"Stop doing that. Feeling sorry for people. Feeling responsible for things that have nothing to do with you. Life is good for Alexandra. She's probably about to inherit a whole lot of money, and she can afford to get her head screwed on straight. If you're going to feel sorry for someone, feel sorry for yourself. She *might* go to jail. You, on the other hand, are *definitely* going to jail."

Trying to ignore his intimidation, I wondered how Scythe had pegged Lexa so fast. How long had they been in the House of Horrors before they walked in on me in the study?

"That is," Scythe continued quietly, "unless she goes to prison for life for shooting her mother to death for being a controlling bitch."

"Don't say that!"

"Say what? Bad things about Wilma Barrister or about your friend?"

"About Lexa. She's had a rough row to hoe."

Scythe leaned in so close I could smell that mesquitey scent of his. "Don't be so blindly loyal. It just might kill you one day."

He strode to the door, where Harland appeared. They talked in low tones that even my eagle ears couldn't make sense of. He handed Harland a voice recorder out of his pocket and the younger man took it with shaking hands. Then Scythe looked pointedly at me over Harland's head. "I'm leaving you to give your story to Officer Harland, Miss Sawyer. Make sure to tell him everything just as you *remember* it." He walked away.

I was insulted that he was leaving me with Harland, who seemed very sweet but probably had the IQ of the village idiot. I'd rather him than Officer Bad Breath, but still . . . Then the point of Scythe's look hit home—he was letting me tell my story without a whole lot of intense grilling. I could sway it as far in my favor as the facts would allow. Later, I would likely be tortured by a defense attorney on the stand, but the initial statement given to police was always considered the most plausible, the most accurate.

The long-limbed young cop stumbled once on the carpet, then began to test the voice recorder. It took him about ten minutes of "testing one, two, three" to get it all figured out while I critiqued his over-gelled dirty-blond hair, which was spiked but missed being hip by needing to be shorter on top and a bit longer on the sides. Maybe I would offer to fix it for him while I was lingering behind bars. The adrenaline began draining

from my veins, and I felt myself droop. It was somewhere around three o'clock in the morning. I was about
the drift off to sleep when Harland finally was ready. He
sat on the love seat across from me and set the recorder
on the coffee table between us.

"Okay, ma'am." Boy, did that make me feel old.

"You can call me Reyn."

His Adam's apple bobbed. "Please state your name
and address."

"Reyn Marten Sawyer, Number Twenty-two Magnolia, San Antonio, Texas."

"So, tell me what you did this evening prior to coming here to the Barrister residence."

I took off there, running my mouth, beginning with
my refrigerator cleaning and telling the story in a way as
sympathetic to me and Lexa as possible. Harland let me
talk on, encouraging with sympathetic noises and even
an "I understand" when I explained why I felt so sorry
for Lexa.

"And the rash on your hand?" Harland interrupted,
surprising me. "Where did you get that?"

I was about to be impressed with this sudden show of
sharp thinking when I looked down and saw the index
card in his hand with Scythe's writing on it. Jerk. "It's
not a rash. It's an abrasion of sorts. Or maybe you could
call it a series of small punctures." I mulled this for a
moment, rubbing my fingers along the bumps as if they
could tell me since I couldn't see them with my hands
behind my back.

"A defensive wound, then?" Faithful Harland was
still reading from the card. I wondered what other
goodies were waiting there for me, courtesy of Scythe.

"Defending myself from boar's bristles? Lexa handed me a brush, and she slapped it down on my palm with a great deal of force, enough to break the skin."

"She must have been very angry."

"No, I would say confused, frustrated, frightened."

Harland really didn't know how to handle this, which made me realize how lucky I was. Another cop might have hammered away at me to get to the motivation for her emotional state. As he pondered his index card and how to proceed, I turned on the charm. "Hey, Harland, what was the big deal in there a little while ago? Everyone was pretty worked up about something."

"Oh, yeah." He leaned forward, excited. "The vic's fingertips were chewed postmortem. We were trying to figure out if it was the suspect—you know, the guy's got to be a whack-job if he painted her up like a clown."

"It wasn't the suspect," I said, disappointed that I already knew this juicy tidbit of information.

"How do you know?"

"Unless the Barristers' cat's a marksman."

"Her own cat chewed her? Eeuw!" Harland jumped up and shook his hands as if he could shake off the whole idea. He ran out of the room. "Hey, you guys, I found out who chewed . . ."

I was left in the room with the tape recorder running and the index card on the table. I stared at the card and squinted, trying to decipher Scythe's handwriting from four paces. It looked like chicken scratches. When I was a teenager, I used to be able to see across the hay field at home and into Errol Standard's bedroom. That'd been better than TV. I sighed. I was getting old. I looked around the half-lit, dreary room. I couldn't stand

it—I had to know what Scythe had written on that card.
I lifted my right leg and grimaced when the right side of
my gluteus maximus clenched painfully. I pointed my
toe and twisted my hip and stretched until the sole of
my Tony Lama skimmed the card. I bore down and,
even though my hamstring began to cramp, dragged the
card close enough to read.

Remember name/address.
Sequence of events.
Ask about her relationship with Wilma Barrister.
Ask about her friendship with Alexandra Barrister.
Ask about her personal life. Barrister has a son
about her age. Kermit. Are they involved?

"Oh, please, Scythe," I muttered. "With someone
named Kermit?"

If not, whom is she involved with? Remember,
most crimes are about sex, love, or money.

"Sneaky bastard."

"Who? You?" Scythe's voice called my attention to
the door.

My leg was still hiked up on the table; since my hamstring had locked, it would have to stay there. I tried to
look cool. Scythe tried not to look up my skirt.

"No. You."

"I'm not the one who's snooping." His laser blues
drifted to my exposed thigh.

I snapped my knees together. "What about those personal questions you sent your lackey in here to ask?"

"That's called investigating."

"Different word for the same action."

"Another difference: I'm trained and paid to do it, you are not." Scythe snatched up the card and shoved it into his jeans pocket, which made me look places I shouldn't be looking if I wanted to hang on to my high-and-mighty attitude.

"It's none of your business whom I'm seeing."

"It is police business—you are a material witness. You may be an accessory to murder. You may *be* the murderer, for all the Terrell Hills PD knows. Remember the gun. The only witness to your innocence is Wilma, and she's not talking."

Gulp. My fingerprints *were* on the gun. I supposed I could be considered a valid suspect. I didn't want Harland and Officer Bad Breath poking in my private life. I wanted Scythe poking around in it even less. "Okay, I don't know Lexa's brother, and I'm not seeing anyone currently. For your information, I took a vow of celibacy."

"Really." Those eyes danced as they zeroed in on mine. He took a step forward, then another, then leaned forward and whispered low into my ear, out of recorder range, "I do love a challenge."

 six

DESPITE ALL THE PROMISE behind the "I love a challenge" thing, it was nothing more than talk. I should've known better than to expect more. Scythe did this with regularity, got me all weak-kneed and fidgety, then walked off into the sunset. You know, if he got me weak-kneed and went in for the kill—I'd be supper that night. He probably knew that and was scared. Sure, that's it, he was scared he'd fall head over heels with me, and life as the happy-go-lucky bachelor would be all over. Either that, or he was just using his effect on me to his advantage—for whatever he wanted me for at the moment.

Yeah, I'd vote for that one too.

And right now, he wanted me out of the way.

So, there I sat, having regained strength in my knees, handcuffed in the armpit of the suit of armor, waiting for Scythe to return to transport me to jail. And that was when the bathroom door opened.

Now, as far as I knew, no one had heeded the call of nature while I'd been there. This was either Wilma's ghost, or a strong gust of wind—or, perhaps, the murderer.

A rather shaggy brunet head belonging to an average-size androgynous body in a white T-shirt peeked out, saw me, swallowed an outburst, and retreated back inside. Going for the murder weapon, no doubt. I was dead. I thought longingly of jail and how I would never get the opportunity to experience it. Now fully depressed and regretting that I hadn't planned my funeral in detail, I saw the door ease open again.

From the shadows, either a high tenor or a low alto murmured, "I guess now you know I'm in here."

"Um, not necessarily." *My answer would depend on whether you have a gun or not.*

"It was stupid of me to open the door so soon. I just thought that policeman had taken you with him."

"No, he's waiting until he can take me to the big house."

"A bigger house than this one?"

I rolled my eyes. A dense criminal. Great, maybe he'd be less bloodthirsty. "The big house, as in slang for 'jail.'"

"Oh. Why? You didn't kill Mrs. Barrister."

"How do you know?"

"You weren't here earlier."

"And you were?"

"I work here."

"Okay." The Shadow worked at the House of Horrors. That was good. "What do you do?"

"I'm the gardener. No, actually, I work for the gardener."

"The gardens are lovely." It's good to give homicidal maniacs compliments. I read that somewhere.

There was a long pause. I wondered if the Shadow was contemplating ways to kill me to keep me quiet. I decided now was a good time for a distraction technique.

"So, did *you* kill Wilma, then?"

"Of course not!"

"Who did?"

The Shadow sighed. "I wish I knew. While I was weeding the rose garden about seven-thirty, I saw Mrs. Barrister in her evening gown through the kitchen window. She was pouring herself a glass of what looked like wine. Later, I heard a couple of cars come and go while I was finishing up planting impatiens along the back wall. I didn't think anything of her having visitors. It happens often. The cars were gone when I came on up to the house about nine. I rang the bell. No one answered. Mrs. Barrister was expecting me, and the door was unlocked, so I came on in."

"She was expecting you at nine in the evening?" Oh, no, not another matron having an affair with a gardener. I'd been through this not long ago with the other murder investigation I'd bumbled my way into. Just as I was about to form a husbands-whose-spouses-left-them-for-the-gardener support group, he chimed in, "It's not what you think. Mrs. Barrister was helping me get my GED so I could go to college."

Wilma, a hands-on (figuratively, that is) philanthropist? Well, go figure.

"But when I saw she was . . . so weird-looking and dead, I panicked. I had some trouble with the police a couple of years ago—not this kind of trouble, though. I ran in here. I don't know how long I stayed in here, wondering what to do, when I heard Alexandra's voice, and then yours. Please don't turn me in."

So he had an even lamer story than I did. I should've been thrilled there was some dumb schmuck to take some of the pressure off me, but instead I felt sorry for him.

The Shadow stepped out of the bathroom, and I felt even sorrier for him. His dark brown hair was months from its last cut; probably meant to hang one length at his chin, it now sat on his shoulders. He was a slim-built twentysomething, about five-foot-two and probably a hundred pounds soaking wet. I wondered if he could handle pulling a patch of crabgrass, much less give cops any real run for their revolvers. "What kind of police trouble are we talking about? Running red lights? A plethora of parking tickets?"

"Not exactly."

"What . . ." I paused to fortify my patience. ". . . exactly?"

He cleared his throat. "An assault charge. Assault with a deadly weapon."

Oops. I tried not to laugh because it seemed so preposterous. But then, three-year-old kids had been known to pull a trigger. Sobering up, I scanned for the bulge of a concealed gun butt under his Hanes tee. "Not a revolver, by chance?"

"No." He held up his hands. They were disproportionately large on his sticklike arms. "These. I broke an arm, a nose, and five fingers. Someone was after my girl."

I had to bite my tongue to keep from laughing out loud this time. I wondered how surprised the Lothario had been when someone built like a midget scarecrow pummeled him good. "You know, your crime was one of spontaneous defense. The one against Wilma is definitely one of psychotic premeditation. Two different MOs entirely. The cops will question you and let you go. If I were you, I'd go turn myself in—be honest, tell them what you saw, and be done with it."

He hung his head. "You're going to turn me in, aren't you?"

I cocked my head back toward my shackled hands. "Look, you and I are on the same side here. I don't want to see you get in trouble, but, hey, what if I'm not the only one who knows you were here? The cops are going to come after you to question you because you work here. Having no alibi and a . . . history with the police won't help you a bit. I say tell the truth now and you'll be better off. And maybe you saw something important you don't realize. Maybe your information will be what catches the killer."

"You're right, I guess." He sighed, rubbing those giant hands together.

"Get your hands up!"

The Shadow swung his head to the door, his small brown eyes filled with terror, and his hands flew into the air. I couldn't see past the suit of armor to see who'd arrived, a logistic that Scythe doubtless planned when he put me down here. But if I didn't recognize the voice, I'd recognize the breath anywhere.

"Officer Manning," I called past the metal elbow going up my nose, "this gentleman was about to turn himself in. I don't think you need to hold him at gunpoint."

Manning and all his muscles stepped into the room, training his gun and gaze on the Shadow, but talking to me: "You're just mad I broke up your strategy session. You don't have to tell me: You are the brains and he's the brawn of this criminal operation."

Manning must have caught my raised eyebrows in his peripheral vision. "Okay, maybe you're the brawn and he's the brains."

"Or maybe he's Tweedledee and she's Tweedledum," Scythe's voice interceded in our tête-à-tête. Leave it to him to worsen any insult. "What the hell are you talking about, Manning?"

"Lieutenant, sir, I caught these two getting their stories straight, before he likely escaped out the balcony doors."

"There's balcony doors in this room?" the Shadow asked, confused. Yikes.

"He's definitely the brawn," Manning concluded with an officious nod.

"Yeah," I said with exaggerated pride. "Look at those hands. Brawny."

In answer, the Shadow smiled shyly at me and shook his hands where they were suspended in the air.

Manning, observing the big hands for the first time, looked duly impressed. I winked. Scythe sighed. Big and loud. "You two know each other?"

"We do now," I offered.

"We met ten minutes ago," the Shadow clarified. "Except I don't think we ever formally introduced ourselves. I'm John Tanno."

"I'm Reyn Sawyer."

"Good to meet you, Reyn."

"Same here, John."

"Wait," Harland interrupted, coming into the room. "If they only met ten minutes ago, they couldn't have murdered Mrs. Barrister, because the medical examiner just said she died about seven to eight hours ago—"

Scythe cut him off with a glare. "Thanks for relaying that vital information to potential suspects, Officer."

"Oops." Harland blushed. "Sorry, Lieu."

Scythe slid his glare over to me. I grinned. He leaned over me on the pretense of checking the fit of my handcuffs. "Leave it to you, Reyn, to manage to bollix something up even when handcuffed and behind a closed door."

"That's where I do my best work. Behind closed doors." Hell, I was already in trouble, I might as well have fun with it.

A flare sparked in his laser blues for an instant before he stepped back and cleared his throat. "Manning, take Mr. Tanno here into another room for an interview. Cuff him if he's uncooperative. Harland and I will stay and try to figure out how he got into the guarded room with Miss Sawyer. And what went on after he was in."

"I'll make it easy for you boys." I nodded toward the table, where the tape recorder was still running. "It's all on tape."

I figured that after Scythe listened to the tape and saw how I was trying to help instead of hinder the investigation, he'd soften up and let me go. No such luck. Without a word, he and Harland exited again, sending a uniformed officer with the personality of a mannequin into the room to watch me. Guess I was considered a

high security risk now that I'd managed to produce a
live body from an empty room. I sneaked a look at the
monolith sharing my air space. I wasn't sure he was even
breathing. Just as I was about to miss Officer Halitosis,
Scythe returned, unlocked the handcuffs, and pulled me
to my feet.

"Let's go to the car."

"Is Lexa okay?"

"None of your business."

"Murder solved yet?"

That earned me a glare. Well, anything was better
than the none-of-my-business thing.

I shook the hand of the suit of armor. Scythe nudged
me in the small of my back. "Come on."

"Sorry. In case you didn't notice, he and I got close."

"You're punchy."

"And whom do I have to thank for that?"

"Yourself. You could be home snug in your warm little bed with your dogs—"

"Hey, who's to say I wouldn't be snuggled up with
someone else?"

"You're the one who said you took the vow of
celibacy."

"Well, some vows are made to be broken."

"I'm glad to hear that." Scythe flashed a devastating
grin. For a moment, the world fell away. It took me another moment to catch my breath. I'd have to start
wearing some sort of protective sunglasses around him.
Some of his expressions were just too much for me to
think through logically. We walked out of the bedroom,
down the hall, past the crime scene techs bustling
around with their bags of equipment and cameras.

Chief Ferguson crossed the massive foyer and looked up at us.

"Chief, I'm taking her downtown," Scythe said, trying a little too hard to act like he was a hard-ass. "I'll be back shortly."

Ferguson threw me an apologetic look. "Is that really necessary?"

"Is what necessary? Him coming back?" I quipped.

Ferguson failed to hide a grin.

"Yes," Scythe said tightly, ushering me down the stairs. "It is necessary to book her."

Ferguson shrugged and followed a crime tech into the kitchen. Scythe opened the front door and led me to a Terrell Hills Police Department sedan. He opened the back passenger-side door.

"You're really going to make me ride in the back?"

"We have to do this by the book." His cocked his head toward a second-story window, where Harland, Manning, and half the crime scene techs were gathered, gawking. They scattered when I looked up. I got in the damned car. It smelled like athlete's foot meets a week-long Thunderbird drunk. "You really need to start wearing deodorant, Lieutenant," I said.

Grinding his teeth without answering, Scythe fiddled with the handcuffs for show but didn't put them back on. Then he slammed my door shut, slid into the front seat, locked the doors, and turned over the ignition.

He drove out the gate before breaking the silence. "If you are so intent on helping your friend, tell me all you can about Alexandra."

I began chronologically, which most of my tales do, but I digressed as bits of information floated to the top of my mind like a chaotic computer screen saver. I told him about Lexa's drive to irritate her mother, how I learned this after she started coming to get her hair done at Transformations. How this showed me how ambitious she was, but how misguided that quality was and how I longed to redirect it to more fruitful pursuits. About how basically she was a good person, fun-loving, with a quirky sense of humor. How she rebelled against her parents by driving an orange Pinto instead of the year-old Mercedeses they tried to hand down to her and refusing to go to law school because she didn't want to be an attorney, even though she was plenty bright enough. Yet, she was proud of her mother's accomplishments and her father's success. It was obvious when she spoke of them.

"It's enough," Scythe said more to himself than to me.

"Enough? You don't want to hear any more?"

"No, go ahead. It's just enough to motivate her to murder her overbearing mother."

"Come on. Lexa wouldn't murder anyone, especially her mom." I employed my pop psychology. "They were too codependent."

I expected an eye roll, but instead Scythe bought into my theory and turned it to his advantage. "Maybe Lexa finally was ready to be free. It's probably a lot easier to pull a trigger to cut the cord than stretch it emotionally."

Uh-oh. "Prove it."

"That's not my problem. It's the district attorney's."

"You just used me to make your case against Lexa!"

"Get used to it. It's what cops do. Plus, it's better than trying to make a case against you, which would probably be a helluva lot easier."

"Oh, yeah? What would my motive be? Maybe I thought by killing a famous society matron and doing her hair postmortem, I'd get some extra business from all those crime scene photos. . . ."

"You *are* sick."

"I'm ambitious. Others could testify to that. You might be able to sell that story. Okay, you come up with something more plausible."

"Maybe you and Lexa are having an affair and you are taking revenge for your lover."

I shook my head. "Weak. You guys all have those lesbian fantasies. It's really sad. You think a woman cop would ever come up with that one out of the blue with no supporting evidence? No way. If you got a woman on the jury, that one would be toast."

In the rearview mirror, I could see him grimace at the road.

"Have you arrested Lexa?"

"None of your business."

"I guess it's also none of my business that you let some hack chew on your hair the last time it needed a trim, huh?"

"Damn right," he snapped. Then his gaze went reflexively to the rearview mirror for a quick check before he caught himself and stuck it back on the road. He ground his jaw and tried not to ask. A minute ticked by before his ego couldn't stand it anymore. "What's wrong with my hair?"

"Nothing's wrong with your hair."

His shoulder muscles dropped as he relaxed.

"It's your cut that's embarrassing."

Oops—those shoulder muscles rose, higher than before. It's fun to mess with the mind of an egomaniac, which is, of course, most of the male species. They can't help it, it's testosterone induced.

Scythe held his tongue. He had impressive willpower. I goaded him more. "Number-two clipper cut on the sides, and long enough in back to maybe make a pony-tail. I don't know, maybe you want to look like a Bubba who lives in a trailer park and has a rifle rack on the rear window of his Ford. Hey, have you been working under-cover?"

I really had to remember the guy was armed. Still, I knew that cut and who did it. I just wanted him to admit it. Just one more try.

"Or maybe you're dating the girl who cut it. You know, when a man loves a woman . . ."

He shook his head, but didn't open his mouth. We were between streetlights and I couldn't read his ex-pression in the reflection off the dash, so I didn't know whether to push a little harder or drop the subject alto-gether. It was that touchy with Scythe. Not that I didn't usually enjoy pissing him off, but his current state of mind might make the difference in the kind of jailer I got for the upcoming strip search.

I decided changing the subject would be the safest course of action.

"I took a couple of shots of Wilma—" He nearly ran off the road. Oops, leave it to me to pick the wrong word. "I mean, shots with a camera." Scythe shook his head and got us back on track. I continued, "Anyway, I took the pictures for you guys before I fixed her hair. It was straight out like this." I pulled my artfully messy locks out by their ends in a poor illustration. He cocked his left eyebrow. "Oh, well, you'll see in the photos. I hid the camera back in the bookcase. Don't tell Lexa I took them, she'll freak out. Oh, also, I recognized the kind of hairspray the killer used—it's Main Mane by Hair's Breadth."

He sat up straighter and shot me a glare through the rearview mirror. "Why didn't you tell me this before?"

"I forgot. Apparently, being handcuffed and stuffed into the armpit of a suit of armor impairs my memory."

Scythe grunted. "While you are in the remembering mode, why don't you tell me what the Carricaleses told you before I noticed they'd arrived home?"

I shook my head. "I don't think so."

I watched his jaw flex. "Why not?"

"It really wouldn't help you any. It was all a bunch of small talk. You know . . . 'Why are you here?' 'Oh I'm kind of locked into the situation, ha-ha-ha'. . . . That kind of thing." The truth was, I didn't know what to tell Scythe. He could use any of the "hims" and "hers" in the servants' scenarios to make his case against Lexa. And while I thought *some* of the "hers" the Carricaleses mentioned might be her, I knew not *all* the "hers" were her. Got it? Until I understood more of what they meant, I wasn't telling Scythe jack. Plus, there was the open gate thing. I wanted to make sure Lexa didn't open it before I blabbed about it.

"Sure." He knew I was lying by omission, but didn't call me on it. Not yet. "You knew this servant couple? Or was it like our friend Tanno and you'd just met?"

"I'd met Maria once when she brought Lexa to a hair appointment months ago. I'd never met her husband."

"Uh-huh." He didn't sound convinced.

"Look, I am not a friend of the family. I am Lexa's

friend. I was Wilma's enemy." Oops, that was a bad
word choice. Again.

"Really?"

"Well, she thought of me that way. Once she came
and tried to talk me out of doing Lexa's hair. It was more
a control thing than anything about me. I knew that."

"So, how does her brother feel about you?"

Was he still stuck on that? Geez. I was tempted to
tell him about some wild sex orgy we'd shared, but I
doubted I could do it without spoiling the fib by bursting into gales of laughter, so I fell back on the truth.

"Hairdressers aren't the focus of long-distance family
conversations, so I doubt the guy knows about me and I
wouldn't know him if I fell over him. From what I'm
told by Lexa, he's gay. He lives his own life in Houston
with a devoted partner and has as little as possible to do
with his parents. He's friendly but not close. Lexa re-
spects him for that, envies him for it, too."

"What about Mr. Barrister?"

"What about him? Lexa never says much about him
except to mention his lifelong disappointment that she
won't be a lawyer or marry one. I've only seen him once
before tonight, and that was at a charity function a date
dragged me to."

From my rearview mirror perspective, I watched
Scythe's eyebrows shoot up. I wasn't going to tell him
that had been my last date and it had been a year ago.
Let him think it had happened last week.

"You might be interested in my opinion, as a beauty
professional, of the way the victim was arranged. I think
it shows a great deal of hostility, and the killer was making a statement about appearances."

"You might be interested in my opinion, as a law enforcement professional, of the way you were found in the presence of the victim, carrying what might prove to be the murder weapon, all on the pretense of helping a friend."

I was ticked off he was ignoring my evaluation of the situation. After all, I knew a helluva lot more about the aesthetic industry than he did. We exited the freeway, and I could see the high-rise that was the Bexar County Jail about two blocks away. "And your opinion is?" I finally asked frostily.

His voice was hot and tight when he finally spoke. "Reyn, you need to learn to say no. If you'd said no when Lexa called and asked for help, then you wouldn't be in trouble. I wouldn't be forced to take you to jail."

"Good advice. I'll start practicing saying no to you."

The way his neck stiffened, I knew I'd hit home.

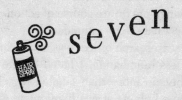

seven

DON'T LET ANYONE TELL YOU that going to jail is no big deal. Every emotion imaginable mixes thick in the stale air of the bullpen that is the Bexar County receiving room. Cops laugh with each other over their children's latest escapades as they register the effects of a one-legged Vietnam vet booked for vagrancy. Street-walkers hike up their spandex skirts to show they have nothing on underneath to the officer taking down their vital information. A deputy sheriff flirts with a rookie SAPD officer. A detective argues with a social worker as they fingerprint a sobbing teenage mother arrested for letting her boyfriend drown her baby. A man arrested for five rape/robberies stares at a lovely heiress klepto-maniac shoplifter, planning his sixth. A Boy Scout troop leader falsely accused of fondling a charge stares hope-lessly into space. A goth freak details his latest cult ani-mal killing to his benchmate, who looks ready to vomit.

This or another version of it happens every minute in the room where Scythe led me. I knew he'd taken me to

jail to teach me a lesson. Emotionally, I learned it in the
first thirty seconds. Intellectually, though, I refused to
let it change my future course of action. I'm hardheaded
that way. I hate to be intimidated.

The strip-search officer was kind, which made it mar-
ginally less humiliating. I hated Scythe about that moment, but no more than I hated myself for answering
my damned phone at nearly midnight and for not being
able to say no. But what if I hadn't? Lexa would be getting searched now, and she'd be having a harder time
handling it than I was.

The fingerprint ink was cold. When I fought off a
shiver, someone asked, "Do you need a blanket?"

I didn't think the processing cops were usually so so-
licitous of their charges. I slid a glance at Scythe, who
was talking to another detective as they leaned against
the wall. I wondered what he'd said in undertones to the
cop in charge when we'd walked into the bullpen.
Scythe was ignoring me now, but a couple of times I'd
caught him shooting me a glance, flexing his jaw, and
balling his fist in the pocket of his jeans. Guilty? I was
getting the impression this was harder on him than it
was on me.

Good.

Finally, the woman officer who'd been processing me
turned to Scythe and said, "I'm taking her to get her
picture taken."

"Don't let that dumb hairdo break the camera," he
quipped.

She stared at him, aghast. "What are you talking
about? Her hair is awesome. Meg Ryan messy is the
best. And the color, that amber brown, is so rich. Look at

all the cool highlights, a little blond, a little auburn . . ."

"Thanks," I told her. "Now, about *his* hair . . ."

"Oooh, girlfriend. Trailer park trash."

I grinned. Scythe rolled his eyes up to the ceiling, shook his head, waved at the buddy he'd been talking with, and stalked off. I did notice him looking at his hair in the glass as he passed through the door.

As soon as I sobered up, I felt alone.

I smiled when the flash went off anyway. My mother taught us always to smile for a camera, because you never knew where the picture might end up. I might be wrong, but back in the seventies, I don't think she was being prescient about the Internet and digital imagery. Still, that was today's reality, so if my face was going to end up on some porn site on Pamela Anderson's body, I might as well look happy about it.

For all the apparent chaos, they were pretty darned organized at the jail, so I didn't wait long to be arraigned. I wasn't sure what charge I was being held on. The fact was, it could be a host of them. Scythe had promised to call my next-door neighbor Tessa Ugarte, who was an attorney, to help me through the process. I wondered what the hell was taking her so long to get there. I mean, I knew it was early (or late, considering your point of view)—almost six o'clock in the morning—but still. After all, I did feed their cat, Merlin, when they went out of town.

Time to return the favor.

Scythe had been MIA since before my photo session. I really hated to miss him, but, damn it, I did. Of course, I was sitting in night court between a twitching, sweaty crack addict going into DTs and a chanting street preacher wearing nothing but a grimy gunnysack that read IDAHO GOLD POTATOES, so I probably would be missing Jack the Ripper as long as he wore antiperspirant and real trousers and could carry on a semblance of a two-way conversation.

The bailiff called my name and I was led to the judge's bench. Still no Tessa. The damned cat could starve the next time they flew to Cozumel.

I kind of missed the beginning as I was plotting how pissed-off to be at Tessa, but I did hear: "Reyn Marten Sawyer. You are being released." The gavel went down. The bailiff tried to shoo me out the door. I ignored him and stood stubbornly in front of the bench.

"Why?"

"What?" The judge looked up from the next file on his desk.

"Why are you letting me go?"

"Not enough evidence to hold you over for arraignment. You are free to go. This arrest will be expunged from your record."

"But how come?"

"Miss Sawyer." He sighed heavily, reminding me of Scythe. I have a way of rubbing the justice system the wrong way. "I have never in a decade of sitting on the bench had anyone argue with me over being released."

"I just want to know if someone pulled some strings—"

"I don't know and, furthermore, who cares? You are free to go. If you argue with me any more, I will hold you in contempt of court for your stupidity and then you really will be arraigned!"

I hate to lose an argument and I especially don't like

being threatened, but it occurred to me that now was probably not a good time to stand on principle. "Thank you, Your Honor."

The bailiff shook his head as he led me out the courtroom door. He stopped dead in his tracks in the hallway, and I bumped into his back. I don't think he even noticed because all he could see was Trudy. In his defense, her knockout body in an orange and white polka-dotted mini-suit cut down to here and up to there and over-the-knee white patent-leather boots would've stopped the President on his way to pick up the red phone. She's a tall, lithe redheaded beauty who would make my more athletically built freckled self feel like a troll if I thought a lot about it. Which I don't. Not unless I'm prepared to have a whole carton of Häagen-Dazs that day. Today I wasn't. I had way too much on my mind to feel sorry for being shorted in the looks department. I eyed her boots. It was only early April. "Did I miss Easter?"

"Whoever said white was only a spring and summer color was a close-minded fool." Trudy was never a slave to fashion rules. And anyone who ever saw her forgave her.

The judge bellowed for the smitten bailiff. Trudy waved at him as he left, and I thought he might faint with pleasure. "What are you doing here?" I asked. I was glad to see her, but this was no coincidence. As an interior designer, Trudy hung out at antique auctions, fabric stores, and chandelier bonanzas, not the jailhouse.

"Jackson called me."

"Did he, now?" I shoved my hands on my hips. "What did he say?"

"He told me to get here as fast as I could to take you home once the court released you."

"So he knew the judge was going to release me?"

Trudy nodded. "I got the impression he arranged it."

"So I was right. It was all an idiotic stunt. I'm going to kill him!"

The hallway full of arrestees went silent. A jail officer in the corner straightened to attention, hand on gun butt.

Trudy threw an absent smile at the sudden audience and waved off the stunned silence. "Oh, it's just a lover's spat. Her boyfriend's a cop. Jackson Scythe. That's who she wants to kill." She giggled.

"Really?" The jail officer took a step forward, not giggling.

"He's not my boyfriend," I argued—the wrong point, of course.

"But I bet you're gonna kill him anyway?" the jailer inquired.

"Of course she is." Trudy added helpfully, "She'll try to, anyway. Likely with torture involving his genitals."

The jailer took another step forward. I finally heard our conversation from his perspective. Uh-oh. I put a hand up. "It's not what it sounds like. I'm just joking." I patted Trudy's arm, a little too hard. She winced. Okay, maybe I whacked her. "She's just joking. It's all a joke. Ha-ha."

Trudy finally caught on and added a weak he-he to my ha-ha.

The jailer was suddenly in front of us, not sharing our chortling. He pulled out a notebook, pen poised. "What's your name?"

Double uh-oh. "Zena Zolliope," I said quickly, pulling Trudy past him and down the hall before he could finish spelling Scythe's hairdresser's first name.

"Reyn," Trudy admonished as we made our way through the parking lot to her bubble-gum-blue Miata, "you really need to learn to curb that temper of yours or you'll end up in jail for good."

"Trude, you really need to learn to turn on that brain of yours or you'll help me get there. What's with the genital and boyfriend comments?"

"Well, you could've come up with a better assumed name. Zena Zolliope." She gave her giggle-snort. "Who'd ever believe that was someone's real name?"

"It *is* a real name. It's the woman who got her hands on Scythe's hair and Lord only knows what else." I tried to keep my voice neutral, but I think I failed. I think I might have sounded a tad bit jealous.

"Neon newts and kinky kangaroos, no kidding?" Trudy giggled. She snorted. She stopped in her tracks and looked at me. "He *told* you that?"

"No, of course he didn't tell me. I recognized the cut."

"You can't do that," Trudy scoffed, blowing the whole idea off with a wave and a flutter of her peachy perfect fingernails.

"Hairdressers have signatures just like you interior designers do. Don't tell me you can't place who designed what room."

She acknowledged that with a nod and deactivated her car alarm. It beeped back at her. "I can."

"There you go. I was assigned Zena as my partner at

the last two hairstyling workshops. She is stuck on this goofy cut for guys who have natural wave in their hair. No matter how many cuts she was shown, by how many experts, from 'Om to Paul Sasson's clinician, her attempts always ended up the same—looking like Scythe's does now."

"Still, that doesn't prove—"

"And," I interrupted, "five feet of her five-foot-ten is legs. Her sheet of honey-blond highlight-foiled hair reaches her size two hips. She favors three-inch-long crimson fingernails and four-inch strappy gold sandals. Her head would float away if not attached to her neck."

"That would be the clincher." Trudy nodded. "I guess you're right." Over the course of the last murder we'd been unwittingly mixed up in, Trudy had seen the various women Scythe dated. They pretty much could be summed up thus. Around the cop shop, his women were called "Flavor of the Week." "Flavor of the Day" might be more accurate, but nobody asked me.

We lapsed into silence as we sank into the miniature seats of her sports car, and she buzzed out of the parking lot. The horizon showed the promise of dawn as Trudy drove past the ragtag group of mostly Hispanic men, many of them from Mexico, on the corner waiting to be hired as day labor on various construction jobs around town. As we angled onto the interstate, Trudy pursed her glitter-peach–glossed lips and threw me a sidelong look.

"I can't believe you lied to me. I should've let you catch the bus home."

She was so steamed that the bus was sounding pretty damned good about now. "What do you mean?" I asked.

"I mean, you promised me less than eight hours ago that you wouldn't get involved in another murder."

"I can't help it that someone offed Wilma. I can't help it that Lexa called me."

"You can help what your answer might be."

Was this a recurring theme or what? It was beginning to piss me off.

"I didn't know that Wilma was dead when Lexa called, Trude."

"That's what Jackson said."

" 'That's what Jackson said,' " I mocked in a nasal tone as she exited the freeway. "If you know the whole story, why are we discussing it?"

"We aren't *discussing* it. I am giving you a piece of my mind."

"You don't have enough to spare," I muttered. "And I don't like it that you're doing whatever Scythe tells you to."

"Hey, that's not fair." She braked too hard at a stop sign. "I don't need Scythe to tell me that you ought to mind your own business and stop nosing around in other people's problems."

"This is more than a problem, Trude. This is a murder."

"All the more reason to keep out of it."

"Well, it's too late now. I'm in it, and nosing around is the only way I'm going to get out."

"Rabbits' rumps and possums' pissers, Reyn!" Trude nearly missed my driveway and had to do a one-eighty to miss an oncoming car. I was waiting for what came next with a certain trepidation, since the only time Trude used body parts in her colorful expressions was when she was royally ticked off. "Hasn't it occurred to you that by letting you go, you *are* off the hook? Duh! Do some cuts and colors today, talk about the latest hot affairs in high society, and stay out of the Barrister business."

"Okay, okay." I held up my hands, ready to give in.

"Besides which, the cops suspect Alexandra. It's on the radio."

"What?" I shouted, slamming the Miata door. Gingham curtains ruffled upstairs at the house catty-corner to mine across McCullough Avenue. Uh-oh. I'd woken Mama Tru, the quintessential nosy neighbor, who just so happened to be Trudy's mother-in-law. She was probably wiggling into one of her infamous rainbow caftans right now as she hurried down the stairs. I lowered my voice as I marched to my kitchen door. "Lexa didn't do it. And if they think she did, then I'm toast because it looks like I helped her cover it up."

Trude pulled her eyebrows together in concern. She really couldn't argue that point, which scared me, since she seemed bent on arguing me out of the situation at any cost. I guess I did look guilty from that perspective, even to someone biased in my favor. "Maybe the news guys got it wrong," she offered weakly.

"No, they didn't. Lexa is Scythe's suspect numero uno."

"But he'll do anything to keep you out of it."

"Why do you think that?"

"Because you turn him on."

"Torturing me turns him on. Tonight is a case in point." I paused. "Zena Zolliope is the one who's turning him on from the waist down and off from the neck up; otherwise he'd never put up with such a lame haircut."

Trudy didn't want to agree with me, but had to, with a noncommittal shrug. Then she grinned. "I wish I could be there on their next date, after he's heard she's threatened to mutilate him."

The scenario played in both our heads and giggles turned into gales of laughter as Trudy let us into the kitchen with her keys, since mine were in my purse in my truck parked behind the Barristers' servants' entrance. Trudy put her keys on the table. I waved at the girls, who were begging with whines and yips to come in. I was starving as usual, so I made a beeline to my refrigerator. I swallowed a shriek when I opened it and glimpsed the back wall of the Frigidaire. I thought for a moment someone had robbed me of half its contents. It was traditionally full to bursting. One never knew when one might need something, and I despised being halfway through a recipe only to have to go to the store for a missing ingredient.

"You were cleaning it out, remember?" Trudy deadpanned, reading my panicked expression.

"Oh, right." Actually, the Brie in the trash can should have been reminder enough; it was stinking to high heaven. I tied up the bag and hauled it out to the big can in the alley, three hopeful dogs at my heels. I let myself out the gate and lifted off the trash can lid.

That's when a figure lunged out of the early dawn shadows, blocking any hope of a swift retreat. I screamed, swung the metal lid reflexively, and then dropped it, sending my Labs baying until no one was left sleeping on Magnolia that morning.

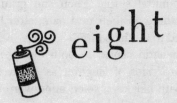

eight

IT TOOK ME HALFWAY into my fifth sopapilla before my heart rate returned to normal. Mama Tru had offered to make my favorite food in the world to make up for scaring me half to death in the alley. I had agreed to eat them to make up for the bump I'd put on her head by beaning her with the trash can lid. The fried sweet tortillas dripping with honey were more than worth my fright. Once I'd rationalized that all that blood pumping surely increased my metabolism enough to burn off an extra sopapilla, I reached for a sixth.

"Wilma was such a *jefe fuerte*. I could see how she might make someone mad," Mama said, pausing to lick honey off her fingertips. "She took no bull, demanded more than people's best, and expected miracles."

"All for a good cause," I offered diplomatically.

"I think that was her cover. You can abuse if you do it for the right reasons, no?"

"The means justify the ends," Trudy added, nibbling on her second sopapilla.

"*Si*. It was her argument often, as well as that of those who supported her," Mama added.

"Who were those who supported her?" I asked, listening carefully now. Esmeralda Tru was nothing if not the best gossip west of the Brazos River. If anyone in San Antonio even thought something, Mama Tru had heard it.

Mama stood to refill her coffee cup with some freshly ground Kona roast as she answered. "Foundation chairs, nonprofit managers, boards of directors—anyone who benefited from her hardhanded tactics and was above being recruited into the trenches. Now, those girls, they despised her."

"Maybe they were just jealous of her power, her money."

Mama emitted a "humph." Trudy sipped her coffee. "Maybe."

"Who are they, the ones who hated her?"

Trudy looked into the depths of her cup. "Library volunteers, hospital candy stripers, animal shelter dog walkers . . ."

"Junior Leaguers," Mama added into Trudy's silence. Trude flashed her a warning look. What the hell was that all about?

"I knew Wilma was a bigwig in the Junior League, but I thought it was just another in a long list of projects."

"Oh, no. It was her pet project," Mama Tru clarified, sliding Trudy a look as she did so.

Trudy was definitely squirming. I raised my eyebrows, and she reluctantly elaborated on Mama's statement. "Wilma Barrister held the record for being an active member of the Junior League of San Antonio for the most number of years."

I narrowed my eyes but continued the line of questioning. "I don't get it. I know women a lot older than Wilma was who surely joined long before she did and are still in the Junior League."

Trudy looked deeply into her now-empty coffee cup again. As she watched her, Mama Tru's face screwed up in apology. What was she sorry for? I let the silence drag on until Trudy finally felt compelled to fill it. "They would be sustainers. All members of the Junior League have to go through a probationary year where they learn the ropes and make sure they are committed; then the ten years following that they are required to do active community service. After that period, they can go 'sustainer,' which means they pay dues, donate items or cash to the rummage sale, and buy tickets to other fundraisers, but they don't have to donate their time anymore. Wilma, she never went that route; she maintained her active status from the age of twenty-one until the day she died. Other sustainers donate time, but of their free will. Wilma still held to the active requirements. We never could believe it."

"Who is 'we'?" I jumped on the slip. Mama cringed.

Trudy blushed and stammered. I'd never seen that happen to my smooth-tongued friend, not ever. "Well, uh . . ."

"Oh, *Dios mío*, Trudy." Mama put her cup down too hard on the table. "She's onto you now. Might as well tell her."

I stared at my best friend, stunned. I couldn't believe it. "You were in the Junior League," I intoned.

She stared back, acutely embarrassed and vaguely guilty.

"*Is* in the Junior League," Mama corrected.

I've caught a boyfriend or two cheating on me, but this felt worse. Much worse. This was my girlfriend, my best friend, a woman I thought I knew. To find out she was a member of a group I thought was nothing but a bunch of shallow social climbers masquerading as do-gooders seemed the ultimate betrayal. Knowing her upbringing as one of three daughters of an old-money San Antonio family, I shouldn't have been surprised. Her mother, Daffy Richardson, a nipped, tucked, and teased fiftysomething airhead if there ever was one, could be a poster child for the image I had of the typical Junior Leaguer. But I'd thought Trudy's surprise marriage at eighteen to Mario Trujillo, an ordinary son of Mexican immigrants, marked a certain rebellious streak in Trudy that would defeat any further attempts at trying to get her to rise another rung. Guess I was wrong. I felt sick.

"How could you have been my friend for five years and not told me?"

"I really didn't think about hiding it from you until Buffy Peters and Candy Streskoff started coming to you. You went on and on about how disgusted you were when they told you they had to join the Junior League to find the right middle-aged mom to impress so she'd take them home to meet her son. It made the whole thing sound like a twist on the archaic arranged marriage. Then when Zoe Severson told you she joined so her kids could get into a better private school, I knew there was no use trying to explain to you that some of us do it just to help the underprivileged in the community."

"There are lots of opportunities to do that without the Junior League."

"Ever heard of strength in numbers? It does make a difference."

"Not when Buffy and Candy and Zoe are in the numbers."

"Sometimes going to help the underprivileged helps change the perspective of the privileged doing the helping."

"I bet that's a line they make you rehearse until they release you from Junior League probation."

"I wish I could think of a way to prove it to you." Trudy's green eyes flashed. She was angry, an emotion rare to her. The second time this morning I'd made her mad enough to spit. I was going for a record.

I'd been thinking about the resentment against Wilma in the ranks of the hypocritical socialites. What a great source of information about Wilma the Hun and her enemies! Maybe I could use Trudy's crusade mentality to my advantage in ferreting out the real killer. "Okay. Take me to a Junior League function. Let me mingle and be enlightened."

Mama Tru nearly choked on her last sip of coffee, spewing it across the table. I ducked, and it sprayed the window. Guess my capitulation surprised her.

But my best pal was no pushover. "I'm onto you, Reyn. You just want to go nose around in Wilma's affairs. Maybe you'll learn we're not all social-climbing creeps in the Junior League. Here's the deal. Today is the deadline for nominating new members. I'll nominate you and get Charlotte Holmes to sign on for the second sponsor, and my mom can be your sustainer sponsor. We can go to the new-member mixer tonight."

Whoa. The vision of me dressed to the nines with

Trudy's mom, Daffy, at my elbow was more than I could take. What a nightmare. "Hold on a minute, Trudy. How about you just have a little party with a bunch of your Junior Leaguer friends, and I can get the skinny there?"

"It wouldn't help you investigate Wilma's murder," Trudy said lightly. "I'm a little fish in that big pond. Wilma and I didn't move in the same circles in the JLSA."

Sneaky little rat. I had no way of disproving that. "But I don't want to be a member."

"It's not like you're signing up for the Marines. You can decide you don't want to join anytime in the process, and they won't rip off your right arm."

"Unless it's wearing a David Yerman bracelet they covet," Mama Tru chimed in, answering her daughter-in-law's glare with an unapologetic grin and chuckle. "It was just a joke, my dear."

Trudy looked thoughtful for a moment. "Of course, Reyn, a withdrawal is not without its drawbacks. It would make it more difficult for you, if you ever did decide to join the Junior League again."

She read my look and shrugged. "Okay, so that's not an issue. Let's get busy, then."

We all have moments we aren't proud of. For some reason, I think I have more of those moments than other people my age. Maybe there is a big universal embarrassment bank in the Grand Scheme of Things and once our account gets full, we don't have any more of these moments. That way I could be a really cool old lady who did nothing but the perfect thing, admired by all. Maybe, but I doubted it.

As I looked in the mirror in bathroom number four-hundred-fifty-two of the Hanson luxury compound, I hoped I would never have to live this down. Trudy's legs were too long, her boobs too big, and her hips too small for me to borrow any of her clothes. Daffy, unfortunately, was more my size, although everything was still too big across the chest. Her closet was full of only this season's hottest fashions and nothing else. None of it was practical in any way and most of it was horrid. She made a big deal about her generosity in allowing me to wear her latest purchase from London—a suit in a color that had no name and was impossible to describe. Think cat barf after a garbage-can raid behind the nearest Thai restaurant, and you might be close. It was a lumpy, tweedy thing the texture of barf, too. It was trimmed in real raccoon fur and the fur went around the bodice, so I looked like the raccoon was hugging me. Did I mention the fur was tinted aqua and fuchsia so you could still see the ghost raccoon stripes? Daffy's Manolo Blahnik fuchsia leather pumps with clear Plexiglas three-inch heels had clear windows at the tips that showed my white squished-together unpainted toenails. The final insult was that my Meg Ryan messy cut had to be "toned down." Trudy said I would stick out like a sore thumb, so she suggested a flipped-out bob that half the zip code was wearing now. Trudy stuck a jeweled barrette in above my left ear.

As I futilely patted down the fur that tickled my chin and prayed no PETA member would be attending the mixer, I realized that I not only clashed with myself, I clashed with the peacock-feather–looking wallpaper. With a sigh, I turned on the peacock-tail–shaped spigot at the sink and picked up the peacock-molded soap to wash my hands. I dried my hands on (you guessed it) a peacock-embroidered towel and steeled myself for going out in public. I'd escaped to the bathroom as soon as we walked in the door. Now I couldn't put it off any longer.

"Reyn!" Trudy hissed through the door. "Get out here right now."

"I'm primping."

"Save it for someone who'll buy it. You've never primped in your life."

True. I hated when she was right. I emerged. "How did you find me?"

"I've checked at least a dozen bathrooms. I figured you'd gone into hiding."

"Hiding? Why is she hiding? Isn't this fun? I'm having so much fun. And I know you are, too." Charlotte Holmes stopped to take a breath, which was always the best time to stop her incessant flow of chatter.

"Yes, Charlotte," I interjected quickly. "I'm having more fun than I can stand."

"Let's get you back to the action, then." Trudy led the way back down the hall.

"It's going to be so cool to have you in the League, Reyn," Charlotte began before we could take two steps toward the cavernous sunroom that opened into the gardens where most of the platters of hors d'oeuvres and fruit lay. "We'll do our community service together."

As we wound our way through the assembled group, it seemed half the women were already drunk, while the other half were either pregnant or nursing and held tight to virgin mint juleps. I was so overwhelmed that I was ready for an IV line of Chardonnay. I stopped myself from reaching for one of the glasses being circulated by the tuxedo-clad caterers because I wanted to stay sharp while I got the dirt on Wilma.

Charlotte hadn't stopped talking, but that was her way. In the two years since she'd started coming to me to get her brunet curls trimmed, I'd mastered the art of listening to her on two planes. I could take in only certain words, enough to provide a believable answer, which freed me up to think of other things. Charlotte had a heart of gold and an unenviable life as the daughter of filthy rich, emotionally absent parents. I'd heard all about the nannies who'd raised her and even met the one the Holmeses kept on the payroll even though Charlotte was well into her twenties. She arrived to her appointments at Transformations in a chauffered white Mercedes. When I'd asked what the special occasion was, Charlotte looked at me like I'd spoken Chinese. Finally, she explained she had a driver because her parents considered it "too dangerous" out on the road for her ever to be behind the wheel. She was book-smart, having graduated from the top private school in San Antonio two years early as a CPA, but had been taught absolutely no common sense, which, personally, I considered more dangerous than driving.

"So, do you want to, Reyn?" Charlotte popped an orange-glazed cookie in her mouth. She was a hundred pounds overweight because when she didn't have anyone around to talk to, she ate. "Huh? What do you think about that?" She snatched a petit four off a passing tray and swallowed it without visibly chewing. "I think that would be the perfect place for you to meet new people."

"I'm sorry, Charlotte, what did you say?"

Her brown eyes chastened while looking sorrowful. How did she do that? I wanted to learn how to do that. She sniffed. "I guess I was talking too much."

"Oh, no, Charlotte." She was prone to erupting into fountains of tears. That was the last thing I needed. "You just have to forgive me. This is a whole new world, and I'm just trying to take it all in."

"I understand. I grew up with it, so this is nothing new, and I know how someone who really didn't have money or social position or marry well would have a hard time getting with the program here."

Did I mention Charlotte didn't have any couth either? Money, social position, and marrying well weren't ambitions of mine, so what she said didn't really bother me. Now, good legs, that was another thing entirely.

Speaking of good legs, the best pair I knew had wandered off to talk to a trio of women. Trudy laughed at something one of them said, and I felt a pang of jealousy that she would fit in so well in a world I was not comfortable in. It was silly, I knew, to feel that way, but emotions were rarely logical. Bad luck for me, since emotional was my middle name.

Charlotte dove back to the table for another meatball, and a pair of twentysomethings who had on more gold than was held in Fort Knox paused before me. "Isn't that a Mitchell Saunders?" the blonde asked.

I tried to look encouraging, when in fact I could not for the life of me remember if that was the name of the designer Daffy was so proud of.

"Of course it is," the brunette answered. "Jerry Hall was wearing it in the last issue of *W*."

The blonde eyed me critically. "You know it's not

appropriate here, but I guess if I could afford it, I would've worn it, too, just to make everyone else sick with envy. I'm sure a lot of girls here will be scrambling to catch up with this by tomorrow."

The brunette nodded in agreement, and they walked off while I wondered what planet I was on. Who wanted to "catch up" with a fashion disaster besides Joan Rivers and Mr. Blackwell?

I looked around and noticed that, like the Bobbsey Twins who'd just critiqued me, most of the women my age were wearing some combination of black pants or skirt and denim. It was so prevalent it almost resembled a uniform. Well, damn, someone could have told me. Why hadn't Trudy told me wearing her mom's suit would make me overdressed? For punishment, no doubt. Someone walked by wearing a denim jacket trimmed in ostrich feathers. That made me feel a little better. I didn't think I looked quite that goofy.

"Serena." Charlotte, having reappeared with her mouth half full of meatball, clamped a hand on Ostrich Feather's forearm. "You have to meet a friend of mine, Reyn Marten Sawyer."

I nodded politely. Serena Ostrich Feather looked irritated, but nodded back and smiled stiffly. She extended her perfectly manicured hand and fluttered it amid the feathers. It never touched my hand. A handshake version of the air kiss. "Nice to meet you. Are you joining us?"

"Ah, yes, I guess so."

"You'll meet so many people who can help you. You're not married, are you?" She looked at my left hand, and I felt like I was in a singles bar. "No, you're not. Great. See that woman over there, the one in the

Valentino, with the Gucci purse and that David Yerman we are all dying for? She's got a son who just got out of A&M med school after getting his degree from Harvard Law. Word is he's going to go with the number-one medical malpractice firm in the nation—they offered him more than he'd make as an M.D., even one with a specialty. He's visiting home for two weeks before he gets started with his practice. You've just got to meet him. Makes me wish I weren't married; an architect really doesn't measure up to that."

The ostrich feathers flew off. I was just getting ready to beg off sick when I passed a group of three women and heard Wilma's name.

"I hate to say she deserved it, but Wilma was so mean, especially to the provisionals. I bet she ran off half of each year's potential League members."

"She said she was practicing Darwinism, survival of the fittest. By giving them a hard time, she weeded out the weak provisionals, making the League stronger."

I sidled up to the group and tried to look innocent. "Uh, I'm going to be a provisional. Is she someone I should look out for?"

"Not anymore. We're talking about Wilma Barrister. She was murdered last night in her house. And it's good news for you," added the caramel blonde with the hairdo Trudy had tried to get me to emulate, her critical sweep of my outfit telling me I'd have had a lot to worry about if Wilma were still around.

"Now, Charis, don't be so heartless," the pal to her right with the same hairdo chimed in, although I wasn't sure whether she was chiding her for her comment to me or the one about Wilma. "She was an amazing leader."

"Like Stalin," Charis said under her breath.

"Mrs. Barrister was an icon," put in the third woman, also with the flip-out hair and a barrette like mine. "The fund-raising projects she headed up made more money than any others in the history of the JLSA. Programs she started had record-setting results."

"What about the programs she killed?" asked a short, dumpy woman who'd come up beside me. She was about my age and dressed worse than I was, in an off-the-rack suit that was ill-fitting in a way that made me think either she'd had it a long time or she'd lived with the tight shoulders and loose skirt because she got it cheap at a secondhand store. Her flyaway frizzy black hair was starting to spring out of its super-sprayed bun at the nape of her neck. She nodded and smiled, then extended her hand to me, which was more than the three others had done. "Mitzi Spagnetti."

I ignored the way they were looking down their noses at her, introduced myself, then asked, "What programs did she, uh . . ." I couldn't use the word "kill." "Eliminate?"

"Anything that didn't directly have to do with children under the age of ten," Mitzi said with more venom than seemed necessary.

Before I could get to the source of her anger, Trudy appeared at my elbow. "Hi, Mitzi, I'm sorry I missed your meeting this morning. I'll try to make the next one."

"Good news. We might not have to go underground anymore with the program. I just talked to Sonya, and she says we can present it again to put on the community service slate."

"What program?" I asked.

"Outreach on preventing teenage pregnancy." Mitzi lit up like a proud parent talking about her child. The sudden animation made her almost pretty. "Trudy worked with me when I chaired the program for a couple of years before the League pulled the plug on the money."

My friend in her micro-miniskirts counseled teens on abstinence? What other surprises lay in store for me?

"The program was killed," Mitzi continued, "but now it might come alive again."

The symbolism was a bit creepy, but she seemed so excited I didn't comment beyond "Congratulations."

The three fashion stooges drifted off just as Charlotte bounced up. "Aren't you having a blast, Reyn? Isn't it fun? Isn't this just the greatest, Trudy, having Reyn here with us in the League?"

Trudy looked at me and raised her eyebrows in question.

"I'm glad to meet someone like Mitzi. Someone who really wants to use her membership to make a difference."

"Not all of us think community service means taking the best eligible bachelor out of circulation."

I smiled at what I thought was a joke, but Mitzi wasn't smiling. She seemed to take just about everything a little too seriously, but that probably boded well for the programs she worked on. No teens would dare get pregnant on her watch. I drew in a deep breath to bolster my good manners and caught a whiff of her cologne. It smelled vaguely familiar.

Before I could place it, Daffy tip-tapped up on her

four-inch black lizard-skin heels. Her perfectly liposuctioned hips and model C cups undulated beneath a gold and black checked dress that was surely out of place in the land of the denim and black uniform. Somehow it seemed to work for her as well as the rainbow raccoon *wasn't* working for me. Go figure. Her five face-lifts had left her skin so tight across her cheekbones that I cringed when she blinked her false eyelashes. It looked like it might hurt. "Thank Gucci I found you, Reyn, dahling. The membership chair just asked me for your application. Did you remember to bring it?"

"I left it in the car. Let me go get it."

I wound my way back through the throng to the front door, pausing only a couple of times when I heard Wilma's name mentioned. One group was reliving the gory details of the murder according to the gossip mill, which had her possibly dismembered after being shot. Someone had heard she was wearing bad makeup, which got answering gasps of horror and one terrible speculation that it was—horrors—Revlon.

I was still shaking my head over that one as I rounded the bush I had parked behind.

Suddenly, I felt a hand reach around from behind me and grab the V neckline of my suit. Fur bunched up my nose. *I knew it.* A militant animal-rights activist had followed me out of the party and was about to strangle me for wearing raccoon.

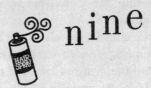

nine

I WAS PRESSED AGAINST A HARD BODY. I wiggled against some interesting testosterone-inspired contours and began to think being assaulted by this particular PETA member might not be all bad.

"Don't move," he warned, squeezing me more tightly. "I think I've got it under control."

"Got what?"

"Don't look now, but you've been attacked by a psychedelic raccoon that's thrown up all over your suit. Oh, wait! I see why he got sick—he ate off the toes and heels of your shoes."

It was just my luck that it was Scythe and not a hunky animal-rights activist. I wanted to stab his foot with my Plexiglas spike heel, but before I could, I started feeling his body heat through the tweed and got distracted. Damned hormones.

"You know," he added thoughtfully, straining to look down around my fur, "I don't think I've ever seen your toes. You always have boots on."

With a herculean effort, I shoved his hand off my raccoon and separated my backside from his frontside. I spun to face him. He looked me up and down, then burst out laughing.

I jutted my chin in the air. Pride comes in handy sometimes, especially when you're dressed like a buffoon in front of the man you have wet dreams about on a regular basis. "Excuse me?"

"I don't know." He shook his head, though the rusty laughter had slowed to a rumbling chuckle. "That's a tall order."

"I don't want you to excuse *me*, you idiot. I was politely asking you to excuse yourself for accosting me."

"I guess we should go in order. Did the raccoon already apologize?"

I arched my eyebrows, folded my arms across my midriff, and tapped my Plexiglas toe.

"Oh-ho. You hang out for a couple of hours with the upper crust and suddenly you're hoity-toity."

"You know what they say about the company you keep," I said archly with a pointed glance at his bad haircut.

That wiped the last vestiges of the smile off his face. He didn't know I'd guessed about Zena. Did he feel guilty about dating her, or was he serious about her? Before I could analyze the issue, he nailed me with his laser blues. I smelled something stinky blow by on the evening breeze and used it as an excuse to look away from him. Had something really barfed on my suit? No, that wasn't quite the odor. Scythe put his hand on my elbow to get my attention again. "What are you doing here, Reyn?"

I smiled. "Rushing the Junior League."

"Right." He shook his head in frustration. "Really. Tell me why you're here."

"I told you. Ask anyone. I'm turning in my application to be a provisional today."

Scythe shook his head and stuck his hands in the pockets of his starched khakis and balled them into fists. He drew them out and ran his right hand through his hair. "You're here nosing around about Wilma Barrister. Reyn, I told you to stay out of it. I let you out of—"

I raised my eyebrows before he could say "jail."

"—my sight for a couple of hours, and you're in trouble again."

"What trouble am I in?"

"Fashion trouble. Look in the mirror."

"With your haircut, you can't give anyone advice about what's in fashion and what's not." I paused while he tried hard not to look insecure.

"With your fingerprints in the victim's lap, you have no cause to sound high-and-mighty," he threw back after a moment.

"Her lap? I swear I wasn't doing anything kinky with Wilma. The cat was the only one in her lap."

"There was a videotape." Scythe arched both eyebrows, and that said it all.

The porn tape. Argh. "I was just trying to get the cat off."

"The cat? One would think you were getting Wilma off, then offed her." Scythe grinned. Big. Jerk.

Uh-oh. "What was the video? I mean, what was the title?"

"*Daring Duos Doing It,*" Scythe answered sternly, then busted up laughing.

I sniffed. The rank smell was nearby, not just on the breeze. It was dog doo.

"Now that you've provided some comic relief, it's time for you to stay out of the investigation," Scythe ordered, completely sobered up from his little titter fit.

"I'll stay out of the Barrister murder when you are on the right track," I put in with a chin jut for emphasis.

"And what track is that?"

"That Lexa didn't do it. That the person who did it is a major whack job who had a personal vendetta against Wilma and wanted to tarnish her image and that of her family. Anyone who would risk the time to defile her with the makeup and sprayed-stiff hair killed her for a bigger reason than just to be rid of her. The case could hinge on whether the makeup and hair job was done posthumously or not. Surely the medical examiner could tell you that."

"Why do you think it matters? Maybe Wilma did it herself."

"Believe me, the woman wasn't flirting with the idea of becoming a rodeo clown, then accidentally met a bullet. When you get to know Wilma, you'll know she'd only look like a clown over her dead body."

"I guess she proved that."

"The hard way," I admitted, then looked at the soles of my shoes and the ground around where we were standing. No poo.

"Is this what you're looking for?" He pulled a Ziploc containing a brush and a bottle of Main Mane triple-super-extra-hold out of his jacket's interior pocket. Some brown stuff was smeared on the inside of the bag.

"Gross!" I backed up a couple of steps and nearly fell

off my Plexiglas perch. "What kind of guy goes around with a bag full of dog doo in his jacket pocket?"

"A guy investigating a murder. It's better than blood."

I grimaced. "I don't know about that."

"Could this have been what was used on Wilma's hair?"

"Where did you get this?"

"From inside a doggie-doo scooper sitting next to a trash can in the alley a block from the Barrister home. An enterprising patrol officer found it."

I wrinkled my nose harder. For some reason, knowing what was smelling made it stink worse. "I hope he got a commendation for reaching in and getting it."

"He called Manning to take care of that."

That made me smile.

"Check for Wilma's hair." I studied the bristles through the plastic. They looked like they'd been picked clean, but I saw a couple of potentially conclusive broken strands of hair. "The hairspray will be a match, though. No question, this is what lacquered her hair to a standstill. It's a shame the company couldn't use this as a selling point."

"What did you find out in there?" Scythe nodded toward the house.

"Tears and sneers."

"Sounds like a rap song."

"Wilma was a fund-raising icon who was universally respected and just as universally hated. Your list of potential suspects could probably include everyone attending the party in there. Except I did hear one woman say Wilma deserved to be killed, although I'm skeptical she had anything to do with something that could lead to a broken fingernail."

Scythe whipped out his notebook. "What's her name?"

"Charis. I didn't hear her last name, but how many Charises could there be?"

As Scythe scribbled, I watched a car ease up next to where his Crown Vic was parked a few cars from mine.

"You know you're being followed?" I cocked my head toward the dark sedan, where a man at the wheel was studying me intently.

"Yes." Scythe looked sheepish, then waved his hand in the air. "It's one of our guys. My boss ordered it. Apparently there's some buzz around the jailhouse that my life's been threatened."

"Oh, really?" I said casually, praying that the pounding in my chest would not vibrate the raccoon hairs enough for him to notice. I strove to hold a convincing look of innocent interest. "A perp you locked up?"

"No. Someone I have some, ah, personal history with."

Personal history? Leave it to a guy to come up with that euphemism for doing the nasty.

"I see," I said with a little too much knowledge in my voice, because he narrowed his eyes.

"What do you see?"

"That it's something you can't really talk about."

"Exactly," he answered, relieved to be rid of the subject. Hmmm.

I really should've been feeling guilty for framing Zena for my crime-of-the-big-mouth, but I wasn't. If life were fair, she would be locked up purely for giving Scythe that bad haircut. My gaze must have lingered a little too long on his sideburns, because his right hand flew to his hair. "What?"

"Oh, I'm just thinking."

"About what?" Defensive. Down, boy.

I was really thinking about all the "hims" and "hers" the Carricaleses had mentioned. That still didn't make sense. "Do you think Wilma had a boyfriend?"

"No, but Alexandra does. And Wilma hated him."

"How do you know?"

"The Carricaleses told me. They don't know his name, just that he's pale, skinny, wears black, and slinks around like he's crawled out from under a rock. They did add that he's polite. I guess you didn't know this?" he asked skeptically.

"No." On one hand, I was pleased that Lexa had a boyfriend; on the other, I was worried because he sounded a little weird.

"You were good enough friends that she'd call you to come help with her dead mom, but not good enough to tell about her boyfriend? Doesn't sound like any woman I know."

"Maybe you should keep less stereotypical female company."

"Hey, I'm standing here talking to you, aren't I? I couldn't find a less stereotypical female." He raised that right eyebrow in direct challenge. I refused to bite. "As for your friend, she may not be a stereotypical female, but she may be a stereotypical murderer."

"What do you mean?"

"Lots of women have been known to team up with loverboy to off Mommy Dearest, then frame someone else for the murder, especially a sappy, gullible pal."

"Oh, get creative, Scythe. Not every murder is a domestic conspiracy."

"This one is shaping up to be. Did your friend call to see if you'd gotten out of jail? Or to apologize for getting you in this pickle? No?" He reached over and plucked the barrette out of my hair and stuck it in his pocket. I was so distracted by his inference that I didn't react. "Since I can't snap a photo of your toes, I need some souvenir of my visit to Reyn in the Land of the League." Scythe strode away, pausing as he reached his car to throw over his shoulder, "Maybe your friend Alexandra planned for you to take the fall from the get-go."

I knew what he was trying to do. He wanted to raise suspicions between Lexa and me so he'd wriggle all the secrets out of both of us. Maybe he wanted me to get so mad or scared I'd rat on Lexa. He ought to know me better than that.

Scythe said something to his bodyguard as he reached for his door handle. Well, he wasn't the only one who could play head games. "Scythe, watch your back."

He froze. The bodyguard drew his sunglasses down his nose and stared at me. I smiled apologetically. "Considering the threat, that is. Just be careful. I'm worried about you. Of course, the smell of the evidence in your pocket is enough to ward away predators for miles."

The bodyguard winked at me. Scythe shook his head and got in the car.

It nearly took an act of God to extract Trudy and Daffy from the party. Trudy was deep in conversation with a woman who'd grown up in the projects and was now in her second year in the League. Trudy had mentored her in the pregnancy prevention program, had helped her get into community college, and now was her sponsor in an advanced-degree fashion design program. She and Trudy were planning on presenting an idea for a mentoring program to reach more girls in the projects. I had to admit, Trudy was right. Not all the members were hypocritical airheads. I remembered Charis and her buddies and Ostrich Feather. Well, partly right, anyway.

I left Trudy to wrap things up and went, application in hand, in search of Daffy. Charlotte found me first. She had a salmon taquito half in her mouth. She bit into it and offered me the other half. I shook my head and tried not to gag as she waxed poetic about the chow. "Isn't the food the best? I love the Brie. Have you tried the Brie? I had to have about a pound of it and I just want more. Oh, there's Berry Wiendsterger. She is the coolest. You know *In Style* magazine came to her house to see her jewelry collection and did a whole spread that's going to be in the next issue? Oh, and the chocolate mousse cheesecake is the bomb. I mean, it is so good I feel like I *died* and went to heaven."

We were just passing a group of sixtysomething women huddled together, speaking in low tones. They stopped and glared at us.

Charlotte flushed and stammered. I apologized for her. "It was just a figure of speech. I know, probably ill-timed, considering the Barrister murder."

"Wilma," one woman wailed, blowing her nose into a silk handkerchief. "She was a saint."

Saint of hell, maybe.

"With all she had to deal with at home. She certainly is sitting at the right hand of God."

Huh? "Oh? I thought she had a nice family life."

"That son of hers, he was always her favorite, and always such a perfect angel as a child. To have him be what he is now . . . well, it's just sacrilegious. Wilma doesn't deserve this. And that girl. She breaks her mother's heart. She won't do anything she was raised to do. You know, she even refuses to . . ." She paused for dramatic effect. I leaned in for the great sin, which I was sure would be not wearing underwear or something like that. "Refuses to join the League."

"No!" I shuddered in mock horror. They all nodded solemnly.

"Poor Wilma. I wouldn't be surprised if she'd killed herself, with all the burdens she had to shoulder."

I couldn't even conjure an image of dictatorial Wilma as a pitiful victim of circumstance. The only way that woman would have killed herself would be to get someone else in trouble. Hmm. I hadn't considered that.

"And that husband of hers."

I perked up, temporarily abandoning the suicide theory. "Percy?"

"He's a flirt. After he hit middle age, he became quite the ladies' man, that one."

For what kind of ladies was the unibrowed, garlic-scented troll a flirt? Blind ones born without olfactory nerves?

"So he had girlfriends," I offered.

All their hands went to their chests. They did a silent vote, and the one who'd spoken first shook her head. "No, but his roving eye, well, that did weigh on poor Wilma's heart."

I was just glad to hear Wilma had one. "Did she ever

do anything about it?" Maybe the eye candy got even
when Percy couldn't do any more roving.

"Oh, no," said Silk Hanky with a sniff. "She just suf-
fered in silence."

Apparently not too silently, because these old gals
knew all about it. I suppose everyone's character was automatically elevated upon death by those feeling guilty
about not treating her well enough in life. I reviewed
the assembled matrons. Hmmm.

"Thank Gucci, Reyn! I thought you'd never get back
with the ever-important *documento*," Daffy sang in my
ear. I noticed the matrons had recoiled. I'd guess Daffy
wasn't their sort of woman, since from a distance she
could pass for Trudy's younger sister instead of her
mom. Besides which, she wasn't wearing support hose
or carrying a Coach bag. For an instant I was proud of
Daffy for being different. It only lasted a moment.
"Look at you," she fussed. "You lost your barrette. Your
fur is ruffled and I daresay you've scuffed my Manolos."
Heavy, ominous sigh. "You're going to need a lot more
work than I thought before we can take you anywhere
and claim you."

Snatching the paper out of my hand, she hooked her
three-inch nails in my raccoon cuff and dragged me away
from the gaggle of grannies. "*Excusez-mois*," Daffy called
back. "I've got to make this provision-al offici-al."

Oh, dear. This was worse than that year my friends
dared me to try out for a part in the school production
of *National Velvet* and I didn't make it, which was
probably a good thing because Midge Cassidy who got
the part of Velvet tripped on her cardboard horse and
broke her leg in four places. Had it been me, I proba-

bly would've broken both legs. I hadn't wanted the part then, and didn't want to be in the Junior League now, but I have this irrational fear of rejection. Even when it involves things I don't want. I took a deep breath and reminded myself how all usually works out for the best.

Except maybe for Wilma.

The membership chair took the application with a fake smile that made me want to yank it back out of her hands. I resisted the impulse and left Daffy to talk me up. "Reyn is world-renowned for her creativity as a beauty consultant . . ."

Hey, Daff, I just dye, cut, and curl hair.

". . . and is incredibly eloquent . . ."

Especially with those four-letter words.

Thankfully, I got out of earshot before I could elaborate eloquently about my worldwide renown. I'd negotiated through the maze of fiberglass nails, David Yerman jewelry, and Chanel No. 5 and was almost to the front door when Charlotte caught me. Damn.

"Reyn, you can't leave yet!" She was holding a cup of cappuccino and nibbling a biscotto. "The party's not over. There's some pâté left."

"Charlotte, I have to go see a friend of mine."

"What friend could be more important than this?"

I hated to burst her bubble and give her just a glimmer of painful life perspective, but, hey, I was in a hurry. "Alexandra Barrister is the friend I have to go see."

"Oh." Charlotte swallowed the biscotto whole. I wondered if it would travel down her throat like a snake's dinner, but I couldn't see a thing. And I looked. "I'll go with you."

"No, Charlotte, that won't be necessary."

"I refuse to let you go alone."

Swell. I wish I were meaner and tougher, but the truth is, when it comes to hurting someone's feelings, I am an absolute wuss. Sighing, I opened the door and let her bounce along next to me, talking a mile a minute about everything and nothing.

I was sure Lexa wouldn't open up to me with Motor-mouth around. Oh, well, I'd go by and see how she was doing, and then maybe drop Charlotte off and go back to the House of Horrors.

We pulled out past the limestone barrier that rivaled the Great Wall of China, and I negotiated the twenty thousand stop signs in the one-point-three miles between the two homes. We were almost to Guaraty Road when I heard Charlotte say, ". . . works for Percy Barrister."

"Who works for Percy Barrister?"

Charlotte looked slightly miffed, her expression telling me I'd missed a lot of the conversation. "One of my friends from high school, Annette Hastings. She took a year off before law school and is working as his paralegal–slash–executive assistant to make sure she wants to specialize in tax law when she graduates. And to ensure she gets a scholarship. Mr. Barrister is a big alum at St. Mary's Law."

"She's smart," I said, and Charlotte brightened with the knowledge that I'd actually started to listen to her again.

"She says Mr. Barrister has been so edgy lately, and he's overtired, falling asleep in his office."

I thought about his arrival time that morning. All those late nights. Hmm.

"And then he started getting weird packages."

"What kind of weird packages?"

"I don't know. I didn't ask."

Even if Charlotte had asked, she probably wouldn't have shut up long enough for poor Annette to answer. She must have seen the look on my face, because she rushed to trivialize it.

"Come on, it's a tax law office. After all, anything not shaped like an eight-by-fourteen-by-three legal document is probably considered weird."

"Probably, but you really should tell Annette to talk to the police about the packages."

Charlotte whipped out her phone and dialed while I negotiated the Barristers' intercom. Maria Carricales had doubts about letting the woman she'd last seen being led out by the cops back into the compound, but her husband prevailed on her to have mercy on me. Meanwhile, Charlotte held her finger over the receiver, her smooth, guileless face rumpled in worry.

"Annette says she can't talk to the police. Mr. Barrister ordered her not to tell the cops anything or else she'll lose her job and her chance to get back into law school. And, worst of all, her scholarship."

Percy, not a smooth move.

"But she says she's worried enough about what's gone on that she'll tell you what she knows."

Enough to worry Percy.

"You have to swear not to tell anyone where you found out. I told her you were the most loyal person I knew, that if you made her a promise, you'd keep it to the death."

I repressed a shiver as I noticed Wilma's luxury sedan

parked in front of the house. How odd. "Hopefully, it won't come to that."

Charlotte had the grace to look embarrassed that her runaway mouth had added that tidbit.

"Tell her to meet me at the salon in an hour."

As we pulled even with the Jaguar, the front door flew open. Lexa skipped down past the bloodthirsty lions, waved at us, flashing a diamond-studded Rolex, and hopped into the front seat.

She was wearing Chanel.

She was carrying a Prada purse.

And in her hair was a jeweled barrette.

 ten

I'D HAD TO NEARLY THROW MYSELF in front of the silver Jag to keep Lexa from driving off. Now she refused to get out of the damned car.

"Come on, Alexandra. Let's go inside and have scones." Charlotte almost licked her lips. "And a cup of Earl Grey."

"Or a brandy," I offered, figuring that's the type of thing they likely had in this Scottish barbarian knockoff. With the white-knuckled way Lexa was gripping the steering wheel, it looked like she needed something stronger than tea, too. "Or a shot of tequila," I added, ever helpful.

Lexa shook her head. "I'm not hungry or thirsty. I'm fine. Just fine."

Uh-huh.

"Well, I need something. Something *strong*," I emphasized, and, after the last twenty-four hours I'd had, that was no lie.

"Make yourselves at home, please," Lexa said, turning the key in the ignition, staring hard out the windshield. "The bar is fully stocked. Dad's out, but the Carricaleses are in."

I wondered where Percy could be during what my gran calls "dark-thirty," the night after he came home to find his wife had been murdered. Hmm.

"Lexa," I said, putting my hand on her forearm. She jumped like I'd scalded her. She'd never been a touchy-feely person, but that reaction was extreme. "You need to talk, to cry, to grieve and be around people who care about you."

"Actually, I think I need to let loose on the road. Alone. That should clear my head well enough."

"Your head doesn't need clearing. Your emotions do."

"How would you know what I need?" she snapped, still staring straight ahead. I was glad to hear it. I hoped she unleashed a whole lot more.

I prodded her. "I suppose I *would* venture to know what you need after I helped you fix up your dead mother and then spent all night at the jailhouse, thanks to you."

"I'm sorry for what happened," Lexa whispered. A single tear trailed from the outside corner of her eye. "It's my fault. It's all my fault."

"No," I jumped in, even though I knew I should let her keep talking. Her face just broke my heart. "I could have said no when you called for help."

"You don't understand. It is all my fault that Mother died."

Charlotte's eyebrows rose so high that, if they could have levitated above her head, they would have. For once she remained speechless. My heart caught in my throat for a moment, and I couldn't even grunt. Was Scythe right after all? My tongue finally came alive. "Did you kill her?"

"I might as well have."

"What do you mean?"

"I should have been here with her that evening." Lexa paused. A tear leaked out the other eye. "But I wasn't."

"Why weren't you?" I asked carefully.

She just shook her head.

"Were you with your boyfriend?"

She stiffened. "I don't have a boyfriend."

I sighed. "Lexa, the police know you have a boyfriend."

"A lot of people who live in this freakland are going to say a lot of things about me," Lexa said, defensiveness dripping from each word. "Some of it true and some of it false. The cops are just going to have to sift through it on their own."

"That's the problem, Lex," I put in gently. "The cops around here probably aren't real good at the sifting process. No practice."

"Too bad."

I looked at Charlotte, but she just shook her head helplessly. Great, just when I needed a verbal boost, Motormouth went mute.

"Okay, Lexa, let's say you don't have a boyfriend. Then tell me why you've gone designer on me."

Unexpectedly, Lexa opened the door and put out a leg. "You like it?"

On closer inspection, the suit's mango-colored silk was even finer than I'd thought. Certainly no ordinary

Chanel. Or was that an oxymoron? As I debated that, I noticed Lexa's calves. Had they been shaved? She was wearing actual pantyhose and mango and black Ferragamo pumps. The Prada bag of many colors looked brand-new.

"Mother always wanted me to dress this way, so now I'll dress this way. It's the least I can do for her. It will be my own personal memorial."

"I don't think they'll let you wear Chanel in jail, Lexa," I pointed out.

She shrugged.

Uh-oh. Guilt was setting in. But guilt for what? Not being there to prevent the murder, for never being the daughter Wilma wanted, or something more sinister? "Where did you get all this stuff?"

"I went to Saks Fifth Avenue today."

Shopping instead of planning the funeral. I'm sure that looked good to the police. No wonder Scythe was after her ass.

Charlotte was nodding. "Therapeutic shopping. I do that all the time."

Along with therapeutic eating. But, hey, I did that too, along with therapeutic snipping sometimes. Face it, we were all head cases in one way or another. Some of us just hid it better than others.

"But I doubt the visit to Saks made you feel any better, did it, Lexa?"

She drew her mouth into a tight line and pivoted on the seat, slamming the car door. "I'm going to do what Mother would've wanted me to do. I should have done it all while she was alive. Then maybe she'd still *be* alive."

"What else are you going to do now—go to law school or marry a lawyer, or both?"

Lexa threw the Jag into drive. I knew I was being pushy, maybe a bit cruel, but I had to be. The police thought her behavior was something like that of the Munchkins in *The Wizard of Oz* who danced around singing "Ding-dong, the wicked witch is dead," but this weirdness was really something else altogether. She felt terribly guilty, that was clear, but I could've sworn her actions were atonement for past sins, not for the murder. How could I explain that to the domestic-murder fans along with whatever she was hiding?

"I guess your boyfriend could go to law school and solve the whole dilemma for you."

The tires squealed on the cobblestones as she peeled out. Charlotte, ever the overly dramatic, screeched and jumped back. I just stood there and nearly got my toes run over, watching her zoom down the driveway only to have to wait for the gate to open with the speed of a sloth. Kind of ruined the effect of a burned-rubber getaway.

Reality. Sometimes it really sucked.

Especially when I was gypped out of my shot of Cuervo Gold.

The Carricaleses were no help with clarifying the hims and hers who were doing this and that to each other. Maria looked nauseated that she'd blurted out the whole thing in front of the potential murderer (me), and José looked sorry that I cared what any of it meant (because I was a nice girl and needed to be home doing cross-stitch or something, whatever nice girls do). Even emphasizing that I was trying to use their information to help keep Lexa out of jail didn't sway them. I guess they trusted the guys in blue more than they trusted me. Or maybe Percy paid them to keep their traps shut. Go figure. Oh, well, we got something out the deal anyway. I got to taste some hundred-year-old brandy, and Charlotte got to eat a couple pieces of chocolate torte.

I delivered Charlotte back to her car at the Hanson compound and headed home to meet her friend, who'd stipulated that Charlotte not be there. She won big points with me for that, since Charlotte had a mouth with no sensors. If she'd been present, whatever this girl told us would end up as part of gossip central in no time. I pulled up in front of my house, and felt that little rush of pride I still got whenever I saw the sign for Transformations.

I'd let the dogs in, underwent Char's guilt trip, Cab's adulation, and Beau's studied apathy, and fed them when the doorbell rang. The dogs went wild, nails scraping on my polished oak floors, racing to be the first at the front door.

I held them back and opened up to see a tall young woman whose skin was the color of my morning coffee with a generous splash of cream. She wore her hair about a quarter-inch long, which just complemented her flawless features. By anyone's standards, Annette Hastings was lovely, even though her tight expression and severe dress set her beauty on edge. She wore a heavily starched white cotton blouse tucked with military folds into tailored black slacks so sharply creased they looked capable of slicing cheese. She wore no makeup or jewelry other than a stainless steel watch that told time in at least four time zones and probably went on the Internet, too.

"I guess you've never had a break-in," she observed as she entered, kicking out at the dogs as they tried to greet her. Cab and Char kept trying, but Beau looked slitty-eyed at her and hung back, keeping the unfriendly interloper in her sights.

"You'd think that," I said, closing the door and ushering the group down the hall in the kitchen. "But I have had a guy break in."

Her eyebrows rose, but she didn't ask for details. That was good, since she'd never believe how it happened, anyway.

Annette refused my offers of a drink and asked me to close my wooden blinds. I thought it was a little paranoid, but I complied.

"No one can know I came here."

"Charlotte knows."

"I'm aware of that, but she'll keep quiet."

I must have looked skeptical, because she added, "I have dirt on her."

I held my look. She added, "I had a dozen bagels same-day FedExed from Brooklyn, then videotaped her eating the whole package. Her parents think she's on the Atkins diet. If she falls off the wagon, they say they'll send her to that famous fat farm up in Dallas."

"That's cruel," I said, aghast, and she just nodded.

"Mr. Barrister told me not to tell anyone what's been going on at the office. Not even the police," she said as she claimed the window bench. She had a model's body but moved like a toy soldier. I'd say Annette had issues. Driven to a fault would be one of them, I imagine. Having no perspective beyond her own goals would be another. I certainly would not ever want to be in her way.

"Why did Percy say that?"

She looked down at her watch. Wondering what time it was in Bolivia, maybe? "I don't know. He is a secretive man with an extremely controlling nature. I imagine the fact that the police and media will be into his affairs because of Wilma's murder is making him nervous."

"You think that's all it is?"

"Maybe. Or something he did led to her murder."

"You think so? Why don't you contact the police anonymously?"

Annette shot me a glare that made me flinch. Then, when I didn't back down, she shook her head. "I can't. I know Mr. Barrister has at least one cop on his payroll. Don't ask me why—I won't tell you. Don't ask me who—I don't know. But I can't risk Mr. Barrister finding out I talked. I grew up on the east side without a dime, raised by my grandma. I'm saving money to get into law school, and with my college record, my test scores, and his recommendation and contacts, I'm a shoo-in for a full scholarship at St. Mary's. I will *not* jeopardize that. Not for anything."

I believed her. Percy could come in and murder Annette's grandmother in full view, and Annette wouldn't rat on him and mess up her plans. She was going to make one helluva lawyer. Compromise wasn't a concept she understood, even in conversation.

"Come on, Annette. Why not come clean to the cops now and get it over with? After all, do you really think you're going to get that scholarship if your mentor is arrested for killing his wife?"

"You didn't grow up here in San Antonio, did you?"

"No." I watched her closely, not sure where this was going.

Annette sniffed. "No wonder you don't get it. In the circles we're talking about right now—big-time back-scratching, oh-nine zip codes, and eight-figure net worths—life is very incestuous. Everybody owns every-body else somehow, whether it is through marriage, knowledge, favors, sex, or money. What happens be-tween the cops and my boss won't change what happens inside the circle. Whatever he is owed and how the scholarship pays that particular debt won't change. If he knows I disobeyed his orders, however, he will find some other way to call in payment that doesn't benefit me."

"So why talk to me at all?"

"Because, despite what you may think, I do have a conscience."

No she didn't. She was telling me this for some other reason. Annette saw skepticism in my face and shrugged. "Fine. I have to protect myself on all sides. If Percy Bar-rister is arrested and convicted, then I want to look like I told the truth to someone. I can always say later—after the scholarship is mine, after he is behind bars—that I didn't go to the police because I'd been threatened by him. If what I tell you prevents any more murders, then it makes me look even better in the end."

She was using me, but finally being honest about it. Okay. I could live with that. "You think there are going to be more murders?"

"Maybe. They say things happen in threes."

Now, that creeped me out. The superstitious statement was completely out of character for this woman. She knew something. Probably not what she was about to tell me, but she had juice, no question.

"Okay, Annette, you can tell me whatever you want the police to know, and I will make sure they won't find out where it came from. You have my word."

"I checked you out by another source, or I wouldn't have come."

"Who was the other source?"

"Jon Villita."

"How do you know Jon?"

The way she smiled, I decided I didn't want to know how she knew Jon, my gentle friend. The thought of him knowing this tough cookie was scary.

"I have something on him, too," Annette said with a cold smile, "something that, if you turn on me, I will make public."

What could she have on Jon, a Boy Scout if I ever met one? I had a fertile imagination and I couldn't conjure a single possibility, that's how squeaky-clean this friend was. I guessed by checking me out with Jon and Charlotte, she'd determined that I was fiercely loyal. An Achilles' heel I was proud of. An Achilles' heel that had almost killed me once.

Before I could mull her threat any further, she got down to business. "So we understand each other?"

Annette apparently understood me better than I understood her, but I nodded. She began: "About a year ago, Mr. Barrister started to get what became a series of odd packages. In retrospect, they started coming after his first visit from a pair of men from south of the border—they were well dressed but low-class."

"Trying to make themselves silk purses out of sow's ears?" I asked.

Annette cocked her head at me. Oops, sometimes you couldn't take the country out of the girl. Maybe she understood me less than she'd first thought.

"Anyway," Annette continued, "despite their designer suits, these cats were dangerous. You could feel it when they walked into the room."

"The kind that carry guns under their coats?"

Annette shook her head. "The kind who carry switch-blades in their shoes."

"I've only known one man like that. He was caught gutting small animals for fun."

"Uh-huh. I think that was just a warm-up for these cats. Anyway, they arrived unannounced and met with Mr. Barrister, and he was a nervous wreck for a week after they'd gone. Then a couple of weeks later I go out to lunch and a package is outside the door to our office. It's addressed to Mr. Barrister, but it hasn't come through the mail system. With all the mail bombs. I thought I better not pick it up, even if he is only a tax lawyer. There's not much people get more worked up about than money, which is what taxes are all about. I called him. He went ghosty white, picked up the pack-age, and locked himself in his office without another word. I have to admit, I didn't wait to see if it was a mail bomb or not, because I figured I'd hear it from the restaurant if it was."

"That's cold," I couldn't help saying. "You didn't care if he got blown up?"

"I guess that's the difference between me and you. You'd probably blow yourself up before you'd stand around and watch someone you know get rearranged, huh?" Her tone said I was an idiot.

"That's true. I'm proud to be that way."

That set Annette back a second or two. I'd bet she wasn't used to people getting one up on her, especially idiots. She cleared her throat and continued, "When I got back from lunch, there was no sign of the package. We got a couple more visits from a pair of Mexican men, different ones, but the same in that they were dangerous and well dressed, and one spoke impeccable English, the other none. The packages would come a short time later. Same scenario, but twice Mr. Barrister called me to dispose of something in a garbage sack that felt like animal body parts. The last package I did see by accident, because I walked in when he was opening it. . . ."

Annette paused and swallowed hard. Even the memory rattled her. That was saying something, as she was the most self-possessed woman I'd ever met. I gave her a minute to compose herself. She cleared her throat and straightened her spine. "It was a photo of the Barrister family when the kids were in high school. The glass on the frame had been shattered, blood splattered over the photo."

"Uh-oh, that sounds like a threat to me. Are you sure these Mexican guys were the ones who sent it?"

"Where and how they left it, the brown paper wrapping, even the writing was the same."

"Did you tell Percy he ought to call the police then?"

"I did. He just shook his head, went into his bathroom, and vomited for about ten minutes, then told me to throw the thing away in a Dumpster on my way home, which is what I'd done with the other packages."

"When did the bloody frame arrive?"

"Less than a week ago."

"Where did you drop it?"

"At a strip mall across from the theaters along I-10. You know a lot of those places lock up their Dumpsters, so I had to wait until someone came out to dump something and went back in for more. That's when I slipped the frame in there. It was the third Dumpster in the row."

"So it sounds like these Mexican guys were the most likely suspects—either they were blackmailing Percy over some secret, or he was involved in some dealings with them that went sour."

"Maybe." She reviewed her perfect, unadorned nails.

"You don't sound certain. You have a better suspect?"

"Well, I have to say that Mr. Barrister's girlfriend—"

I slapped my hands down on the table in surprise. "Percy has a girlfriend?"

"He always has a girlfriend."

The unibrow troll must have some major pheromones I didn't detect. Or maybe a lot of women were in dire need of some free tax-law advice. Wouldn't the old gals from the Junior League be surprised that Percy did more than look? "Any of his old girlfriends jealous of the new one?"

"They aren't bitch-slapping each other in the lobby over his affections or anything like that. Frankly, if they won't let go when he's done with them, I think he threatens to send the IRS after them."

One way to cut off an affair. "How chivalrous."

She shrugged. And waited.

I had to nudge her again. "I'm sorry I interrupted. You were saying about his current girlfriend?"

"She may be the real deal. He's been different with her. He's really in love this time."

"So maybe Percy took care of Wilma to clear the way for happily-ever-after for him and his sweetie."

Annette shook her elegant head. "Mr. Barrister wouldn't have done that. He was too afraid of Wilma and too used to having all her money. Tax law doesn't necessarily pay well enough to keep up the standard of living that Wilma's family inheritance did. I overheard him on the phone a couple of weeks ago, telling his girl-friend that if Wilma preceded him in death, all but an allowance for him and the children goes into a trust for future grandchildren."

I'd bet Annette overheard a lot that went on in Percy's life. Poor man had better nominate her for the scholarship, or else. "Kind of an odd conversation to have with a girlfriend. Although if she was considering killing Percy's wife, I guess that would've thrown a damper on her plans instead of inciting them."

"Not necessarily," Annette argued. "She might have just wanted Wilma out of the way. And when you think about it, Mr. Barrister's allowance and salary probably are enough for her, a working-class girl. The news said Wilma was shot and left in a degrading position. While it could've been Mr. Barrister's Mexican visitors, I also think Shauna Rollins could've shot her with no compunction."

"Where can I find her?"

"She's got a converted cottage she uses as an office on North New Braunfels. From what I hear, she's an expert of sorts, plans to start traveling all over the country."

"Expert in what?"

"Makeup."

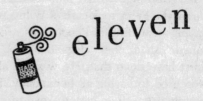

eleven

BY THE TIME ANNETTE LEFT, in her convincingly coldhearted way reminding me she knew where I lived, how much I loved my dogs, and who all my friends were, it was after midnight. I was itching to go see Shauna Rollins, but doubted that she'd be doing somebody's makeup at the witching hour, unless it was another customer in Wilma's state of unbeing. And if that was the case, I didn't want to be walking in on the two of them.

Besides, when I sat down on the couch to plan my sleuthing around my next workday (hey, I had to make a living) and how I should diplomatically relay all the goodies I'd learned to Scythe, I zonked out. After all, I had been awake about forty hours straight. Even the leftover moo goo gai pan I'd taken out of the freezer to thaw couldn't keep me awake.

I dreamed about mutilated animals with clown makeup, Lexa in Valentino in a Jag running the Junior League, and Scythe marrying Zena Zolliope. When I woke up surrounded by my dogs on the couch, I was humming a song that had something to do with an armadillo, a cowboy boot with a golden heel, and a palomino Appaloosa in a limo stocked with Perrier on their way to Bismarck. I was a little afraid that somebody had slipped something funny into the canapés I'd tasted at the Junior League function when I heard the second verse of the song and realized I wasn't crazy or high—it was coming through the half-open window on the Ugartes' side of my house. Rick Ugarte had evidently been up working all night, and this was the result. My neighbor was a songwriter, once of rock but now, thanks to my complaints, of country. He'd sold one about me and my mostly fictional shenanigans. Lyle Lovett was said to be interested in a couple of others, including this one. I'd bet money.

I threw a grumbling Beau off my legs and stretched. Her two daughters jumped up and licked me before running to the door to go out. In my bra and panties, I shuffled over and opened the door, then ground some Costa Rican coffee beans and set the pot to brew. I wandered back into the living room and swore. I'd shucked the designer raccoon wear before passing out, and Char had apparently slept on it, chewing a little on one cuff sometime during the night. I grimly examined the dog-slobbered fur and knew my first stop had to be the miracle-worker dry cleaner. I could guess how much outfits straight off Milan's catwalk cost, and I'd have to sell my truck to replace this hideous thing.

What a great start to a Monday.

Sipping my coffee, I found the address of Shauna's business, Makeup Magic with Shauna, in the yellow pages. Reviewing my appointments, I decided I could pay her a visit about ten that morning between a perm and a foil highlight. As for Scythe, I hadn't quite decided how to tell him my treasure trove of information. Maybe Shauna would implicate herself or, better yet, confess, and I wouldn't have to tap-dance around Annette's involvement. He could pull out my toenails, and I wasn't ratting her out. I'd decided that when she pulled out her key ring with a black and white rabbit's foot. When I'd asked where she'd gotten it, she flashed this queer little smile that reminded me she'd disposed of Percy's mutilated gift animals. Uh-oh. Maybe she was into recycling.

I hadn't completely disposed of the notion that she might be on Percy's list of girlfriends and was setting me off on a wild-goose chase with the story about mean Mexicans and sexy Shauna. Frankly, ambitious Annette scared me a little, so I was hoping someone else would pan out as a murder suspect.

The doorbell rang me out of my reverie. I grabbed a gingham tablecloth out of the buffet drawer and wrapped it around me. As I passed the mirror, I saw my reflection and yipped out a short scream. My plastered-down flip-out do had, with eighty percent humidity, ten pounds of hairspray, and six hours on a couch pillow, morphed into something out of *Aliens Among Us*.

The bell was ringing wildly, then something thumped against the door. It flew open and my new receptionist, Bettina Huyn, having shouldered open the door, stumbled into the foyer. The door latch hung at a funny angle. So much for the lock. I guess I'd have to get Bettina a key to my house as well as the salon if she insisted on doing any more Rambo imitations. "Are you okay, Reyn?" she asked in a deep baritone. "Why did you scr—" Then she saw me and, hand to chest, screamed before she could finish.

"What the hell happened to your hair, girlfriend?" Bettina moaned, having recovered her feminine alto. Bettina (aka Bert) was an attractive Korean undergoing a series of operations to change her into a woman. She worked as a dancer at a transvestite club at night and for me during the day. Trudy said she gave my salon's name, Transformations, a new meaning. As a small-business owner, I had bad luck with receptionists—I hadn't been able to keep one more than six months. My last one, Sherlyn Rocca, was getting close to setting a new record when I found her doing the nasty on the reception desk with the Redken supplier. That might not have been a firing offense, except that the Biolage supplier walked in on them and got jealous—it was apparently his "turn"—and knocked the Redken guy through the original front window of my historic residence, which cost a fortune to replace. It had pissed me off.

Bettina needed the money, so I was giving her a go. So far, so good, except for the days she didn't wake up early enough to put her woman together and had to come as a man. Some of my clients thought I had two receptionists. Some thought they were brother and sister. Some just stayed confused.

"The line at Starbucks was ten miles long, so I came over to get a decent cup of java so I could function this morning. You know"—she paused—"gingham really isn't your pattern." Bettina eyed my makeshift shift, then reviewed the wreck of my living room, waving toward the suit on the couch. "What died?"

"A raccoon. I had to go to a Junior League party last night with Daffy, Trude, and Charlotte."

"Hey, maybe those society girls are a lot more interesting than I gave them credit for, what with animal sacrifices, New Age hairdos, and gingham togas."

"Very funny." I rolled my eyes. "The corpse on the couch is part of Daffy's million-dollar designer suit that Char got a bit too friendly with."

Bettina scooped it up. "I've got a tailor who can do wonders. I'll make it right."

"Thank you. I owe you."

"What you owe me for is not taking a blackmail photo of you right now, girlfriend." She chuckled. "Wouldn't Scythe pay the big bucks to see you this way!"

"Don't even think about it," I warned. I had enough trouble getting him to take me seriously.

"Nah, I like you owing me. I'll take this over at my lunch hour." With a wave, she vanished into the salon.

In the shower, I shampooed my hair fourteen times to clear it of the hairspray, then re-created my Meg Ryan messy with a sigh of relief. I'd tried for years to cover up my freckles, and at thirty gave up. Now I just wore the minimum of makeup. I dabbed on transparent foundation that I used just for the sunscreen value, and mascara, a must, because God shorted me on eyelashes. If you want proof that life is not fair, just look at my brothers, Dallas and Chevy. Their lashes are so long they brush their eyebrows. Grown women swoon when those boys blink. Without mascara, no one could tell if I blinked. They got the thick, black, naturally curly hair, too, the bastards. My sisters and I got the fine, straight, dirty-blond hair. I find being naturally blond terribly boring, so I dye it various colors. Right now I was going conservative.

I gave the girls their breakfast and let myself into the salon through the kitchen. A couple of the stylists who work with me were already on the brush. Enrique was rolling a blue-hair's perm. Cameron was doing her weekly style on a local newscaster. Uh-oh. I'd forgotten Amethyst Andrews came in on Mondays. I tried to slink by. Too late.

"Reyn?" That fakey newscaster voice always sounded wrong coming out of anything but a TV. The bobbed brunette with the Pan-Cake makeup spread her rose-red lips in a semblance of a smile. "Reyn Mar-ten Saw-yer. I need to talk to you."

I'd refused to turn on the television or radio this morning because I really didn't want to hear my name associated with another murder. Being mixed up in Ricardo's was bad enough, although, ironically, it did increase my business. Life's warped.

"How are you, Amethyst?" I'd found in my brief dealings with the on-air talent that shifting the focus back on them was sometimes an effective distraction technique.

"Fabulous! Thanksforasking! Ratingsareup, you know."

She talked that way, running four and five words together to sound like one. I don't think she ever took a breath.

"We are now number one at six. Our consultant says it's the new set and our new investigative segment that he recommended but I think it's that viewers are tuning in to see the rapport between me and Mark. We've developed a trust with the viewership and something strong like that takes time to develop, longer than one rating period. Don't you agree?" I would've liked to see Amethyst in a conversation with Charlotte. They'd probably talk right over one another like my mother's sisters.

"Oh, yes." I nodded sagely. "Without a doubt."

Bettina stuck her head around the corner and called down the hall, "Your eight o'clock is in the chair, Reyn."

That wo-man was getting a raise.

"Oops, gotta go, Amethyst. Talk to you later."

Poor Amethyst's face clouded as she realized that her ego had eaten up her opportunity to get the scoop on Wilma's murder. "Can I call you later, Reyn?"

"Anytime." *Call all you want, I won't answer.*

Jessica Szabo sat in my chair studying a chemistry textbook. She was a hardworking, hard-partying college student who was going to make a great physician someday. She'd been accepted into medical school and was just trying to tie up her hours as an undergrad. Jess always asked for the style worn by the girlfriend of her favorite member of the group Limp Bizkit. Since he always had a different girlfriend, we were always changing her hair. Today she presented a photo from the Internet—I recognized the color as RubyRedSlipper and the cut as a graduated buzz. There was no use trying to talk Jess out of it. I'd tried that before. Instead, I got to work mixing the color.

"What did the on-air-head want?"

I smiled at her pun and whispered back, "I never let her get to it, but I'm guessing she wanted to ask me about Wilma Barrister's murder."

"Probably."

"Was my name mentioned in the news this morning?"

She nodded. "They had a view of this grim-looking house and a Terrell Hills cop car out front. They just said she'd croaked, likely from a gunshot wound, and that you were a friend of the family and among those brought in for questioning."

Hmm. Could've been worse and could've been better. I didn't know whether to thank Scythe for masking the arrest or holler at him for getting my name involved. Oh, well, I guessed I'd gotten myself involved, so I couldn't expect miracles.

I was thankful Jess was my appointment this morning. She was not a gossip, too busy with her own life to want to dig around in other people's, unlike most of my clients. I worked in silence while she went over chemical formulas. As I began to rinse out her color, she asked, "How's Alexandra holding up?"

"You know Lexa?"

"Vaguely." Jess shrugged. "She was three years ahead of me at Alamo Heights. I hadn't seen her in years, and met up with her backstage at a Limp Bizkit concert a few months ago. We talked for a few minutes."

"Was she there with a bunch of scuzzbags?"

"No, she was there by herself."

"She went by herself to a concert?" It sounded odd.

"Well, she wasn't there for Bizkit. She said she was there for one of the bands that opened for them. She was pretty cozy with the bassist, little skinny guy—real polite, though, with old-world manners you usually don't find at one of those things, believe me."

Lexa had done a lot of things to bother her mother,

like hang with creeps and listen to headbanger music, but I'd never known her to date any of the pals she picked up. Frankly, I think the idea scared her, like getting romantically involved would be getting in over her head. My heart was pounding at the possibility of another break in the case. One minute I'd had no suspects; now I had at least three. I swallowed and tried to resist hyperventilating. "So they were going out, you think? Lexa and this guy."

"The vibes were definitely there."

"Do you remember his name? Or the name of his band?"

She shook her head, and I nearly drowned her with the spray nozzle I'd forgotten to move away from her rotating head. After we'd dried her off, she continued, "I don't think she ever said his name. And the name of the band escapes me, too. I'm sorry, when I'm around my man I just lose my mind. The name of her boyfriend's band was something gruesome, though—had to do with death."

Swell. I wanted to make sure it was the same guy the Carricaleses had seen. "Dark-haired, pale, thin guy in all black?"

"Yeah, I guess."

Well, that was definitive. I gave her a thumbnail sketch of Lexa's general mental state and she only half-listened, with one eye on her book. After I'd shaved her temples one last time and was sweeping her newly red hair off the floor, Jess turned to me as she shinnied into her ripped jean jacket and said, "Oh, yeah, I remember that the band was a regular at Bangers, a club on Sixth Street in Austin."

Now, with that, I could go somewhere. Bangers, here I come. But first, a makeover from a potential murderess.

I'd called Shauna Rollins and asked for an emergency makeover. I'd just wanted to make sure she'd be in her office and alone. But she had been so sweet and agreeable on the phone that I felt guilty for falsifying my reason for seeing her. I reminded myself I was lying for a good cause, clearing Lexa and myself in the process, although the more I found out about Lexa and her secret life, the more I wondered if I shouldn't stop digging. A couple of reporters, who'd likely gotten run off from the Terrell Hills PD by Manning's halitosis, were sitting in front of my salon. I escaped through my kitchen and borrowed Bettina's puce sports car just in case any of the reporters knew my truck.

Since Monte Vista is adjacent to Alamo Heights, another small city within the big city of San Antonio, I eschewed the highway that ran between the two and cut through neighborhoods. Alamo Heights, like Terrell Hills, is real Old San Antonio and very high-society. It makes historical sense, I suppose. The headwaters of the San Antonio River were the place to be in the seventeenth century, serving as an Indian campground for decades, and later European explorers, missionaries, troops, and visitors congregated there. The area is now home to Brackenridge Park, named after one of the original settlers. To the south is downtown, and to the north are Alamo Heights and Terrell Hills. San Antonio was established as an official city in 1718, but it wasn't until two hundred years later that the city tried to annex

Alamo Heights. The residents wanted to remain unique, so they voted to become a private municipality. It still carries a strong religious influence from being home to Incarnate Word College and the headquarters of the Episcopal Diocese of West Texas.

I imagined Shauna chose to work where the money for luxuries was, hence the quaint little cottage that housed her business on one of two main drags in the posh 78209 zip code. I parked in front and knocked on the fancy stained-glass door as I let myself in. I walked toward the sound of someone humming "You Are My Sunshine." A caramel blonde in her late twenties came from the back of the four-room cottage, ponytail swinging, jeweled zoris twinkling, tiered rainbow minidress floating. She smiled, her wide blue eyes guileless, her face open and sweet. Shauna Rollins looked more like an overgrown child than any adult I'd ever seen. She stared at my outstretched hand for a moment, as if she wasn't sure what to do with it, like she might have hugged me hello instead of giving me the awkward, limp handshake she finally performed.

"I'm looking for Shauna Rollins," I said.

"I'm Shauna. You must be Charade."

When I'd heard that my name was in the news again in connection with Wilma's murder, I knew I had to use an alias to see Percy's girlfriend. On the phone with Shauna earlier, I'd given my sister's first name off the top of my head, not realizing what a double entendre it was. "Yes." I fought to keep a straight face. "That's me."

Her gaze flicked over me. "Boy, you were right. Do you ever need a makeover."

I know that sounded rude, but this girl was so

damned sweet that it didn't come across that way at all. It just seemed refreshingly honest. How come it didn't work that way for me? I said honest things all the time that offended people.

"Why don't you have a seat in here"—she waved an arm toward the kitchen she'd converted into makeup central—"and we'll talk about what kind of lifestyle you lead, so the make over is something that mirrors your personality."

Devil horns and Pinocchio's long nose would work right now. This girl made me feel positively evil for duping her for information.

"I just want something simple."

"Makeup is never simple, Charade. Even the most subtle of cosmetics take a great deal of artistry. Everyone is beautiful in their own way. Bringing out that beauty is just my joy in life." Smiling, she studied me for a moment, humming a bar of "Everything Is Beautiful." I felt a little like I was in *The Twilight Zone*, then felt guilty for being so cynical. "Your hazel eyes are your best feature. I bet we can make them look green or gold or brown depending on our surrounding color choices."

I was beginning to think that Annette definitely had some ulterior motive in putting the heat on sweet Shauna. If Percy was having an affair with her, I couldn't blame him. She was the polar opposite of his demanding, controlling wife. Even if she was the impetus for Percy blowing Wilma away, this girl herself couldn't have killed a fly, much less a human being. I was here, though; might as well try to dig up some more dirt on Percy. Shauna deserved better than a unibrow troll whose kisses undoubtedly tasted like garlic.

"Are you cold?" Shauna asked when I didn't properly suppress my shiver of revulsion.

"I'm okay. I guess someone just walked over my grave, as my gran used to say."

She wrinkled her pretty brow. "Huh?"

"Oh, it has something to do with alternate universes and our souls existing throughout time."

Her brow wrinkled tighter. "I don't understand."

I was afraid she was going to hurt herself. "Never mind. I'm not cold."

"Oh, okay." She nodded, then started humming another bar of "Everything Is Beautiful" as she spun through a color wheel, finding a color and holding it up to my face.

"How long have you been doing makeup?"

"As a business?" she asked. I nodded, and she smiled that wide, hapless grin of hers. "About two months now. My boyfriend set me up in business. It's a good thing, too, because I didn't know what I was going to do to make a living. But he said, do what I was good at. I didn't really want to charge guys for what he always tells me I'm best at"—she paused to blush prettily and giggle—"so I decided to do what I was second-best at— makeup."

Okay. Shauna was sweet, but Shauna was stupid. It was beginning to get on my nerves. Thankfully, the telephone rang in another room. She excused herself to answer it.

I rose and began to scour the room for any clues that Percy was the boyfriend she'd mentioned. I wondered how I could get her to cough up his name. How tricky would I have to be? If it weren't such an unusual name,

I could pretend to have a boyfriend named Percy. I ambled down the hall, looking at the photos presumably of makeover customers. I noticed a room that looked like an office and had nearly passed it by when I did a double take. Was that who I thought it was in a framed photo on the desk? Looking down the hall both ways, I ducked into the office and peered at the photo. It was Annette, arm in arm with Shauna. They looked younger, high-school age, perhaps. Shauna was exhilarated. Annette had forced the smile. Why?

The girls weren't talking. I'd have to get the answer elsewhere. No other photos in the room held any familiar faces besides Shauna's. No Percy. Damn, that would've been too easy. I retreated to the hall and peeked into the next room and nearly had a heart attack.

Clowns.

Photos of hundreds of clowns lined the walls from ceiling to floor. I walked into the dim room and tripped into a clown dummy. I grabbed him by his stuffed shoulders to keep him from sliding off the hat rack where he hung, and came face-to-face with a familiar face.

Wilma's, to be exact.

I screamed.

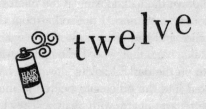

twelve

OKAY, SO IT WASN'T WILMA'S FACE. To be precise, it was a face done in the same clown makeup I'd seen on Wilma's corpse.

It was still freaky.

"Are you afraid of clowns?" Shauna asked as she rushed into the room.

"Of clowns?" I still gripped the poor dummy by the shoulders. "Of course not. I love clowns. In fact, I grabbed this clown for dear life because I saw a . . ." I paused. "A mouse."

"A mouse?! Shauna's hand went to her throat as she jumped backward. "What happened?"

"Well," I explained, making it up as I went along, "the mouse, he ran over my toes and I grabbed this friendly clown to fend off the marauder."

Apparently easily distracted from her rodent paranoia by her clown passion, Shauna smiled as she flipped on the light and gazed around the room. "Yes, that's how I feel about clowns, too. They are wonderful. That's why

I made clown makeup my specialty. I do all the rodeo clowns in South Texas and I'm setting up a schedule of clinics around the country next year."

The room was even more shocking in full Technicolor, with the recessed lighting arranged to spotlight the rows and rows of framed photos. My clown friend was still swinging eerily from his hat rack. I shivered again.

"You *are* cold. You're just too polite to admit it. I'll turn down the air-conditioning."

Shauna disappeared again. The phone rang. I willed the thousand clowns to stop staring at me. Just between you and me, clowns gave me the creeps, always have. She only spoke for a few seconds before she returned. "That was my boyfriend again, just making sure we were okay. I hung up on him when you screamed. Percy is a little sensitive to disaster right now because he just lost his wife. She was murdered."

My eyebrows flying up to my hairline was probably an appropriate response by a stranger to that out-of-the-blue statement. The "hot damn" I was about to say was probably not, so I bit my tongue. Hard.

Those azure eyes blinked at me. Either she'd made me for a fraud and was trying to psych me out, or she was clueless that it might be bad form to admit to an extramarital affair with a dead woman's husband.

"I'm sorry," I finally croaked out when I realized she was waiting for a verbal response.

"Yeah, it's been a real bummer. I haven't been able to see him much with the funeral plans, the police stuff, and all that."

"I imagine."

"Oh, by the way, Percy thought he might know you."

Uh-oh. My breath stuck in my lungs. I felt dizzy. How would Percy know me under my assumed name? Had Shauna described me well enough that he'd caught on to me snooping into his affairs? Had Annette set me up, sending me straight into a trap?

"But then"—Shauna giggled—"I realized he heard me wrong. He thought I said Sherry Aid when I said Charade."

Sherry Aid? Sounded like a stripper who dressed like a nurse. Perhaps one of the stars of the video library in his office?

"You don't dance for a living do you, Charade?"

"No, no. Can't keep a beat to save my life."

Shauna shrugged. "Wrong girl, I guess."

Okay, panic attack averted. Now to figure out how this ding-a-ling and her honey figured into the murder. I sucked in a deep, cleansing breath. Had Shauna had something to do with Wilma's death and had no conscience or apparent fear of discovery? Was it a coincidence that she was interested in clown makeup and had a clown identical to her lover's dead wife's face? Or was someone trying to frame the sweet, empty-headed girl?

Someone like Annette? I wouldn't put it past her if it forwarded her ambitions. Someone like Percy? It might be a way to get away with murder by fobbing it all off on a jealous lover. Someone like Lexa?

I refused to consider that.

I knew I had to get Scythe over there to collect the clown dummy as evidence. I didn't want to leave for fear it would disappear. Maybe I could take Shauna to lunch while the cops got a search warrant. I considered several scenarios.

"You didn't say, Charade, what happened to the mouse? I guess you could tell, I'm deathly afraid of rodents."

"The mouse?" I'd forgotten all about my fib. That was the problem with fibs, you had to keep such close tabs on them; it was just easier to tell the truth. "Uh, the mouse." I did a visual survey of the hardwood floors and the surprisingly tight molding. No potential mouse holes. The clown had a hole in his bootie, however. "The mouse ran into the clown."

With a small yip, Shauna snatched the clown off the rack with lightning speed, raced out the front door, and cocked her arm to throw the clown into the yard. I saw evidence about to take a tumble and, on impulse, grabbed at her arm. My interference sent the clown careening toward Bettina's car instead of the grass, where its porcelain face smashed into a thousand pieces on her hood.

Oops.

"I'm so sorry about your car," Shauna apologized. running to collect the pieces of the clown face off the scratched puce paint, humming "Send in the Clowns."

"I'm so sorry about your clown," I said grimly, meaning it more than she knew.

"I wish you hadn't grabbed my arm," she said, poufing her lip out in a pout.

I had to think fast. My evidence was shattered. The clown shrine might be enough to throw suspicion on Shauna, but it was very circumstantial.

"Let me make it up to you. You could make me up just like your clown dummy. Then you'd at least have a photo to put on your wall until you can get a replacement."

Shauna brightened. "Really? You'd do that for me?"

I gulped. "Sure. I'd love to."

"I'm a clown," I said reluctantly into my cell phone two hours later. I tried to ignore the vanful of toddlers kicking their legs in their car seats, laughing and pointing at me as I sat at the world's longest stoplight.

"I was wondering when you'd admit it," Scythe answered dryly.

"No, really, I look like I'm ready for Ringling Brothers." A man to my left was shouting, "Hey, Bozo!"

"Good for you. Maybe they're hiring. Since you aren't ever working at your real job, might as well get one you're probably more qualified for."

"How do you know I'm not at my job right now?"

"Because I just left there looking for you."

"Why were you looking for me?"

"I'm not telling now. You don't get any goodies if you go sneaking off."

"What kind of goodies? Another set of handcuffs? Another trip to the pokey?"

"Watch out what you say, you're turning me—"

"Besides which," I interrupted, "I didn't sneak off."

"What do you call running off in another vehicle to throw me off?"

"I wasn't trying to throw *you* off, stupid, just the media." I shook my head and the wig went a little askew. I glared at the light through the red curls.

"If you'd stay out of trouble, you wouldn't have the media on your butt."

"If I stayed out of trouble, *you* wouldn't be on my butt, either," I pointed out, my voice rising. I noticed out of the corner of my eye that the toddlers had stopped laughing and instead were looking concerned.

There was a long pause. "You don't know that."

"Yes I do. I was out of trouble for several months, thank you, and heard from you twice." I flipped the receiver the bird. Oops, I'd forgotten I had an underage audience. I smiled benignly at the kids. One of them stuck her tongue out at me.

"I'd think you'd like that," he snapped defensively.

"Like it? I loved it!" I shouted. One of the toddlers started crying and his mother shot me a wicked look as she zoomed off.

"Hmm." Another long pause, during which he was probably thinking about Zena Zolliope's legs.

"Are you going to come to my house right now or not?" I said impatiently before I started to imagine what he was imagining he'd like those long Zolliope legs to wrap around.

"Not. If you have something to show me, come to the police department. You can't be far."

Actually, I had just driven within a block of the Terrell Hills PD, but I wasn't telling him that. "I'm not showing this in public."

Scythe's baritone dropped to a tigerlike purr. "Oh, really? Now, this *is* getting interesting." I squirmed in my seat.

"Interesting enough to come to my house?"

"It depends. If you're ready to culminate our deal, I'll come. If not, I won't."

Damn. I squirmed harder. The temperature of this typical South Texas spring day had climbed from the morning's midfifties to the midnineties by the time I'd gotten out of Shauna's shop. The topic of our conversation drove my temperature up an additional ten degrees. Bettina's little car didn't have air-conditioning. I refused to roll down the windows because the obnoxious guy was keeping even with me, shouting lewd things he'd like to do with clowns. I could feel the oily makeup starting to melt off my face. It was now or never.

"Okay, okay, Scythe. Come get your end of the deal. And bring a camera." I rang off before he could heavy-breathe any harder into the phone.

I tucked my wig under my arm and made a mad dash for the door. I thought I'd made it into my house unseen, but of course I am the unluckiest woman on the planet (not counting Wilma), so I was wrong. My songwriting neighbor appeared at my elbow as I was unlocking my kitchen door.

"You've got to start shaving your armpits, Reyn," Rick teased as he tickled my red curls. He followed me in, shadowboxing with the dogs all the way to the kitchen.

I threw my purse and keys on the kitchen table. "I'm not in a mood for jokes."

"What are you in the mood for? Your boyfriend on his way over?"

Uh-oh, what was he going to think when Scythe *did* show up? Probably the same thing Scythe would be thinking when *he* showed up. Both were going to be sadly disappointed. I sighed. How did things get so ass-backwards in my life? Did I naturally complicate things, or did they just work out that way accidentally?

"I don't have a boyfriend, Rick."

He reviewed my clown face with raised eyebrows.

"Maybe you could get one with a different makeup technique. This color scheme seems a little extreme."

I glared. He put his hands in the air. "Hey, it's jolly. I guess I'm wrong. Perhaps it's better to clown around when it comes to romance."

Rick grinned, and I tweaked his beaked nose. He was an irrepressible goofball, albeit a creative one, and the antithesis of his wife, a deeply serious, intensely intellectual criminal attorney. I adored them both, but never would've put them together in a love match. Sixteen years later, they were still as happy as newlyweds. Maybe that's why I didn't have Cupid's job.

"The makeup is a long story I can't explain right now."

"I bet you've gone undercover to work for the cops—something sinister at the circus." He started to hum a tune, throwing out a few lyrics.

Time to distract him. "I'm glad you're here, Rick, I have a question. But you can't stay long."

"Aha! I knew you were having company. A nooner, huh?"

I ignored him. "Have you ever heard of a club called Bangers on Sixth Street in Austin?"

Rick pulled a kitchen chair around and sat on it backward. "Heard of it. Know the manager."

"Great!" That was better than I'd hoped for. "You think you can call him up, ask if someone in a band playing there, or that once played there, that opened for Limp Bizkit recently, is dating a friend of mine, or at least had a recent romantic involvement with her?"

Rick rolled his head around, letting his tongue loll out of his mouth. "That was worse than a promo for *All My Children*. Look, my guy wouldn't be able to follow the first quarter of that question, much less the whole thing, and especially not over the phone. What does the band player look like?"

"Pale, skinny, wears black."

"Swell, that's half the rockers in Austin."

"Is exceedingly polite."

"That ought to narrow it down some. Of course, polite is relative. Not sticking your hands down your pants to scratch could be considered polite in some circles."

"These circles?"

"Definitely." Rick shrugged at my grimace and stood. "Look, if you really want to find this guy, your best bet is to go in person. Why don't I round up Tess early from work tonight, and you ask Trudy and Mario to come so Mama Tru will watch my kids."

"Mama Tru will watch your kids anytime until she gets grandkids of her own."

"Hmm, I think I'll be slipping Trudy lots of birth control." Rick grinned. "Now, to find you a date. How about the police dude?"

I was already shaking my head before he got the words out. "No can do. He's working that murder case."

"This trip is about the murder case, isn't it?"

I hadn't said that. Sometimes I wondered just how much Rick heard about my life through his open office window. Maybe I talked in my sleep.

"What's his name—Jackson something?"

I shook my head harder. "He cramps my style."

"What is it with you two?" Rick sighed heavily, and fingered his goatee. "I'd suggest the vitamin salesman you've been panting over—the guy who lives down the street—but I think he's still pretty steamed about his baked Porsche, even though that wasn't your fault."

I had no response for that one. Another case of circumstances killing my love life. My friend Ricardo's murderer had torched the Porsche to create a diversion when he came after me a few months ago. Rick pressed on. "Okay, what about Jon Villita? He used to come around all the time after your last brush with the law. I haven't seen him lately."

"He's been working long hours—he's expanding his business into Dallas and Houston."

"There you go, invite him to come along so you won't have to dance alone. All work and no play makes a boy a dull drip, and that boy has a tendency to be a bit drippy anyway. Consider it your community service."

I agreed readily, mostly so that Rick would drop the Scythe suggestion, but also because I liked Jon. He was a kindhearted young man who'd survived some difficult revelations in the past year, including the fact that he was really Ricardo's son. He was only a handful of years younger than I was, but for some reason I felt decades older in wisdom. Scary, I know.

I was flipping through my Rolodex for Jon's number when Rick let himself out the kitchen door with a warning to be ready to leave by eight o'clock. When I finally got Jon on the phone, he was surprisingly game. Trudy beeped in, having ascertained with her uncanny buddy ESP that she might be missing out on some action. I'd just finished juggling their calls when I heard the door open behind me.

"They said they'd come," I threw over my shoulder, assuming Rick had come back to check on the status of our plans.

"Hopefully, *they* won't come until I've collected on my deal," Scythe purred as he wrapped his arms around my midriff and kissed my neck. I have to admit, I swooned a bit. Just for a few seconds, understand, but it was enough to forget everything but the moist caress of his lips at my nape, the heat of his body through my jeans, the press of his fingertips on my hip bone.

I turned around, already tasting the kiss.

His eyes widened as he gasped and stumbled back.

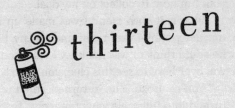# thirteen

IT TOOK SCYTHE, the jerkasaurus, a good five minutes to stop laughing. I mean, that's when he could actually finish an entire sentence without bursting out into gales of laughter or having a chuckle rumble up out of his chest.

"When you said you were a clown, I didn't think . . ."

He-he ha-ha.

I crossed my arms over my chest. "You got that right. You didn't think."

". . . didn't think you actually meant the red rubber nose. This wig goes with it?" he asked, clearing his throat, probably to drown another guffaw. I nodded sullenly. Scythe plucked it off the counter, perched it on my head, and considered me from top to toe.

"You're kind of cute as a clown." He studied my glower. "Athough with that expression on your face, you look more like Curmudgeon Clown."

"If you're finished having your fun with me—"

Scythe reached over and tickled my ear with his fingertips. "I'm not anywhere near finished having fun with you. I'm here to collect on my deal."

What is it with men? I was made up identical to the murder victim—major clue and creepy, besides—and all he could think of was nookie. "I just used the deal to get you over here to see this clue, you bozo."

"You're Bozo," he returned, then a deep chuckle turned into full-scale laughter again. Tears were forming at the corners of his eyes. I'd seen Scythe always masculine, often sexy, forever intimidating, once vulnerable, but never cute. Right now, all six feet of his muscular frame were vibrating with pent-up giggles, and it was cute. Too bad I was too pissed-off to enjoy it.

"Scythe, I'm going to wash this clown face off, if you don't whip out—"

"Whip out what?" he interrupted eagerly, looking like a puppy hoping for a scrap of dinner.

"Your camera, you pervert. You did bring it like I told you to?"

"Well, of course, since I thought we were doing the deal." He pulled a Nikon with a telephoto lens out of his jacket.

"Why did you need a telephoto lens for our deal?"

He just grinned wolfishly.

Hmm. The deal had been struck months ago between Trudy and Scythe, my best friend apparently pimping me out, albeit in a creative way, for help from the cop in the last murder investigation. I knew the general concept of the deal, but maybe less than I thought I did, I decided as I eyed the long lens nervously.

"Maybe I don't know all the details of the deal. Maybe you need to clarify them for me."

"You'll know when you're ready to go through with it," Scythe offered with a wry smile. "Which may not be until we are both in a nursing home. Then it will require some Viagra."

"It might require some Viagra anyway, Scythe," I quipped.

He raised that left eyebrow.

I raised my right eyebrow.

"Reyn, why don't you call me Jackson?"

"I prefer Scythe."

"Why, because it keeps your defenses up?" He took a step toward me. I retreated, bumping into the counter behind me. "Are you afraid—deal or no deal—that if you relaxed your defenses, you would be unable to resist my charm?"

"What charm?" I jutted my chin up.

"This charm," he said, snaking a hand around my waist and pulling me to him.

His lips just grazed mine before I put my finger on his chest and pushed him away. Boy, did I have willpower or what? "You're going to compromise the evidence."

Heaving a big sigh, he stepped away and grabbed the camera off the kitchen counter. "Why can't you be like a normal woman and have problems with your own hair instead of a corpse's, gossip with your girlfriends instead of murder suspects, get your makeup done so you can go on a quiet date instead of to use as evidence in a murder investigation?"

Why didn't he just say, *Why can't you be more like Zena?*

I smiled blithely. "If I did that, you wouldn't find me nearly so interesting."

"I wouldn't find you nearly so aggravating." He sighed again and snapped a few photos. Then he had me sit in one of the kitchen chairs and close my eyes. I tried to look as dead as I could.

"That's good enough," he barked out gruffly. Gone was the playful man; the all-business cop had taken his place. I wondered what had caused the switch. Had I looked too dead and scared him a little? For some reason, that made me happy. I'm twisted that way.

Scythe reached under my sink and handed me a roll of paper towels. He sat down at the table. "Take off your clown face while you tell me what rocks you've been busy turning over and who crawled out from underneath them."

"I did a cut and color this morning," I began as I wiped at my gooey cheek, smearing the red and white and blue together.

"So you won't be bankrupt and dead at the end of the investigation, just dead."

"Thanks for your optimism."

"It's called realism, and you need a big dose of it."

"Anyway, after that I went to see Shauna Rollins, makeup artist extraordinaire, who has a shop at North New Braunfels and Townley." I recounted my escapade with Percy's girlfriend, only altering the story somewhat so I didn't look so culpable for the mannequin's demise.

"You think she was onto you and was destroying the evidence on purpose?"

"Well, no, because I imagine it would have just bounced off the grass where she was aiming."

"And why didn't it go where she was aiming?"

"Because I kind of grabbed her arm to save it."

Scythe emitted a growly sound and buried his head on his forearm for a moment. He lifted his head and rested his chin on his wrist. "Still, maybe Shauna did whack Wilma just to get the old bat out of the way so she could have Percy, that stud, all to herself."

I shook my head. "I don't think she has enough ambition to be that mercenary or enough emotion to be that passionate. Besides, she is not the sharpest knife in the drawer, as Gran used to say. I don't think she could've figured out how to kill her even if she considered it. I don't think she has a mean bone in her body, besides. Now, I *do* see her being sweet enough to have helped someone who asked her, and being dumb enough to buy whatever story they concocted to explain why Wilma wasn't breathing."

"Who would that someone be? Percy or Alexandra?"

Or Percy's Mexican business associates? Oops, I couldn't mention them without getting into Annette.

"Not Lexa."

"Of course. How did you find out about Shauna? Maybe Lexa set up the poor girl, coerced her into helping, let her leave her fingerprints all over the place, then got you in and culpable so you would nose around and find Shauna to take the fall. I gotta hand it to her. It's well thought-out. Neat and tidy. Isn't Alexandra the one who told you her father was having an affair?"

"No!"

"How did you find out, then?"

Double oops. I was nailed. His laser blues were boring into me from across the table.

"It came to me in a dream?"

He shook his head.

"I smelled her signature cologne on him and put two and two together?"

His head shook harder. "Can't smell anything on that man but garlic, remember?"

"Okay." I blew out a breath. "I have a confidential source."

"They are called informants. Police are the only ones who can use them. When a member of the public uses them and doesn't give their name, it's called obstruction of justice, which is a felony. In case you hadn't noticed lately, you aren't a cop. Which means I'll probably have to arrest you. Again."

"Look, can't you use me as an informant mediator?"

Scythe rubbed his forehead with his palm and made another growling noise.

"I'll tell you everything I can, and, in return, I keep the identity of the person secret. How about that?"

"You tell me everything *and* the identity of the person, and, in return, I keep you out of jail. How about that?"

"I'm a person of my word. I guess you'll just have to cuff me, because I don't break a promise."

He muttered unintelligible words, but then the corners of his mouth turned up for an instant. "That bodes well for our deal."

Hmm. Sneaky bastard.

"All right, Reyn, how about this? You go back to your informant and convince him to come forward with his information on his own. I'll give you two days. Meanwhile, is there anything you can tell me without implicating this witness?"

I dismissed the possibility of describing the packages in general and the visits from the south-of-the-border duos. No one knew about those but Percy and Annette. I thought about the bloody photo. Workers from the store could look into the Dumpster as they were throwing something away and recognize Wilma from the media. It wouldn't necessarily point the finger at Annette. I gave Scythe the location of the Dumpster and mentioned that he might look for something like a picture frame.

"And are you checking Percy's phone records?"

Scythe nodded grumpily.

"Okay, pay special attention to calls to or from anywhere south of the border."

Scythe growled again and blew out a huge sigh. He ran his hand through his hair. I winced. I'd pretty much gotten to where I could ignore his haircut, but sometimes I couldn't help noticing it, especially when he ran his best feature through his current worst one. Then he pinned me with his laser blues.

"Look, Reyn." He put his hand on my shoulder and played with the tips of my Meg Ryan messy under the wig. "You be careful with this secret informant business. It is always dangerous. If they have a reason to stay anonymous, they have a reason to be desperate. Even trained professionals have trouble with this. I have a death threat against me involving an informant right now."

"Really? Another death threat?"

"What do you mean, *another* death threat?" He leaned in and turned up the heat of his gaze. "How do you know whether the first one involved an informant or not?"

Oopsy. "Uh, I don't, of course. I guess I just assumed it didn't. I mean, you know how your mind does funny

things, and I guess I was frightened on your behalf
and—"

He took his hand off my shoulder and put it on my
lips to stop them. He shot me another penetrating look,
and I smiled, unconvincingly, I'm sure.

"I have a date with a Dumpster. Then I'm going to
meet the clown queen. Try to behave yourself. Use your
best pitch to get the tipster to talk to me, even if it's just
over the phone. I'd feel a helluva lot better if you were
out of the mix. I'll check on you later."

Ha, he could try. I was going to make sure Lexa's
boyfriend was on the up-and-up before I mentioned
what I knew about him to Scythe.

You know, a night out on the town isn't what it used to
be. I remember the good old days when my girlfriends
and I would decide to paint the town red and our
biggest dilemma was having the cash to do anything.
Surprisingly, a lot of things in life are free. I hardly ever
went out at night anymore, and now that I had to and
had rounded up my collection of grown-up friends, we
had more serious dilemmas than cash. First, we had to
dislodge Rick and Tessa's two-year-old son from his
dad's femur. We had to convince their worried six-year-
old daughter that we weren't taking a spaceship to pop-
ulate Mars, which was what Mario, kid idiot that he was,
told her for fun. Then we had to talk Trudy out of a
mental meltdown because she thought that the lines on
her legs from sitting on a chair were the beginnings of
varicose veins. Then I had to refuse for the seventeenth
time to restyle Mario's hair to look like a Hispanic Sting.
Thankfully, Jon was pretty low-maintenance, standing in

a corner of the Ugartes' house waiting for the chaos to die down. Finally, we had to decide which vehicle to take. It wasn't easy. The Miata was out of the question, my crew cab would have the six of us entirely too friendly during the hour-and-a-half drive, and the Ugartes had a purple kidmobile, a minivan. Practicality made the decision for us, and we were on our way in a sexy oversize eggplant. Watch out, Sixth Street.

Being the obvious brain trusts of the pack, Tessa and I claimed the back of the van so we'd be as far from Rick as possible. Rick tended to try out all his new lyrics on captive audiences, especially when he was driving. While there were numerous problems with this, the biggest was that he often got so involved in the singing that he forgot to look at the road. It made for a suspenseful ride for the person in the death seat. It was a damned good thing most other people were defensive drivers. His wife and I knew from experience it was best just to be in a position where one couldn't watch.

Trudy and Jon sat in the middle seats, leaving Mario the front. It was for the best, really. Of all of us, Mario was the one who would never notice if Rick nearly sideswiped an old woman sitting at a bus stop or caused a ten-car pileup behind us. My best friend's husband loved Trudy with his whole heart and was good to her, which made me forgive him for being a total dimwit.

Rick began to sing, "The armadillo in a stretch limo . . ." until Mario begged him to do "Reyn on the Run." Tessa and I rolled our eyes and ignored Rick's musical take on my last brush with the law. Trudy and Jon were deep into discussion about the interior redesign Trudy was doing for his hair salon chain.

Tessa turned to me and whispered, "If you need any representation during this fiasco with the Barristers, let me know. We'll work out a babysitting trade."

Ugh. From the way the kids had acted tonight, I thought I'd rather go to jail. Still, I smiled and thanked her. "I almost needed you yesterday about dawn, but they let me go without arraigning me."

"Yes, Rick tells me you have a cop on your side. He says he reminds him of Toby Keith. Lucky you."

"Why don't I feel lucky?" I asked.

"Forget feeling lucky. How about getting lucky?" Trudy threw into the backseat without missing a beat in her own conversation. Elephant ears. Jon slipped me an embarrassed look. What did *he* have to be embarrassed about? Humph.

Tessa smiled indulgently but, ever serious about business, returned to her subject. "Well, it's good to have friends in the local cops, but before this Barrister affair is done, you may need more than just the guys in blue."

"Why is that?"

"Rumors. The legal community is a big hotbed of gossip, and the hottest bed lately is our boy Percy's."

I waved off her intensity. "Oh, I know all about the girlfriend."

"Which one?" Tessa asked.

"Is there more than one current one?"

"I don't know about that, just that he's never at a loss for young female companionship, thanks to the liberal use of his credit card on their behalf. That's not the gossip, though."

"What is, then?"

"That Percy has been laundering money for some

wealthy Mexican 'businessmen,' and that the feds just started breathing down Percy's neck about the funny money."

"What kind of businessmen?"

Tessa took off her glasses and pinned me with her most serious look, the one she reserved for making a point with jurors. "Drug kingpins."

Gulp.

fourteen

"WHICH FEDS ARE WE TALKING ABOUT?"

Tessa shrugged. "There are as many stories as there are lawyers in San Antonio. Some say the IRS got suspicious and is leaning on Percy for unorthodox income. I've heard the DEA is setting up some kind of sting to catch the kingpins. Then there's the one about the FBI putting undercover people in Percy's office building. All or none may be true."

That reminded me about Annette's mention of Percy using the IRS to get rid of his old girlfriends. At the time I'd thought it a rather callous joke, but maybe the IRS was protecting him in exchange for something he was doing for them. I wondered again about Annette's motivation in coming to me with all her information. Was she an undercover federal agent? Was she using me to feed the cops false tidbits to send them on wild-goose chases, or to get me to nose around the investigation more for some hidden purpose? Or did she want to tell someone what she knew in case something happened to her—and why would she think something would? Or maybe she was on the take from the drug kingpins and . . .

Okay, this speculation was getting way too complicated for me. After all, I couldn't even keep up with an innocent white lie or two.

I asked Tessa if she minded if I shared her gossip with the local authorities.

"Go ahead, I'll even talk to them, but what I know is twentieth-hand at best and may be completely spurious. Percy is not the favorite of the bar."

I extracted my cell phone and dialed Scythe. Amazingly, he picked up on the first ring. He never does that.

"Hey, Bozo. You know, I've been thinking that that makeup and wig paired with just the right bra and panties might be kind of a turn-on."

"Charmer, with that kind of comment, you'll be dead before you ever see your deal."

Trudy, talking a mile a minute about drapery fabric, still managed to hear that. She spun around and wiggled her eyebrows at me. Jon's forehead wrinkled in concern. Geez, love affair by committee. I guess I should invite them on our next date.

"Reyn, threatening cops is a felony," Tessa whispered.

Ack, I was surrounded by a pack of well-intentioned busybodies.

Scythe's baritone dropped and smoothed around the edges. "Gosh, and here I thought that telephoto lens had piqued your curiosity. . . ."

I squirmed in my seat. I hated that he could do that long-distance. Trudy grinned. Jon looked like he might start taking notes. Rick increased the volume of his song right at the part about midnight visits from the police.

I cleared my throat and raised my voice. "I'm calling about some important business."

"I thought what we were talking about was important."

Hmm. "I just heard some gossip about Percy Barrister I thought you should be privy to."

"Shoot."

I recounted what Tessa had told me. He asked to speak to her. From her side of the conversation, it sounded like this gossip was news to Scythe. After a few moments, she passed the phone back to me, covering the mouthpiece as she did so. "He told me to try to talk you into taking a trip to the Bahamas for a few weeks."

Getting me out of the way, no doubt, so he and Zena could live happily ever after. I bet she'd wear the clown getup with a push-up and a thong. Humph. "I'm not going to the Bahamas or anywhere," I informed him as I took the phone back.

"That's too bad. I'd hate to lock you up in jail again."

"Why would you do that?"

There was a long stretch of silence in which I thought I'd lost his signal. Finally, he blew out what sounded like a sigh. "Never mind, you're hopelessly hardheaded."

"I prefer to think of it as persistent and committed."

"You need to *be* committed."

"Well, I'm so glad I took the time out of my busy evening to help with the investigation."

"Look, Reyn, all gossip holds a grain of truth. Where the grain is here, we don't know. Is it federal involvement? Is it drug kingpins? It could be that Percy is doing the taxes for a pharmaceutical salesman who is being audited by the IRS, and it got blown into these other stories by the fact that his wife was unrelatedly murdered. You see what I'm getting at? I am concerned that I hadn't heard this before. But, frankly, if the feds are already investigating, they might not tell us. They'd let us turn over the rocks for them and see what crawled out. They are not famous for their cooperation with us locals."

"So, thanks for nothing, is what you are saying."

There was another long pause during which I felt him grappling to control his temper. I got another sigh in my ear. "I like having the heads-up, but it may come to nothing, is what I am saying. And if drugs, Mexican 'businessmen,' and the feds are involved, I like it even less that *you* are involved. All three are dangerous. So get uninvolved."

"Control freak," I muttered. Trudy shot me a glare. Tessa shook her head. Jon got a cat-that-got-the-canary look. What was that about?

"By the way, where are you going?" Scythe asked.

"How do you know I'm going somewhere?" I responded suspiciously.

"You're calling me from your cell phone, and you said you were in the middle of a busy evening. What are you so busy with tonight, Reyn?"

"I have a date." I punched the connection into oblivion. Take that, bossy britches.

I hadn't been to Sixth Street in nearly ten years and things had changed. Back when the drinking age was still eighteen in Texas, students from the relatively lib-

eral University of Texas filled not only the sidewalks but
the street itself, drifting from club to club, serenaded by
street musicians, sidewalk circus acts, and palm readers.
Live bands played next door to each other, sending their
music out into the crowded streets. Rock mixed with
country, jazz, and reggae floated together on the humid
night air that was laced with beer and tequila fumes.
You could elbow your way into a club, but half the party
took place on the asphalt outside. It was a Lone Star
Mardi Gras every night. When the state legislature
upped the legal age to twenty-one, more than half the
nightly crowd had to go underground with their party-
ing, so Sixth Street grew up. Downtown Austin was still
a music mecca, just not such a wildly drunken one. Cars
could actually get down Sixth Street on a Saturday night
now, and even though the sidewalks were crowded, it
was nowhere near the chaos of the eighties and early
nineties.

We parked the eggplant and walked three blocks to
Bangers. I kept looking behind us. For some reason, I
was on edge. It was Scythe's fault. He'd made me paranoid about bogeymen. I brushed it off in irritation. I refused to be manipulated. I focused ahead of me instead
and smiled. Tessa and Rick held hands and shared a ten-
der look. They were an odd pair, he tall and gawky, she
short and curvy. But they weren't nearly as odd as Trudy
and Mario—beauty and the beast—who were nuzzling
each other, as usual unable to keep their hands off each
other. If you wanted proof that love was blind, you
needed to look no further than my best friend and her
husband. They had convinced me the whole love thing
was purely chemically controlled—we were at the

mercy of our pheromones. That made me think of Scythe again, an arrogant asshole if there ever was one and still he could make me wriggle just by his tone on the phone.

I was an adult, lots older than either of these pairs of friends when they married. I could overcome some silly hormonal attraction. I needed to find a mate who would be a good life partner, not some package of testosterone who made me hot every now and then and made me mad more often than not.

I smiled at Jon, who walked next to me. With his dark soulful eyes, black wavy hair, and chiseled features, he was handsome and good-hearted, a young man who would make some woman a wonderful, attentive husband. I reviewed the list of my available friends and clients. I thought of a couple of possibilities, including Jessica (if she ever got over her Bizkit obsession), and chastised myself for not inviting one of them to join us. I made a mental note to give him their phone numbers before the night was over.

A pack of giants in letter jackets stumbled out of the club to our right, and Jon grabbed my waist to save me from being trampled. Rick turned around up ahead and motioned us to hurry. He'd found Bangers. We gathered out front. The pounding music was deafening, even outside the door. I winced and wondered if whatever we found out was going to be worth permanent damage to my eardrums.

Rick leaned toward us and shouted, "The manager was supposed to save us a table. We'll get settled, then I'll go looking for him."

We all acquiesced and followed him into the throng

of thong-wearing, gyrating bodies. Jon put his arm pro-
prietarily around me as he forged a path behind Rick. A
band was onstage, and I scanned the members for a
dark-haired, pale, skinny bassist. Bingo. It was hard to
tell about the old-world manners thing right now, however, as he was throwing his head around like he was
having convulsions, his chin-length, sweaty locks slap-
ping across his face. The throbbing, unintelligible music
gave me a headache, but everyone around us seemed to
like it. Mario and Trudy detoured to the dance floor
while Tessa and I sat down at a table that said
RESERVED. Rick waved at us and wandered off toward
the bar. Jon went with him, but returned after a few moments with a vodka gimlet for Tessa and a glass of white
wine for me.

"It's pinot grigio. I remembered you liked it." There
was something stray-puppyish about Jon that was alter-
nately endearing and irritating. I swear, was I never satisfied—criticizing one guy for being too macho, another
for being too cloying? Jon could be forgiven, as he was
just acting with respect for his elders. Even though I
was only seven years older than he was, he was like my
nephew.

"Thank you." I nodded at his glass of clear liquid.
"What are you having?"

"Club soda. I told Rick I'd drive home."

"Good Boy Scout," Tessa said in the dry way she
sometimes had. I gave her a double take, still not sure
from her poker face whether that was slightly facetious
or not. Jon grinned winsomely, apparently taking it as a
compliment.

"Wretched Roadkill!" the man Rick had been talking

to shouted with a sweep of his arm as he jumped on-stage and grabbed the microphone from the lead screecher. "Let's hear it for our Austin boys made good!!! They opened for Limp Bizkit just a few weeks ago, and now they're back at their home bar. Do you know how lucky you are?"

The earsplitting answer was almost more than I could take. I put my hands over my ears. Wretched Roadkill? What the hell kind of name was that? I began to rethink my dismissal of a Wilma suicide. If Lexa was involved with the bassist for a band with that horrid a name, Wilma might very well have ended it all before he be-came part of the hallowed Barrister family.

Nah. I looked at the sweaty, scraggly half-dozen wav-ing at the crowd. She'd be more likely to blow away this whole Black Bart bunch than herself. I thought they wore the color of night to match the circles under their eyes. What would cause those? Living like vampires and singing like dying dogs?

These were all burning questions I wanted to ask Tessa, Trudy, or Mario but it was too damned loud. The screeches had turned into a chant for the name of a song that sounded like "Drag Me Bloody, Love Me Dead." Ack. I thought we'd found a whole new group of murder suspects. What was Lexa thinking? Maybe Jes-sica was wrong. Maybe that wasn't Lexa she'd talked to backstage. Maybe the party animal had nipped into the mushrooms and had been hallucinating.

I hoped so.

Wretched Roadkill started the bloody, dead song. Mario dragged Trude back on the dance floor. Rick fin-ished up with the manager and returned to our table.

"Aaron wanted to make clear that there are a lot of music groupies in Austin, the girls come and go, so he can't be sure. But he did admit that the bassist of Wretched Roadkill has kept one girl in particular around since they started playing here a year ago. The girl matches Lexa's description."

My heart fell. "Is she here tonight?"

"He doesn't know."

"Can I talk to Aaron?"

"I don't think that's a good idea, Reyn," Jon piped up at my left shoulder. Who asked him?

Rick shook his head anyway. "He doesn't want to get involved. He said after the band goes offstage, I can slip back there and check things out."

"Was the band playing two nights ago?"

"Saturday night? You bet. They started at ten o'clock. And, I asked, all members of the band played all night."

I relaxed a little in relief. It didn't eliminate Lexa's boyfriend. After all, a haul-ass drive from Austin to San Antonio could be done in an hour, but it sure would have cut it close. "What's the bassist's name?"

The left side of Rick's mouth quirked in a half grin. "He goes by Asphalt."

"No way." I laughed.

"It's better than Corpse," Tessa offered straight-faced as she sipped her vodka gimlet.

Jon just shook his head as if he was saddened by the creeps of the world in general. Or maybe he was in shock—after all, the boy had spent his entire life in private schools, raised as the son of a U.S. senator. Maybe this dark side was too much to take. If he stuck with me, he'd see more than he knew inside a week.

My throat was beginning to feel raw from having to shout over the music. "How 'bout I go with you to check things out?"

"No way," Rick said. He chugged some beer.

Tessa shook her head once, decisively, and I could see she would be tougher to get through than her six-foot-two husband. Then there was Jon, who'd slid his chair over until it was touching mine. He was probably stronger than he looked, but I bet I could take him. Hmm. Maybe I could find a distraction. Maybe one of the thong-wearers on the dance floor. I would have to get creative once Rick went backstage. I couldn't let him do it all alone.

The wretched bunch had started the last verse of their last song, "Mama in a 'Dillo." The armadillo had actually been flattened by a tractor-trailer rig, but the hitchhiker who had kept it company for hours finally saw his mother's face in the shape of the dead critter.

"Nice," I said, sarcasm thick.

"It's supposed to be symbolic," Rick offered in generous defense of his music compadres. "I think."

"Maybe they'd be a market for your songs," I teased. "They seem to like armadillos. Your 'dillo could fall out of his limo. . . ."

Rick stuck his tongue out at me, and Tessa hid a smile behind her gimlet.

Roadkill sauntered off the stage after a lot of flashing of their wet armpits and flipping of their sweaty, overly long hair. It didn't take much to imagine they were smelling like their name about now. Rick took a final swig of his beer before following them backstage.

Speaking of sweaty, Mario and Trudy returned to the

table, giggling and gasping for air. I don't know if they danced that hard (my bet was on Trudy) or were that out of shape (my bet was on Mario), or whether the pressure gradient of the number of bodies per square inch put the temperature up around two thousand degrees out on the floor (all bets were on this one). Jon rushed to get them a pitcher of water. Then they started telling us about their adventures—how someone had grabbed Mario by his family jewels and wouldn't let go until Trudy agreed to dance with *her*. Okay. Then three women invited Mario to an orgy in the women's bathroom.

"Did you go?"

"Dios mío, Reyn!" Mario blushed and crossed himself.

"Cat's claws and dolphin's dongs, Reyn. Would you have gone?"

"Never been asked," I said truculently.

Jon, returning with the water, drilled me with a questioning look that I ignored. The shocking auntie, no doubt.

But they weren't finished. Apparently, a Hollywood talent scout was here visiting his sister-in-law and had seen Trudy. He'd tried to convince her during the squished armadillo song to move to Hollywood and work as a body double for Nicole Kidman. He named a healthy six-figure salary for official features, with more off the books for whenever Nicole might want to use her to fake out the media in order to sneak someplace else herself.

"That's something to think seriously about," Tessa said, reviewing the scout's business card Mario had handed her. "That would be a good living."

Trudy looked aghast and shook her head. "Why would I want to go around my whole life as someone else?"

Every now and then, I was reminded of why she was my best friend. We shared a smile.

Tessa put the card on the table and shot a nervous look at the backstage door. I'd noticed she'd been fidgeting, which was unlike a woman who could sit as still as the Rock of Gibraltar. I put my hand on her forearm, and she jumped.

"Are you okay?"

"I'm worried about Rick."

"He'll be all right. You know Rick, he's just palling around before he gets to the point."

Tessa nodded uncertainly. "But it's been a half hour already."

I hadn't realized it had been that long, but the Trujillos could drag out a story. I leaned toward Tess. "We'll give him a little more time, then I'll go looking for him."

"Not much more time, please, Reyn." Tessa was almost in tears. "What I'm going to tell you, please keep between us."

I glanced around and saw that Jon was being entertained by Mario's reenactment of the crotch-grabbing incident. I nodded. "Of course."

"Rick had a problem with drugs, before we got married. In fact, that's how we met. I was assigned to be his public defender on a possession charge. He ran with a bad crowd, but I saw he was a good person. I made him promise if I got him off, he'd go to rehab. He did, and he's never touched them since. But he's avoided the lifestyle since then, too. His agent is the one who deals with the musicians. . . ."

"Oh, Tessa, I'm so sorry I asked for his help in this deal with Lexa. If I'd known, I never would have asked him to go somewhere that might tempt him."

She shook her head, and shot another look at the backstage door. "No, Reyn, it's not your fault. I could've made some excuse. We could've stayed home. I just thought it had been long enough."

"Maybe it has. I'll go find him."

"Will you dance with me?" Jon walked up beside me. I looked at Tessa and nodded our secret pact. I could've asked Jon to go with me, but something told me my watchdog might need saving instead of the other way around.

"Sure," I said, and he led me out to bump and grind to the canned rock music that had been playing since the Wretcheds exited. AC/DC. Journey. At least I recognized some of these songs. One verse into the second song, and I excused myself to go to the ladies' room. Tessa caught on and distracted Jon long enough for me to detour to the backstage door.

The only problem was that there was a man the size of the door standing against it. He watched me with the expression a toad wears when contemplating a fly dinner. None. "Hi, handsome! I need to get back there to see my boyfriend."

No response. I don't think he was even breathing. I reached into my purse to get a mirror, and one huge hand shot out and shackled my wrist in an iron grip. "No monkey business," he growled.

"Oh, no, no, no," I coughed out, and swallowed my shock. "I was just going to, uh, repair my lip gloss before I see, uh, Asphalt."

"Asphalt? He has a girlfriend, and it ain't you."

"Oh, no. Really? How do you know?"

"'Cuz you got a lot bigger tits than her." I looked down at the cotton spandex cowgirl-print blouse I was wearing. Wrong choice. The guard toad had his eyes right between the silk-screened rope and the girl's Stetson. Gross. Wouldn't you know, the only time I out-breasted somebody and the only one who noticed was the most abhorrent human in the place. "Oh, well, gotta go, I guess, if she's beat me to him."

I pried his fingers off my wrist and beat a path to the bathroom to come up with a Plan B. A cretin with greasy blond hair down to his fourth rib pushed out of the men's room. I recognized him as the Wretched Roadkill bongo player, and an idea grabbed me as he tried to slink by. "You are so hot!" I rubbed my hand up and down his right bicep (what I could find of it) and tried not to puke.

"Yo?" For a second I wondered if he didn't speak English; then I realized that rockers probably didn't speak my kind of English regardless—I'd have to use the universal language of love.

I smiled and winked and rubbed. Against other parts. I had to get backstage. His bloodshot eyes tried to focus. I pressed against him. "I wonder if you could get me backstage?"

"No can do, Piece."

I didn't think he was talking about joy-to-the-world kind of peace. Too bad. Where were the sixties when you needed them? At least their free love had some moral high ground. This guy only got on high ground when it flooded or when he smoked some weed. I cleared the gag out of my throat and tried to sound sultry. "I'll give you a piece to thank you if you can get me into the Roadkill dressing room."

His grayish lips spread in a humorless grin. "Now, that might be fun. But I go first."

Whoa. I thought I was starting to hyperventilate. "You go first," I agreed, pushing him off me and turning him around to lead the way around the guard toad. I sneaked a look at Tessa and saw she was desperately trying to keep Jon from turning around to see me. Trudy saw me, though. She cocked her head and opened her mouth. I shot her a warning look.

"Hey." The guard toad grabbed my arm. "I thought you wanted Asphalt."

"I'm moving on. You're the one who told me he had another girlfriend. Were you lying?!" I let my voice rise a little. The toad actually showed an emotion: pissed off.

"Asphalt? Why do you want him? I'm better," blondie whined. "And bigger."

"Prove it," I shot back boldly.

My escort grabbed my other arm, yanked me free of the guard toad, and shut the backstage door behind us. I skittered down the darkened hall. "Hey, wait for me," he shouted.

None of the doors were marked, of course. I paused and he caught up with me, surprisingly fast for a pothead. "Now for that thank-you," he said, pushing me against the door to the left. Before he could collect, the partially opened door slid open. I fell in and was face-to-face with a bigger problem.

A much, much bigger problem.

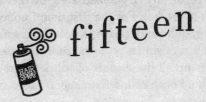

fifteen

RICK UGARTE, surrounded by the members of Wretched Roadkill, had a marijuana cigarette pinched between his forefinger and thumb halfway to his lips. At least, I thought it was a doobie; before now I'd only ever seen one on TV. Hey, I was a good Episcopalian girl from Dime Box, Texas, where a rebellious teenage night out only included some raw Thunderbird and a shotgun. Not that that was a whole lot safer, mind you, it was just different.

Anyway, the doobie looked unsmoked to me, which was good news. But I was seriously pissed, which was bad news. When I get mad I don't see red, I see nothing but my own anger. I was mad at myself for getting Rick in the situation where he'd fall off the wagon after nearly two decades. I was mad at him, too, for doing it when he had the greatest wife and kids in the world.

"You dumb bastard!" It was really meant for both of us—Rick and me. The Roadkill, though, seemed to take it personally. They all jumped up like lions interrupted

from their first kill in a month. I didn't care. Ah, the
armor of fury. I grabbed Rick by the arm and hauled
him to his feet. For the first time I noticed he was looking grateful and, I have to say, a little sorry.

"You ought to be sorry, Rick Ugarte, for wanting to
mess up all these years of sobriety just for a little toke
with a bunch of loser strangers. Loser smelly strangers,
at that—"

"I *am* really sorry, Reyn," Rick said a little too loudly.
What was up with him? Maybe he had taken a toke after
all. His tone of voice was weird. "*Really*, really sorry."
His gaze dropped to his right.

That's when I saw the gun. Duh.

The Roadkill leader—whose extreme height, pro-
truding Adam's apple, and avian eyes reminded me of a
vulture—had a Smith & Wesson double-action nine-
millimeter pointed into Rick's right kidney. I allowed
myself a moment of pride when I realized I could identify the gun. At my request, Scythe had spent an entire
afternoon a couple of months ago with a collection of
weapons testing me on different types before he taught
me how to shoot. He'd told me it was the weirdest date
he'd ever been on, but wouldn't he be pleasantly surprised when I could identify this particular gun? Well, if
I lived to tell him, that is.

"We have to get rid of them both now," the lead
singer grumbled. I noticed the ash sprinkled on his
black T-shirt, which read BLOOD in red. Maybe he'd
been smoking weed since they went backstage. I looked
at his bloodshot eyes. Maybe since he'd woken up that
morning. That boded well for diminished reflexes. I
eyeballed the gun.

"Blood," my erstwhile escort argued, "don't go doing anything without thinking. You, Guts, and Gore always fly off the handle."

What an image. I couldn't resist asking, "You guys call yourselves Blood, Guts, and Gore?"

"That was the name of our first band, man." Guts shoved out his lower lip. He had an electric guitar slung around his neck and talked in a permanent shout, like he'd been playing that guitar a little too loud for a little too long. "We got it legal and all, man."

"Y'see, we played together for years before Asphalt and DD came in," Gore explained, holding a pair of drumsticks, which he air-played for emphasis. He rocked his head back and forth to the imaginary music. "We were awesome, but we needed more zap and bang. And our agent said we needed a more marketable name. He's the one who came up with Wretched Road-kill."

The leader, Blood, bobbed his vulture neck. "Yeah. Killer name. When we expanded, we wanted the guys we hired to get with the whole theme. But Asphalt, our bass guy"—he nodded to the skinny guy in black behind the couch, presumably Lexa's boyfriend—"Ass is such a wuss, he wouldn't take a name that had anything to do with violence. DD, though, our bongo dude, he's really one of us."

"DD?" I was almost afraid to ask as I slid a look next to me.

"Date with Death," my escort clarified proudly.

"Ah." I nodded. "How visceral."

Rick just shook his head, worried, I guess, that my big, sarcastic mouth was going to get him killed.

"Visceral, just like your music," I added helpfully to the group of perplexed, stoned faces.

Rick looked up—toward heaven, presumably—and shook his head harder.

"Did you just dis us, man?" Guts glared at me, then proceeded to mock-pick a manic tune out on his guitar, chanting "Dis, dis, dis."

"She gave us a compliment, you boner," Blood chastised, glaring over his beak nose with those bulging eyes. "It's too bad we have to kill her if she likes our music."

I almost corrected him before a sense of self-preservation stopped me. I smiled benignly instead.

"But we still have to kill her, man," Gore pointed out, crashing a dirge on his air drums, his hair swinging, as stringy and sweat-soaked as the rest of the band's. It was such a uniform look that I wondered if they hadn't found some hair product called Greasy-Sweat: Get the Instant Nasty Without the Hard Work. "Him, too."

Uh-oh. He might beat me to death with his sticks. It was almost scarier than the gun.

"I'm the one you need to kill, not Rick. He came here because I asked him to. He's doing me a favor. He didn't even know Wilma."

"Wilma? Who's Wilma?" Gore demanded, pausing with a stick held high.

"Like Fred's wife on *The Flintstones*, man?" Guts wondered, stroking a last note on his guitar and shaking his body in what looked like an epileptic seizure.

"No." Irritation that these boneheads were terrorizing me and Rick began to overcome my fear. "Like the woman in Terrell Hills you whacked."

"Hey!" My escort, DD, took a threatening step toward me. "The only thing we're whacking is our—"

"Excuse me, miss, but we haven't killed anyone!" came a reedy voice from the back. Everybody froze. The manners were definitely out of context. Asphalt's mournful eyes met mine. Great, leave it to me to find someone to feel sorry for in this sea of scum. Those eyes implored. If he was right, I had to look somewhere else for the killer. That is, unless I got killed myself by a flying drumstick or a bullet.

"Not yet, we haven't." Gore started laughing in short bursts that reminded me of a machine gun. I glanced down at the Smith & Wesson the giant vulture still dug into Rick's kidney.

"Why do you have to kill us, anyway?" I asked carefully.

"If she doesn't know, why do we have to kill her?" Asphalt asked.

"Her buddy here knows," the leader answered, with a twist of the gun that made Rick gasp. "This dude knows unusual quality when he sees it. He noticed right away. We have to off him. Then she'll know he got offed, so we have to off her. Get it, Ass?"

What a nickname. But with a name like Asphalt, what did he expect?

"Get on with it, man," Guts demanded, airstrumming his guitar faster and faster. He bobbed his head to the manic rhythm as he continued, "Maybe I can get a new song out of this. I gotta watch the blood real close. Maybe the look in her eyes when she stops breathing."

"Wait a minute," DD said, grabbing my elbow. I

yanked it out of his hand. "She owes me for letting her in here."

Boy, did I ever. Too bad I didn't have some thumb-screws on me. I could apply them directly to his—

"Can't we have some fun first, Blood? All of us?" DD wheedled, trying for my waist this time. Jumping side-ways, I shivered in revulsion.

Rick stood suddenly, and I thought he was a goner as Blood scrambled to keep the gun on him. "Stay away from her," Rick warned bravely.

Oh, great, chivalry wasn't dead, but I probably would be. And maybe my balding knight in shining leather, too. Why my being raped bothered him more than my getting shot, I didn't know, but I appreciated it never-theless. I smiled at him in thanks.

"No fun," ordered Asphalt, my newest best friend. His bandmates looked at him in shock, but before they could chime in he added, "And we can't kill them here, anyway."

"Where, then?" Gore asked, banging his drumsticks on the top of the couch now.

"Out back, and we'll throw them in the Dumpster, man." Guts strummed.

"That's too close, you boner," Blood told him. "Be-sides, people on the street will hear."

"Let's strangle them instead," Gore offered, tapping a tune on the back of his shoe, and began to sing, "stran-gle, strangle, let her dangle . . ."

"No, that's too hard," Vulture Boss argued. He seemed to be loosening his hold on the gun. I watched for a chance to grab it. "How about those woods behind those tract houses out on the highway?"

"I'm not going in the woods," Gore whined, his drumsticks paused in midair. "There's creepy animals in the woods, like coyotes and snakes and stuff."

"Hey, we don't have a song about a snake, man!" Guts interjected. "We could shoot it, then drive over it, and I could watch the guts come out and write a song about it."

Guts was warming to this new idea, strumming and humming lyrics to himself, and I thought I ought to encourage it. "And maybe it will have recently eaten, and you can have double roadkill."

"Double roadkill, man." Guts threw his head around like he was possessed, but I think he was feeling a beat. "Wow, that is so cool. You're pretty cool, dead girl."

Okay, two compliments in one night. The guard toad thought I was chesty, and now I had enviable roadkill songwriting abilities. At least I was going to die with a healthy sense of self.

"Maybe we'll kill her real slow, and she could write a song about how it feels to die." Gore looked me up and down—apparently planning all the fun ways to torture me. He tapped on my shoulder and my head with his drumsticks until I batted them away.

All of them but Asphalt whistled and nodded to each other. "Cool idea," Blood admitted. "It might work."

A yelp came from the back of the room, and a pale, skinny someone in a black bodysuit streaked out from behind the couch and made for the door.

"Hey, catch her!"

"It's just Asphalt's bitch."

"Start shooting!"

It was Lexa? What had happened to the mango

Chanel? Where'd she come from? Behind the couch?

Asphalt leaped after her, and they both busted out the door and blew past the man standing in the dark hallway.

Scythe? His weapon was drawn and pointed into the dressing room. The laser blues met mine for a second, and all I could see and feel was their intensity. "Police! Everyone, hands up."

Poor Boss Blood was having a hard time keeping up with the action, one too many tokes for him somewhere along the way. He'd waved the gun belatedly toward where Asphalt and Lexa had been, then swung it around toward me. Rick took advantage of the mellow fellow's slow reflexes and knocked it loose.

His long arm dropped.

Scythe fired a warning shot into the upholstery.

We could hear screams in the club.

Scythe stayed in the doorway, I imagined so he could check down the hall to make sure Lexa and Asphalt weren't going to ambush him.

The nine-millimeter had flown toward the couch, bounced off, and landed between me and DD. Now, I might have left it there. I mean, Scythe was in charge of this turkey bake, plus with his muscles all on alert and his laser blues at full blast, he looked scary, and I think he was already mad at me. But when DD slipped me this creepy grin and dove for the gun, my reflexes took over. I dove faster. I grabbed it gingerly, remembering how sensitive the trigger on these babies could be and not knowing if the safety was on. Then a pair of hands grabbed my ass, and I figured out the safety was on or I would've wiped out the entire room as I was goosed.

"Hey, let go!" I kept the gun on the disarmed boss vulture while I tried to yank my booty out of DD's hands. He started kneading. I started doing the mambo to shake him loose. "Right now, buddy. Or your date with death will read today."

"Cover the door," Scythe barked at me, and before I could swing the gun that way, he was gone and so was the vise grip on my ass. I shot a look behind me and saw Scythe holding DD by his long hair. He kicked him in the groin and dropped the now huddled, moaning mass on the floor.

The other wretched members of the decomposing band winced. Guts looked like he was going to puke his namesake out. "Man, did you *have* to do that?"

"*Man,*" Scythe mimicked, "I can do a lot worse unless you drop your guitar, march over to the wall, kiss it, and keep your hands up and on it until the Austin PD gets here."

I heard sirens now and wondered if I could've heard them before. Adrenaline was doing weird things to my perception—it was narrowed, tunneled, allowing me to notice only the things that had direct bearing on my survival. This had happened to me only twice before in my life. Once when I'd almost met my maker, and once when I'd kissed Scythe in my kitchen.

Scythe ushered the men in black over to the wall and motioned me to keep my gun on them. He took Rick with him back to the dressing room door, talking to him in low tones that I strained but failed to hear. Damn. Scythe took his badge out and stuck it in the vee of his white button-down shirt, presumably so the Austin police wouldn't shoot him when they blew in. Hey, I was in all black—except for the cowgirl on my chest—like the bad guys. What about me?

When Scythe got settled at the door and shot me a glare, I thought I should probably be more worried about him shooting me than the Austin police.

Uh-oh.

"Reyn, what the hell did you think you were doing coming here?"

"Um . . ." I tried a weak smile, then let it fade when he frowned deeper. "Trying to help you?"

"How does this help me, Reyn?" He blew out a sigh. He ran his free hand through his trailer-park-trash haircut. He only did that when he was extremely perturbed. This situation qualified as upsetting, I guess, but only by accident.

"I found Lexa's boyfriend. Isn't that helpful?"

"And lost him again, I see." He waved his arm in the direction of the fled pair. "You could have called me with the information. Instead, I had to figure out you were keeping something from me, and spend my whole night following you and your gang of goobers—"

"Sorry to put you out," I said sulkily. He'd probably had to break a hot date with Zena. He was dressed to the nines, in perfectly broken-in Wranglers, a hand-tooled leather belt, and a starched white shirt. A few golden chest hairs sprang out around the badge near his throat.

"You'll be sorry for more than that, believe me."

My gratitude that he'd saved me from DD's clutches and worse was quickly dissipating. I looked across the Smith & Wesson at him with my most powerful glare. "You don't scare me."

"Whu-hoo," the band members chanted from the wall.

Rick looked nervous, like he was afraid that Scythe and I would start shooting each other and he'd be caught in the cross fire. He shifted from foot to foot and implored me with a look. I stuck my tongue out at him.

"I ought to scare you," Scythe shot across the room.

"Whoa-ho," the Roadkill chanted, an octave lower.

"Shut up," Scythe ordered. "You idiots are in big trouble. Don't make it worse."

"Why should I be scared of you?" I was a little scared right now, truth be told, but hell if I was going to show it. I jutted my chin a little for effect.

"I'm going to throw you in jail again."

"For what?"

"Cradle robbing." The muscles along his jaw rippled as he ground his teeth. "I'm not sure your date is of age."

"Very funny. Jon isn't my date. Besides, he's only seven years younger than I am. I guess you think I'm younger than I really am. I suppose I could take your comment as a compliment."

"Don't."

"Come on, Scythe. Jon is my friend. He's a good boy. He's been working too hard at getting the salons back on track. He needs to get out and find a nice girl."

"Looks like he found one. An old girl, that is."

"Ooo-hoo," the Wretched bunch whistled.

"Look, Jon and I are like sister and brother—or, to be more accurate, I feel like his aunt." I don't know why I was explaining this, but a point was a point and I hated not to make mine. "I'd be his mother's much, much younger sister, of course."

"Some guys are into that whole Oedipus thing. He

looks like he's one of them. He's got a thing for you."

"You're being ridiculous. He's not attracted to me, and I am certainly not attracted to him!"

For the first time, I noticed a couple of heads bobbing behind Scythe. How long had they been there? The whole adrenaline-tunnel-vision deal was lasting a little bit too long for my taste. Was it the police? Jon's face appeared behind Scythe's right shoulder. He looked like he was going to cry. Damn. Tessa's face appeared at Scythe's left shoulder. She looked like she was going to kill me. Double damn.

A boom rattled through the room as a door from the alley busted open. "Police. Everybody freeze."

Thank God. Saved by the fuzz. Maybe they really would throw me back in jail.

Considering what awaited me with my friends, it was probably a safer place to be.

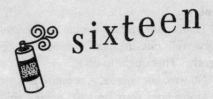

sixteen

"YOU SHOULDN'T ARGUE so much with your copper boyfriend," Gore advised as he was being led past me to the paddy wagon in handcuffs. "Guys don't like a chick with a mouth and an attitude."

"Yeah, man." Guts nodded behind him. He started crooning, "Men just like a soft body and a warm—"

"Whoa." I held up a hand before it got too graphic. "I get the idea."

"I was gonna say warm heart, man," Guts clarified with a pouchy lower lip. Ah, the real romantic of the Roadkill.

"Okay, dudes, I appreciate the advice. I make myself a mute and I've got it made. Right?"

"I dated a chick once that was a mute midget," Gore said, with a visual review of me. "You're too tall for that, but I tell you, she was the perfect girlfriend, better than a pair of drumsticks."

Okay, I wasn't going to think about that too hard.

An officer led a handcuffed DD past me. DD threw

me a wink and a lewd tongue-waggle. "You just want some, hot cheeks, come see me. You still owe me a thank-you."

"Thank you, DD," I said deliberately, moving my booty well out of sight behind the couch. I smiled sweetly. "That ought to do it."

"No way, hot cheeks. A promise is a promise."

"Don't hold your breath," Scythe told him as he sidled up to me. "She doesn't keep her deals."

I looked up at him with a steely glare, crossing my arms over my chest. He raised both eyebrows.

"Oh-whoa," the band bunch chanted from the paddy wagon.

Scythe waved them off. "Enough already."

The officers closed the paddy-wagon doors, and DD pressed his tongue against the back window as a goodbye. I couldn't suppress the shiver.

"Just think, he could've been all yours if I hadn't known you were going to do something stupid tonight."

I stared straight ahead.

Scythe sighed. "So who told you about Lexa's boyfriend?"

I stared at him.

"Have you gone mute?"

"Gore tells me that all dream girls are mute."

"Dream girl is not an option for you, so give up the mute thing."

I glared at him. No, I guess I didn't have legs to there and boobs to here, so I wouldn't be any man's dream. Well, there was my mouth. And, of course, the head-strong personality that I preferred to think of as independence—

"Now, that—what I just said," he said quietly, "you can take as a compliment."

Huh?

He called to the Austin officers to hold the paddy wagon.

Oh, so his strategy was to keep me off balance. Well, I wasn't falling for it.

"So, am I going to have them take you in for obstruction, or are you going to tell me how you found out about the boyfriend?"

DD was doing the tongue thing again. Okay, I'd fall for Scythe's strategy. Just this once. "A customer told me she ran into Lexa at a concert and she was romancing a member of the opening band. I did some sleuthing and we ended up here."

"You didn't think to mention it to me?"

"Well, I knew you were busy, going to see Shauna and checking out the Dumpster. How did that turn out, by the way?"

He lifted his left eyebrow. "We found a body in the Dumpster. Thanks for the tip."

"A body?! It was supposed to be just a little blood on a photo. Now, if it were animal parts, that's a different story. . . ."

Scythe got a little too close and a little too still. He held my gaze a little too long. "If you knew that, why didn't you tell me more specifically what we were looking for?"

"I didn't believe my informant," I said, thinking on my feet. "I thought telling you would predispose you to expect a certain something when it very well could have been anything."

"I don't believe you, but I can't argue with the strategy, and you know it. Sneaky girl. Now, what's this about animal parts? Does this have something to do with Wretched Roadkill?"

"I don't know." I mulled a moment about Annette, her connection, and the possibility the Roadkill had left Percy the parts. But why? They could've done it, but then the threats Percy was receiving were unrelated to the murder. The band had an alibi for the night of Wilma's murder, and besides, I believed Asphalt's denial. Of course, Lexa could've killed her mom on the band's orders. Theoretically. My intuition told me that wasn't true, but I doubt Scythe would buy that reasoning. He was more a facts man. "I can't tell you any more until I clear it with my source."

Scythe blew out a breath and looked at the sky. It must be catching. All the men around me seemed to be doing that tonight.

"Now, what's this about a body?"

He shrugged. "Just a joke."

I looked at him. He was telling the truth. "It's not funny."

"You said it." He put his finger under my chin and forced me to look into his eyes. These weren't just any eyes. Steel blue and strong as a punch, eyes to make the devil tell the truth. "None of this is funny, Reyn. It's not funny that you are so mixed up in this murder investigation that you were close to getting yourself killed. Again."

"Close only counts in the backseat of the car," I quipped to lighten the intensity of his mood.

He held up his right hand. "Don't tell me, your gran used to say it."

"Still does, to my nieces and nephews."

The corners of his hard mouth turned up. "One day, I want to meet this lady."

Ooh, wouldn't that be a field day for Gran? I'd have to sell tickets to that encounter.

Hand on my elbow, he led me over to an Austin patrol car. "But until then, let the detectives talk to you. Give them a complete statement, then go home with your pals and make trouble with hair instead of with outlaws . . ." He paused as he turned to leave. ". . . and little boys."

"Nice boys, don't you mean?" I challenged as he strode away.

He stopped in the middle of the parking lot. He was backlit by the neon sign shining between two buildings, so I couldn't see his face, but I could hear the honey in his baritone. "If nice is what you want, you don't know how *nice* this boy can be."

Austin isn't a big town, but it is the state capital and a hotbed of technology, so there's money and power here. Money and power always breed a different atmosphere amongst public servants. Here the police seemed somehow slicker and less approachable than our hometown men in blue. Scythe was probably the most professional, hard detective I'd run into in San Antonio—I'd accidentally met a few—and, still, he was rough around the edges. He was definitely a cowboy cop, and these Austin guys were more what I'd call calculator cops.

I was sitting in a patrol car, waiting for someone to take my statement, when two detectives walked by. "I've never seen a badge get in trouble from more departments in so short a time as Scythe—the SAPD, Terrell Hills PD, now us."

I sat very still and held my breath as the second detective chimed in, "All because of a meddling girlfriend."

I wondered what Zena had been up to, besides the bogus threat I'd blamed on her. Their next statement made me realize whom they were really talking about.

"I heard her mucking around actually ended up solving that Ricardo's Salon murder, but she nearly got knocked off in the process. Now here she is in the middle of this one, too, mixed up with guns and drugs and killing."

The other cop tsked loudly. "She must be good."

Ha!

"At something, anyway."

At irritating and infuriating, I was sure would be Scythe's answer.

The pair wandered off out of earshot, worse luck. I could pretty much guess why Scythe would be in trouble with the SAPD over the Ricardo deal. I did get a tiny bit overinvolved with that investigation. He'd probably shielded me from a lot of heat then. I guess the Terrell Hills PD, probably just Manning, was pissed that I wasn't arraigned. Maybe Scythe had called in a bigger favor than I imagined in getting me out of that one. The Austin PD likely hated that Scythe had come into their territory, into a situation that would require pulling a gun, without giving them a heads-up.

Okay, I felt properly guilty now. However, I wouldn't put it past Scythe to have staged the whole conversation just to evoke such an emotion in me. It was probably the only one that would make me think twice about meddling further.

And he knew it.

The car door opposite me opened, and I jumped. A woman detective held out her hand. I shook it. She was probably close to forty, her demeanor as no-nonsense as that of my high school math teacher. "Detective Darcy. I need to ask you a few questions."

I nodded. "Go ahead."

She asked me to review the events of the evening, which I did.

"What I don't understand is why they wanted to kill us," I mulled.

"The marijuana is a new strain, super-high quality, traceable to a certain area of Mexico and a certain supplier. Mr. Ugarte apparently recognized the quality, commented on it. They got nervous."

Probably to kill time so he could avoid taking a toke. At least, I hoped so.

"Were you offered any drugs?"

"No, I just saw that one cigarette that I thought looked like what might be drugs."

"What do you mean, 'what might be drugs'?"

"Well, I've never seen drugs before, so I have to guess."

She studied me over her oval, wire-rimmed glasses with a dubious look that said she might discount my entire version of the night's events based on that answer.

"It's true," I insisted.

What is the world coming to when the cops won't believe that a woman without a police record has never laid eyes on drugs?

"I take it back," I put in.

Darcy looked vindicated in her skepticism.

"I've seen them on TV, on an episode of *COPS* once."

She rolled her eyes heavenward. Her too, huh?

"Well, Ms. Sawyer," she said, "while this all might be too much for you to comprehend, having led the sheltered life you have, it seems that the members of Wretched Roadkill were doing some drug running for some businessmen in Oaxaca."

Uh-oh, these businessmen were sounding familiar.

"Do you know who these guys are?" I asked Darcy.

"No." She looked at me sharply. "Do you?"

"I was just wondering how you found out about them. Are the Roadkill rolling on the bad guys?"

"Yeah, some guy named DD in the paddy wagon is offering to tell all in exchange for a prison that allows conjugal visits."

Oh, swell. I hoped DD didn't have my phone number. Of course with my piss-poor luck, he'd blab so much the authorities would be so grateful, they would let him walk and he'd be on my front porch by the time I got home.

"I bet they met these Oaxacan businessmen through Percy Barrister, didn't they?"

"Is that"—she reviewed her notes—" 'Asphalt's chick's old man'?"

I nodded. She shoved her glasses up the bridge of her nose and peered at me through the lenses. "How did you know about the connection?"

"Good guess?" I smiled, shifting like I was going to leave the car. "Maybe I should go buy a lottery ticket."

Suddenly Darcy's posture changed. She was on alert. Damn. I just had to open my big mouth, didn't I?

Putting one hand up, she quashed my plans to win millions. "Not so fast."

She called for her partner on her two-way radio, watching me for sudden moves. I had an itch on the back of my neck, but I was afraid to reach up to scratch it for fear she'd draw the revolver at her rib cage. I fidgeted, but she looked suspicious, so I stopped. Finally, the partner arrived, a whippet-thin fiftysomething who looked like a marathon runner or chain-smoker. He nodded when Darcy did a perfunctory introduction as he slid into the front seat and turned around to face us.

He never spoke. Apparently, the partner was a total trampoline—someone to bounce things off later. Darcy did all the grilling.

"How did you know about the connection between Oaxaca, the band, and this Barrister character?"

"I didn't. I was here looking for Lexa Barrister's boyfriend."

"Why?"

"The detectives working her mother's murder case seem to think she might have had something to do with it. I just want to make sure she doesn't take the rap for nothing." *Me, too,* I added in my head.

"So Lexa told you where you could find her boyfriend, this Asphalt?"

"Oh, no. She won't admit she has a boyfriend to me."

"Why not?"

I shrugged. "Trying to protect me, I guess."

"Or protect him."

I'd considered that, but I didn't like to hear it out loud. I frowned.

"So what makes you think there is a connection between the Roadkill, Barrister, and these Mexican guys?"

"I just happened to run into someone who works in the same building who mentioned that a scary pair who spoke only Spanish, very unlike his usual staid tax-law clients, were visiting Percy Barrister on a regular basis. When you said their suppliers were in Oaxaca, I thought that was too big a coincidence."

The trampoline nodded thoughtfully.

"The Terrell Hills investigators know about this, probably more than I do by now, so you can check with them." She grimaced. I knew about friction between police departments when it came to investigations. They all wanted to run the show instead of cooperate. This one was going to be a royal mess, and I'd just reminded her. It was Podunk PD versus the calculator cops.

Darcy handed me a steno pad. "Write down your contact information. It's looking like the daughter and boyfriend had something to do with the Barrister murder, maybe to protect the drug business. If this Lexa contacts you, let us know immediately."

Tramopline nodded. Bad sign.

I shook my head. "I really don't think that Wilma got killed because she found out about the drug running and put up an argument about it. I mean, if that was the case, why not just knock her off like it was an accident? Run her over, or booby-trap her car, slit her throat and dump her in the river or something. Why would they dress her face up like clown, take half an hour to spray her hair stiff, and leave her dead in her own house? Whoever killed Wilma had a personal vendetta, not a business agenda."

Trampoline's eyebrows went up. The corners of

Darcy's mouth went down. She held out her hand for the steno pad. After briefly flirting with the idea of leaving Zena Zolliope's address and phone, I was a good girl and jotted mine down and slapped it into Darcy's open hand.

"We'll make note of your opinion." I didn't see her taking any notes. "But it's looking like we can wrap these two cases up by the time we find the two missing perps."

Wow, what a fun ride this was going to be—Tessa insisted upon driving even though Rick had only had two sips of his Dos Equis and held a doobie at gunpoint. This had apparently rendered him unable to negotiate the roads in Tessa's opinion, so he sat in the passenger seat up front and withstood Tessa's silent reproof. Reproof for saving me from death, no doubt. I was not number one on her hit parade, having lured Rick back into temptations he hadn't even thought of in years and nearly gotten him killed. I nabbed the middle seat, planting myself squarely in the middle. There was no way I was sitting next to Jon. I felt guilty about what he'd heard, but it was true, and if he was really carrying a torch, it was better he dropped it now rather than later. The man in question threw a tortured look my way as he squeezed past, then hunkered down in the backseat, arms crossed, and looked out the window.

"Where are Trudy and Mario?" I asked. Only Rick, Tessa, and Jon had been waiting for me when I was finally released by Darcy and her trampoline.

"They were smarter than we were and booked it in the bedlam that followed the gunshots," Tessa answered tightly.

That was out of character for my best friend and her husband. I dialed her number on my cell phone. Her voice mail picked up immediately. I left a short, worried message and hung up.

"Did you all see which way Lexa and her boyfriend went?"

"I saw them come out, because I was watching for the two of you," Tessa said, "but just a second later came the gunshot and the crowd ran around bumping into each other like a bed of disturbed fire ants. That's about the time I lost Trudy and Mario, too. I guess they made for the door. Jon and I should've followed and let you two idiots walk home."

Some not-so-latent hostility filled the van.

I tried to lighten the mood. I cleared my throat. "So, how did the interrogations go for everybody?"

There was a beat of silence. Then Rick opened his mouth, but Tessa spoke first.

"This wasn't a job interview. My Lord, Reyn, don't you do anything normal? A simple night out on the town turns into a shootout at the O.K. Corral. First you try to kill my cat, now my husband. . . ."

"I'm sorry, Tessa. If I'd known there was even an out-side chance of that, I would have gone alone." *Hey, get over the cat thing,* I thought. It wasn't my fault he was sitting in the bushes and the murderer had used him as a brick through the window. Merlin had survived with-out a scratch and earned some major cat mojo—he won every fight on the block now.

A small groan in the backseat told me Jon still gripped the torch.

"The lesson here is you shouldn't go at all!" Tessa's

voice rose, then dropped back down as she continued, "Look, I was afraid for you and for Rick. Just promise me you'll stay out of this mess until the police wrap it up. It shouldn't be too long. It looks like the two cases were linked. They'll have everyone who's anyone under arrest within twenty-four hours, I hope."

"That's what I'm afraid of."

"Let it go, Reyn. I didn't see Lexa hanging around to defend you after she got you into this. She's in too deep to save."

Tessa reached over and switched on the news. I guess we were finished discussing our evening. The cellophanish voice of the radio news anchor announced the news at the top of the hour: "An Alamo Heights makeup artist was found dead in her salon just after midnight. An anonymous caller tipped off police to the victim of an apparent shooting. This is the second murder this week in the '09 zip code. The funeral for a Terrell Hills philanthropist found shot to death in her home Saturday night is set for a week from today. Wilma Locke Barrister's mother is apparently on a retreat in the mountains of New Mexico. Family have gone to find her to bring her back to bury her daughter. In other news . . ."

Tessa and I stared at each other via the rearvew mirror, completely mute.

Since coincidence was out of the question, was it my fault the happy, humming dumbbell was dead?

seventeen

FOUR HOURS OF SLEEP isn't good for me. I felt like roadkill, wretched as it comes. My eyeballs felt like they'd been sandblasted, my lungs felt like they'd been blowtorched, and my body felt like I'd been pulled through a knothole backwards. Gran used to say that, and I could never figure out why being pulled through backwards was more of an ordeal than frontwards. Once when I was ten and feeling particularly brave, I'd asked. She told me that I had more balls than a billy goat. I decided to leave that alone, along with the knothole deal. Some things in life you just have to accept and not ask why.

I betcha Scythe would say the murders of Wilma and now Shauna were two of those things in life for me to leave alone, but I was still going to find out why. I guess that meant that Scythe and the murderer(s) didn't intimidate me as much as Gran did.

Enough philosophical ruminating, it was time for action. I eased up in bed and leaned against the headboard. It was no sudden action—after all, I didn't want to hurt myself. The girls didn't look like they felt any better than I did, or perhaps they were acting like that to punish me for keeping them outside until three in the morning. Beau opened one eye, glared at me, and put her head back on the pillow next to mine. I hadn't noticed her getting up on the bed with me, but I probably wouldn't have noticed Ben Affleck on Viagra climbing in with me, that's how worn-out I'd been. Char actually got up from her dog bed, dragged her tongue across my cheek, and sank down on the floor next to me. Cab sniffed at the toes of my right foot sticking out of the covers and raised her doggie eyebrows at me.

I decided to do something drastic. I threw the covers back and leaped to my feet. The girls all jumped up, barking. Mistake. My ears started ringing again after their abuse from the Roadkill. I clapped my hands over them, but it didn't help.

Coffee. It made everything better.

If a man brought me coffee in bed before I got up in the morning, I would probably marry him on the spot. No one I've ever dated has even offered. I know, I pick the wrong men. Tell me about it. I tried to train my Labs to do it, but it didn't really work out all that well. I never did get the coffee stains off my throw rugs.

I wondered if the bald vitamin salesman down the street would bring me coffee in bed. Probably. Once he forgot about my part in his toasted Porsche, I'd see about that. Scythe, I could forget. He was the macho type who'd probably expect me to bring *him* coffee in bed. Besides, he was bringing other things to Zena in bed. Right now, probably. The visual I got with that thought made me feel like a porn pervert.

I considered throwing a robe over my Lyle Lovett "Creeps Like Me" T-shirt and boxer shorts I'd worn to bed, but, frankly, robes are superfluous when in the company of only dogs. When I crossed the threshold, all three were there, trying to muscle their way in front. We nearly got stuck. Then they hauled ass down the stairs, yipping for their kibble in the kitchen. I had to take care of that before I got to the coffee, but finally I sucked in the air full of Costa Rican brew.

Ahh. The world was right again.

That is, until I zapped on the television to see the lovely and beguiling Amethyst Andrews on News4 talking to green–bow-tie–wearing Phil Wimplepool outside a house that looked familiar. Very familiar, as a matter of fact. I peered at the nineteen-inch screen on my kitchen TV. A two-story historic Spanish Colonial. Probably in Monte Vista. I recognized that front porch. Making sure the dogs were busy with their breakfast, I tiptoed to the door that leads to the salon, let myself in, and hugged the hall wall until I got to my dark office, where I could peek through the closed miniblinds.

Yikes!

Three television remote trucks were parked out front. Photographers and reporters were milling around.

Of course, being the visualizer I was, I hadn't listened to a word they were saying on the damned news, distracted by what I was seeing; so I tip-ran back to my kitchen, hunkered down next to the television, and listened.

". . . so here I am, waiting to talk to the city's favorite

amateur detective-cum-hairdresser, Reyn Marten Sawyer, about her latest *brush* with death and how it may relate to the bizarre murder of her customer's mother, famed Terrell Hills philanthropist Wilma Barrister."

I switched channels. The CBS affiliate also had a remote truck outside Shauna's office, which was decorated with bright yellow DO NOT CROSS tape. The reporter was interviewing a neighbor who hadn't heard anything and hadn't seen anything, but wanted to bitch about how the murder was going to "kill his property value." Sensitive sort.

The way the reporter wrapped up his report, it seemed the media hadn't made the connection between Shauna and Percy, only that it was two murders in the '09 zip in a week. I moved to the NBC affiliate, whose anchor was talking to an Austin reporter outside Bangers. Wretched Roadkill were under arrest, allegedly part of a drug distribution ring that must somehow involve Percy Barrister, who was under arrest on drug charges in New Mexico, where he'd gone to look for his mother-in-law to bring her back for the funeral. The funeral had been postponed because Lexa was missing, Percy was in jail, and Wilma's mother wanted to burn her daughter on an Indian-style funeral pyre.

I returned to Amethyst and company, who were listening to their police reporter explain that her source had told her that the Terrell Hills cops had enough circumstantial evidence to charge Percy with his wife's murder and Lexa and her boyfriend, who were still at large, as accessories. The police reporter turned to Manning, who stood stiff as a statue except for the beads of sweat popping out on his upper lip. Leaning toward him, she asked for a comment; then when he opened his mouth, she stepped back. Halitosis must have hit. "I cannot confirm nor deny," he monotoned.

"Come on!" I said out loud to the almost admission. I almost felt sorry for Officer Bad Breath.

The dogs, who'd lapped up the last of their food, now started whining. They were going to have to go out, but then the assembled crowd would know I was home. Damndamndamn. I blew out a frustrated breath and shooed them out the door. It took them all of two seconds to realize we were the most popular kids on the block. They went doggie ballistic. Good, at least it would keep the pretty faces from storming my back door.

That was the upside. The downside hit immediately as all three of my phones started ringing, my cell phone, my home phone, and the salon phone, which I could hear through the wall. Great. I'd been waiting to hear from Trudy and Lexa, both of whom I'd left frantic messages for on our way home last night. I was too cheap to get caller ID so I didn't know who was on the two landlines. Served me right for being a tightwad, but the phone company didn't use this as part of the marketing: *Be sure to get caller ID so if you are wanted by reporters and cops countywide, you can avoid them with alacrity while still taking calls from your friends on the lam.* I checked my cell; it was a blocked number. I had to answer.

"*Hola?*" I screeched with a heavy accent.

"Hello." Cellophane voice. "I am hoping to speak with—" Reporter. I eighty-sixed her but fast.

It rang again immediately. Another blocked number.

I went through the drill another three times before I finally answered and heard: "Gory goblins and geeky ghostbusters, Reyn, who do you think is going to buy that terrible accent?"

"Trudy! Where the hell did you go?"

"Mario and I, uh, left."

"I could see that. Thanks a lot for the moral support."

"We were helping you in another way."

Sure. I know I am a difficult friend to have, being involved in two murder investigations in less than a year, but, hey, when shots are fired and your pal's behind the closed door, wouldn't you stick around to find out if you had to write her eulogy or not?

"Well," I allowed only a bit sullenly, "I'm just glad you two are okay. You *are* all right?"

"We're fine. *All* your friends are fine."

Yeah, whatever. "I'll try to get by and see you later today."

"Just make sure you're not followed."

Huh? Since when was publicity hound Trudy afraid of reporters? Sheesh. "Forget it," I said, and hung up on whatever apology she was whispering into the phone. Just what I needed right now, my best friend to go high-maintenance on me.

My salon phone was still ringing off the hook, probably all my customers who were canceling because they didn't want to go through a phalanx of TV cameras with their roots showing. My cell started vibrating again. I'd kept an eye on the TV and saw News4 return to the live shot of my house with Bettina shaking her booty almost out of her favorite purple suede miniskirt and her lavender satin blouse barely containing her triple-D all-water transvestite bra as she sashayed up the salon stairs. She waved at the reporters and hiked her skirt up a little higher to show more leg. Yikes. That skirt was short. I hoped she'd employed plenty of duct tape this morning or her secret would be out. Literally. That's just what I needed.

As I watched Bettina unlock the salon door with a jaunty wave at the cameras, I looked at the number on my ringing cell phone. Charlotte. I punched the answer button. "Reyn? Reyn! Are you okay? Isn't this exciting? You are famous! I mean, more famous than you were before! Are you going to talk to the reporters at your front door? Wow. I can't stand it, this is so fun! Bettina's on the news! She is so beautiful. Life is just not fair that she's that gorgeous and she's a he."

"You have no idea how unfair life can be," I deadpanned.

"Wow. I mean, really wow. Hey, did you talk to my friend?" I could hear her *wink, wink* over the phone.

"Yes, I did. She was very helpful." Threatening, but helpful. "Listen, can you call her and try to convince her to call Lieutenant Jackson Scythe at the SAPD? She can call anonymously, but he really needs the information she gave me, even if he has to find another source to confirm it."

"Wow. Sure. Then I'd be really part of the investigation, wouldn't I? I'd be assistant to 'San Antonio's favorite amateur detective.' You know the news is calling you that?"

I made a noncommittal sound. It didn't matter. Charlotte didn't ever need an answer. She was a one-person conversationalist. "I'll call her right now and get back to you, boss." She gasped in excitement. "Wow, maybe we can put out our own shingle—Sawyer and Holmes Investigations. Like Sherlock and Holmes. Wow!"

I shivered as she disconnected. That was scarier than anything that had happened so far.

You know, I am convinced that everything in life is timing. Think back on things that have happened to you and what might be different if you had made that green light or said no to the first boy who asked you to the senior prom. I know the answer to the second question: I'd be pregnant with five kids, which is exactly what happened to the girl who went to the prom with the second boy who asked me. I said yes to the pharmacist's son, who was scared of his own shadow and didn't even try to hold my hand, much less anything else. I had to say no to the studliest boy in school, who would've been impossible to resist in a tuxedo. I have an issue with testosterone—I can't resist it in certain quantities. Thank goodness for that particular timing. Whew.

As I was waxing philosophical, finishing my last cup of Costa Rican and wondering what timing would behoove me in this situation, my doorbell started ringing without the accompaniment of the dogs' barking. One of the reporters and/or cameramen (I knew women operated news cameras, too, but feminizing the name was more cumbersome than political correctness was worth) had made friends with the girls, who now sat, tails wagging, tongues lolling, inside the fence along my front walkway, and my level of protection had been severely handicapped. I'd hoped three hundred pounds of teeth-baring dogs would've intimidated the news pretties for longer than that. So much for Labs. I'd have to invest in a pit bull—or maybe a dragon—if I was going to keep getting involved in murder investigations.

Ring-ring. Knock-knock. "Miss Sawyer!"

I leaned forward in my kitchen chair and peered down the hallway to my living room. The door shook with more knocking. "Reyn Marten Sawyer, we know you're in there."

A male face wearing Pan-Cake makeup appeared at my window. I jumped back, chair and all, behind the wall. Had they no shame? Maybe the networks had called. No, probably not yet. If that were the case, the locals would be crawling up through the toilets to get at me for their chance to appear on national news.

Not that I had anything against reporters, mind you. It was the nature of their business and you couldn't hold it against them that the only way to get ahead was to get the story that would capture the most viewers. It was just like traders who wanted to find the best undervalued stock before everyone else discovered it. I suppose you could say I was that day's undervalued stock in the news world.

I called Scythe. "What is going on?"

He sighed heavily, and from the gravel in his voice I could tell he hadn't slept since I'd seen him just hours before. "You heard the news?"

"I *am* the news."

"That's your own dumb fault."

"Did I suggest anything different?"

"Look, the feds have Percy and the THPD have decided to charge him with Wilma's murder. If you hear from Alexandra, talk her into turning herself in, but stay away from her because she is going to be charged with being an accessory."

A rock dropped in my stomach. "What about me?"

"I'm sure the prosecutors want you as a material witness, but as far as I've heard you're just being accused of being gullible for falling for Alexandra's act."

"It's not an act!"

"Reyn"—Scythe's baritone hardened—"if that is the worst you get in this deal, you're ending up damned lucky. Just keep your mouth shut and be grateful."

Grateful to be called gullible? I didn't think so.

"So you really think Percy whacked Wilma?" I challenged.

Another sigh, this one longer. "No, I don't. He's guilty of messing around on his wife and guilty of using his daughter to get to her boyfriend's band to use them as drug runners for some scary kingpins, but I don't think he's directly guilty of murder."

"Then why are you wimping out and letting them do this? The killer is still out there. Aren't you their trusted advisor?"

"Look, Reyn, this is has become a huge clusterf—" He paused. I didn't know why I required a censor, but he apparently thought I did. He continued, "Fairy tale. I've voiced my opinion, but it's being largely ignored. I have no authority in any of the departments involved. There are too many agencies investigating and none of them of cooperating with the others—Terrell Hills, Austin, Alamo Heights, the feds. They'll be lucky not to arrest each other by the time this is over."

"So you're giving up."

"I didn't say that, but you'd better."

"What about Shauna's murder? Nobody is saying anything about that."

There was a long stretch of silence. Uh-oh.

"She was shot in the chest, point-blank range. I think the general consensus is that your friend Lexa was sent by Percy to off her to keep her quiet about her part—doing the makeup—in Wilma's murder."

"And, of course, Lexa has to go running off from us just in time so she has no alibi. Great."

"She hasn't helped herself at all with her recent behavior if she is innocent," Scythe admitted.

"I still don't see what motive they're attributing to Percy and Lexa for Wilma's murder," I mused.

"She found out about the drug money—Percy apparently was depositing his illicit income in a secret account in the Cayman Islands—and threatened to blow the whistle."

"Weak. Why the clown makeup?"

"Results of the autopsy came back. It was done premortem. It's being surmised that it was the girlfriend's idea, to humiliate Wilma."

"Pretty dumb if they didn't want to get caught, considering Shauna's line of work."

"True."

"This doesn't feel right."

"Reyn, it doesn't matter how it feels to you, just as long as you aren't in jail when you're feeling it."

"But what about that Charis girl I told you about from the Junior League?"

"We can't find much of a motive there, Reyn, although she doesn't have an alibi."

"What?"

"I can't say any more."

"How about the rest of Percy's clients? Lexa told me he had a lot of high-powered folks he worked for."

"We have someone working down that list. So far, nothing."

"What about his associates?"

"What kind of associates? He just had a receptionist and a paralegal."

"Uh-huh."

"What are you trying to tell me, Reyn?"

The silence stretched. I didn't want to point at Annette. I just wanted to nudge him in the general direction. "If you get the chance, look at the photos in Shauna's house. Then look at Percy's associates."

"How charmingly cryptic. Reyn, this isn't a game. Cancel all your appointments today. Don't answer your phones or your door. Turn off your television. Read a book." He paused, then added quickly, "Not a mystery. Read a romance. Educate yourself, for a change."

"If I educate myself in that department, I might just have to go looking for a romantic man."

His baritone smoothed around the edges again. "You never know when one of those might turn up."

There was a long pause while I tried to read between the lines of what Scythe had said. Was he trying to put me off on another man? Was he throwing a hint about his own latent romantic abilities?

Finally he broke the silence, his tone hard again, back to business. "Look. Reyn, I'll send my bodyguard over to watch your house so the reporters don't give you too hard a time."

"What about your death threats?"

"It turns out they might've been a hoax. The one who we thought started it insists she was set up. I believe her."

Well, of course you do! With legs up to here and boobs out to there, who wouldn't believe Zena Zolliope?

He continued, unaware of my internal commentary, "The captain has assigned a detective to find out who started it. Don't worry. We'll get her."

Oops.

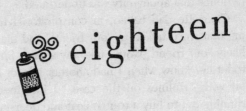

eighteen

I SHOULD'VE READ A ROMANCE. Instead, I picked up my favorite book of all time, *Gone With the Wind,* and started to read it again. I'd long admired Scarlett because she was strong and independent and went after what she wanted. I liked to think of myself that way. Of course, she also fell for the testosterone, and there was no happy ending. I wasn't sure what I would learn, reading it for the twentieth time.

I thought it had something to do with hardheaded survival. I wasn't sure Scythe would have approved.

I'd turned down the volume on my answering machine because it was making me crazy and put my cell phone under the couch pillow. When I finally took a break from reading, both my mailboxes were, thank goodness, full. I listened to all of the messages, deleting none because I didn't want to make room for more. Most were, not surprisingly, from the media. I was tempted to return the call from the stringer for my favorite magazine, *People,* but I resisted. I knew from experience that anonymity was underrated.

Charlotte had called, in conspiratorial tones telling me that she'd talked to "our friend" and that it was unlikely "our friend" would take my advice. She asked me to let her know when I had another job for her, signing off with "Holmes on the case." I imagined Charlotte running out to buy a trench coat and deerstalker hat for her next assignment.

"Miss Sawyer," began the next message in a cellophane tenor that sounded familiar the way all broadcast voices do, "I have something of yours you might want back. It's brown and has four legs. Call me if you are interested in a trade." He left a number.

My stomach clutched. I ran to the kitchen window and peeked through the blinds to inventory my girls. Black and yellow, no chocolate. Beau and Char were posted at the fence, wagging their tails and barking. What a mixed message. Great watchdogs they were, to let one of their own get snatched. I knocked on the window to make sure Cab wasn't napping against the house or under a bush. Her mother and sister came running, but no Cab.

Damn. Someone had kidnapped my dog.

I grabbed the phone and dialed.

"I'm glad you value your pooch."

"What do you want?"

"An exclusive interview. Or I cancel your canine."

I felt like I was in a bad B movie. "Who are you?"

"Come on, now, if I'm smart enough to figure out your prized possession, don't you think I'm smart enough not to answer that question?"

I held my tongue. I didn't want my dog beaten to death with a microphone.

"So, meet me, alone, under the bridge at Woman Hollering Creek and Windy Road in a half hour. Or else."

"Hey, what about the reporters staking out my house? I can't make myself invisible, you know."

"Lose 'em. I hear you're good at that. With men, anyway."

A journalistic comedian. This just kept getting better and better.

After I'd tried calling every friend I thought I had to tell them I was heading directly into danger and got nothing but "Leave a message," I didn't have long to get to the rendezvous spot in the country northeast of the city limits. For the record, my call to Scythe went straight to voice mail, which meant he was probably talking to Zena about their next date. Being the sap I am, I left a message anyway. Quickly, I threw on underwear, jeans, and the Wolverine work boots, camo T-shirt, and camo cap my brother Dallas had given me for Christmas one year. Dallas probably was hoping the ensemble would attract a hunter for me to date so he'd have someone to go to his deer lease with. That's how my brother gave gifts—hoping they would indirectly benefit him. Who would've guessed they would help in this situation? Maybe I'd get the chance to sneak up on the creep through the bushes and nab my dog back without giving the interview.

Journalists made me nervous because many of them manipulated the two things I had in abundance—honesty and emotion. As I approached the bridge, I counseled myself to lie and detach myself from the murder mess my friend had gotten me into.

It had been embarrassingly easy to get by the phalanx of reporters, who just waved without mobbing me as I backed my truck out of my driveway. That made me very suspicious, but perhaps I was just paranoid. Maybe the story had cooled, and they were the B-team assigned to find something for filler. After all, I didn't see Phil Wimplepool anywhere.

I rounded the corner and saw a beat-up sedan under the bridge. There were no bushes or foliage around that could camouflage me for sneaking up. For a second, I battled panic that the real killer had lured me into a trap. But then I realized he would have no reason to come after me now, not with the police trying so hard to wrap up the damned cases and tie them around Percy and Lexa's necks. I supposed it could be a crony of Wretched Roadkill trying to eliminate a witness, but they'd be more likely to take care of Rick before they took care of me. After all, he had touched the weed and actually knew what drugs looked like, not like a piss-poor ignoramus like me. Rick was alive and well; I'd seen him building a deck on the back of his house when I'd left. Tessa had given him a list of home improvement projects that would keep him entirely too busy for the next decade to be led astray, if he was so inclined.

So I guessed the man sitting behind the wheel was really a reporter.

I parked next to the sedan, and the guy cranked his window down. I didn't know what kind of reporter he was, but he had a face for radio, that was for sure. He was an indeterminate age somewhere between mid-forties and seventy, had long, brown Willie Nelson hair held back in a ponytail, and wore a Grateful Dead T-shirt and a quick smile that I answered with a smile. What? I couldn't believe I instinctively liked the guy—after all, he'd nabbed my dog.

"Where is Cabernet?"

"Hey, honey, I don't have any wine on me. I thought we were doing business. Of course, after we wrap that up, if you'd like, I know a nice biker bar not far from here. I'm not sure they have wine, but they have a great brew—"

"Cabernet is my dog."

"Oh, the dog." He cocked his head to the rear of the old Ford. "She's in back."

I looked at the trunk in horror, jumping out of my truck. "She's in the trunk?" I ran over and started pounding on the metal. "Cab, don't be scared. I'm here now. Are you suffocating?"

"Ma'am, ma'am. The dog's in the back*seat*. I'd never put an animal in the trunk. What do you take me for?"

I rushed to the rear window and looked in. Cab was stretched out on the floorboards, a huge, meaty bone between her paws. I called her, and she looked up, tongue lolling, beef scraps between her teeth. She thumped her tail twice and went back to the bone. Traitor.

"Nice look." The guy gave my getup a once-over. "What are you going hunting for? It's quail season, I suppose, and rabbits, they're always good with a little cabbage."

"Why am I here?" I wondered aloud, thinking this

whole escapade might do for another episode of *The Twilight Zone*.

"To get your dog." He smiled.

"Come on, Cab." I reached for the door handle. It was locked.

"After you give me an interview," he added genially, hopping out and coming around the car to open the passenger-side door.

"Why do you even want one?"

"I'm a disc jockey by trade, but I've always had a dream, a dream to be part of the news department. They never would give me a chance. If I get this exclusive interview, they have to give me a chance, now, don't they?"

If it hadn't come at my expense, his determination might have impressed me. I forced my best saleswoman smile. "You know, you really don't have to go to this extreme. My gran always told me that true passion for something is an unbeatable advantage. Surely if you do some volunteering in the news department, they'll recognize your passion for the business. We all had to start at the bottom and work up—"

"I'm too old to start at the bottom," he interrupted. "Besides which, I hand over this interview, and it will say passion with a capital *P*."

I hate it when people turn my arguments to their own advantage.

Grinning, he held out his hand. "Roy Gene, W-H-A-T FM."

I shook it reluctantly. He knew who I was, obviously. "Nice to meet you," I muttered instead. Why do we do that—us well-mannered people? He'd kidnapped my dog, yet my manners were so ingrained I couldn't *not* respond in kind when he was polite. It smacked of parental brainwashing. Beware, all moms and dads, what you drill into your kids.

We settled in his car. He extracted a tape recorder and microphone. "You know," I said, "my aunt Big does a show on radio every Sunday."

"Talk radio? What's her subject?" he asked as he fiddled with some wires.

"*Bertha Talks Big*. She deals with being plus-size in a minus-size world," I answered, remembering the time she took me to the Brenham radio station where it was taped in the middle of the week. It sounded like we were going out live. Then I was taken aback when I heard it on the radio Sunday morning two weeks later. It sounded so live, even I was almost fooled.

Cab was moaning in ecstasy over her bone. I wondered how that would play in the background. I guessed with modern technology, they could delete her before they played the tape on the air. As Roy Gene started his tape, then talked into the microphone about the events of the last couple of days—about the hellacious murder of a society scion, the arrests of a headbanger band on Austin's Sixth Street, and the shooting of a beautiful makeup artist who was rumored to be involved with the husband of the society scion—I got an idea. He had a big, soothing, low tenor, and I imagined he'd be a terrific host for one of those radio call-in shows. Too bad he'd never get his big break, because I was going to nab his tape just like he'd nabbed my dog. All was fair in love, war, and journalism.

I relaxed.

"Reyn Marten Sawyer, hairdresser by trade and

sleuth by accident, finds herself involved in yet another murder investigation involving a friend. You will all remember she tracked down the murderer of salon king Ricardo Montoya last spring. Reyn, how do you find yourself mixed up in another one?"

"Trying to help a friend."

"You'd think you'd learn your lesson."

"Good for you I didn't, since what I'm doing right now is helping you."

"What she means, folks, is helping all of us understand what's going on inside this case. We appreciate that, Reyn, really we do. That friend we were talking about is Alexandra Barrister, daughter of the murdered society woman. Word on the street is she is an oddball who finally cracked."

"I'd say she is a sensitive, caring young woman who had a difficult childhood."

"She grew up in one of the richest families in San Antonio. That's real tough."

"Money isn't everything. You're not doing this for money, are you, Roy Gene?"

"She's got me there, folks. I'm doing it to inform you as a member of the esteemed fourth estate. So, Reyn, you don't think like the Alamo Heights cops do, that Alexandra helped her daddy and his girlfriend get rid of moneybags by dolling her up like Bozo on a bad hair day and spraying her stiff? Or that maybe it was a drugged-up assassin who thought he'd come up with a new hip style along with a body?"

"No, I don't, Roy Gene. I think the killer is someone the police haven't even thought of yet. Someone who hated Wilma Barrister with an uncommon passion."

"But Wilma Barrister was a saint among women, raised money for charities, saved little children from starvation."

"Often, Roy Gene, things are not what they seem. Few people want to look below the surface, beyond the obvious. The police in this case apparently are not willing to do so either."

"Any names, Reyn?"

"If I had names, Roy Gene, I'd give them to the police, not to you."

"Nobody said this girl wasn't smart. Reyn, the two loves of Percy's life are gone, he's behind bars. Do you think it was someone who had it in for the drug-running tax lawyer?"

"It could be, Roy Gene, although it would be someone who'd be inclined to take great risks in order to make him suffer."

"Then it would have to be a woman, because, folks, I don't know anyone more vindictive than a dame who's been crossed."

As I listened to the DJ enjoy his chuckle, I considered Annette again. She was a possibility, although I just didn't see her having enough emotion. I'd have to see if Charlotte could get her to provide a list of Percy's old girlfriends. Maybe angry Charis of the Junior League was on that list.

Roy Gene was wrapping up his report with a great deal of verbosity. ". . . And so, make note, folks, that Reyn Marten Sawyer is standing by the innocence of her missing friend, and thinks the nameless, faceless killer is still on the loose."

He turned the tape recorder off and smiled.

"Can I take my dog home now?"

"Sure thing. Drive safe. Thanks for the interview."

"You bet." I reached back, grabbed the dog bone, and clobbered Roy Gene on the head with it. His eyes went wonky, and he collapsed against the steering wheel. I ejected the tape and jumped out of the car. I opened Cab's door and ran her over to the truck, letting her chase the bone into the backseat. I felt a little guilty, Lord only knew why. I guessed it was another one of those brainwashing things my parents did to me. I ran back to check the DJ's pulse. It was strong. I started to leave, then grabbed his pen and wrote "Sorry" on his blank pad of paper.

Sliding in behind the wheel of my truck, I peeled out, relieved I had my dog and my tape. I turned on the radio in the car and heard my voice.

Uh-oh.

I called Trudy. "I'll forgive you for abandoning me last night if you let me hide at your house. Just for a little while."

"Uh, I'm sorry, Reyn, you can't. Not tonight, anyway. But we heard you, all over the radio and TV just now—"

No wonder the damned reporters had let me leave the house. Roy Gene had made a deal to feed them the interview live.

"—sounded like an orangutan having an orgasm in the background—but, overlooking that, you were so brave and principled to stand by Lexa. She's so grateful. Of course, Scythe is going to kill you, but—"

"What did you say about Lexa?"

"I said she was *going to be* so grateful."

"No you didn't, you said she *was* grateful. How would you know that?"

"Barnacles' balls and jellyfish jowls, Reyn. I've got to go. Talk later. Bye." Trudy was rattled. Little liar.

My cell phone rang before I could get my finger off the end button. It was Scythe's number.

"What the hell do you think you're doing?"

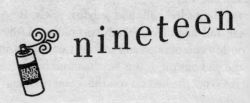

nineteen

"DID YOU THINK you were helping the investigation? Tell me your thought process on this, given you had one to begin with."

Scythe's voice was eerily calm. He was angrier than I'd ever known him to be.

"He kidnapped Cab. That was the deal to get her back."

"You do come up with some doozies, Reyn. Points for creativity. Deductions for not using it properly."

"Really, Scythe. He had her, ask any of the reporters staking out my house. I know they must have seen him do it, probably helped him; then he made the deal to transmit the interview back live."

"Only to you would something like this happen. Who the hell would think of kidnapping a damned dog?"

"Not just any dog. This was Cabernet, Scythe."

He blew out a sigh into my ear. I fidgeted on my seat. His breath did that to me, even over the phone. "Okay, so why didn't you call me when you found out 'not just any dog' was . . . gone?"

"Held for ransom," I corrected. "And, anyway, I did call and had to leave a message because you were obviously 'otherwise engaged.'"

"All you said was 'Please call me back when you get a chance,'" he mimicked. "You didn't say, 'This is an emergency.'"

"I didn't think you'd think it was an emergency."

"Stop thinking for me," he snapped. "You need all the help you can get to just think for yourself."

Showing great restraint, I kept quiet until he finally added, "So why didn't you call someone else in the PD?"

"Because he gave me a deadline and he said he'd kill her if I didn't come alone."

"And you didn't think we badge-wearing types have plans for things like that?"

"I had my own plan." Well, came up with one on the fly, anyway.

"Worked well, I see."

"I stole his tape. How was I supposed to know the interview had already gone live?"

"How did you steal his tape? It sounded like someone was having sex during the interview. Was that how you did it?"

"No, that was Cab chewing! I bashed Roy Gene on the head with a dinosaur-size dog bone!" I really hadn't intended to admit it, but he'd caught me off guard.

"Oh, super." Giant sigh. Louder finger drumming. Pause in which he likely ran hand through trailer-park-trash hair. More drumming. "So now I can expect this

Roy Gene character to come in and charge you with assault."

"Then I'll charge him with kidnapping."

"Good, then we can all spend our time investigating assault with a deadly bone and kidnapping of a Labrador named after a kind of wine, instead of finding the real killer."

"Quit making fun of me."

"Is there a better way to get you to stay out of this? I've tried everything else, asking politely, intimidating, demanding, even arresting you. I'm game for trying ridicule . . ." His voice drifted off, and I heard what sounded like a broadcast turned up and a deep baritone speaking, although I couldn't hear exactly what was said.

"Hello?" I called to Scythe.

I heard voices raised in the background. Then Scythe swore under his breath. I thought he said, "Damn Rangers," but I didn't know why he'd care about the Dallas baseball team in the middle of all this and so early in the season, too. Men, go figure. "We've got a big problem. Reyn, go home. Lock your doors. If you're not home in fifteen minutes, I will send an APB out on your truck." He disconnected, probably to watch the rest of his precious baseball game. I didn't know he was even a fan.

I despise being told what to do. But I believed he meant what he said, which meant I shouldn't give in to temptation and go by Trudy's house, which would've been my next exit off 281. Instead, reluctantly, I headed for home.

No one was waiting for me when I got there. Well, why would they be? The vultures had gotten their pound of flesh out of my Roy Gene interview, headed back to their respective stations to package up their stories for their late-night newscasts, and gone out to celebrate. They'd probably be camped out again first thing in the morning. Meanwhile, I was under house arrest.

Only if I listened to one bossy cop.

Cab and I let ourselves in through the kitchen door. The two outside were whining like I'd abandoned them for years instead of hours. I let them all in for the reunion and a kibble fix, then unlocked the door to my poor, neglected salon to find a note from Bettina about the day's exciting activities. Yes, clients had canceled for today, but all had rescheduled. She'd taken a hundred calls from people who wanted to come to me for their hair because they'd heard my name on the news. What did getting mixed up in murders have to do with doing good hair, anyway? These potential new clients scared me. I read on. Bettina had juggled reporters' inquiries all day, and one talent scout who'd seen her on the noon news told her he could make her more famous than Lucy Liu if she moved to Hollywood. I wondered if it was the same one who'd talked to Trudy. Was someone stalking my friends with offers of fame and fortune? Low blow, since all I had to offer was toil and trouble.

I returned to the part of my house I lived in and debated dinner. Food and I have a lifelong love affair that won't be denied by brushes with death, destruction, or having to fit into Levi's tomorrow. I opened the refrigerator and jumped back, startled again by its semiclean state. I was used to having to catch something falling out every time I opened it. Nothing even teetered this time. I'd forgotten my mission before Lexa's fateful call. I managed a moment of panic when I considered I might not have enough choices to satisfy me for din-din, but then I saw the instant egg foo young and I relaxed.

Popping it into the microwave, I reviewed what my second course might be. Some three-day-old jambalaya might not be bad. I set that out. Then I grabbed some frozen tiramisu to defrost for dessert. Vegetables? Hmm, I hadn't been to the store for four days and had thrown out some half-rotten possibilities the night Wilma was murdered. Veggies might be a problem. Then I brought myself up short. Who said I had to have vegetables at every meal? It was another one of those parental brainwashing things. I was thirty-one years old and wouldn't have a vegetable course. So there.

Feeling very rebellious, I sat down with some chopsticks and dug in. The doorbell rang.

A reporter? Scythe? The newspaper wanting me to subscribe? Roy Gene wanting revenge? DD wanting a quickie?

The last one made me check my peephole before I opened the door. The Marlboro Man stood on my doorstep, minus the horse and the cigarette. Maybe he'd left them at the curb. A Stetson with the perfect crease shadowed his face, but the contours of his chest through his button-down shirt and the bulge of his . . . thighs through his western slacks spoke to me. I decided I ought to let him in.

I opened the door. "Can I help you?"

"Ma'am," he said in a rich, deep baritone that sounded vaguely familiar and extremely toe-curling. He slid his Stetson off and held it. "I'm looking for Reyn Marten Sawyer."

"You found her," I breathed. *And boy, is she lucky, or what?* The Stetson had been hiding thick, jet-black hair just a shade too long to be considered regulation, and just right to be considered sexy. His hairline showed a cowlick fifteen degrees off-center to the right above green-gold eyes that crinkled at the corners, a chiseled face that bespoke some Native American blood, a seven-o'clock shadow, and a mobile mouth with a thin upper lip and plump lower lip that made a girl think about a kiss. And other things.

He reached into his back pocket. I tried not to stare at the way that made his Wranglers pull across his hips. He could've been reaching for a revolver and I wouldn't have cared. He flashed a badge instead. "My name is Clint Calhoun, ma'am, with the Texas Rangers."

Oh, were *those* the Rangers Scythe was so worked up about?

No wonder. This Ranger had me pretty worked up, too.

I hoped I wasn't panting.

I stared at him a beat. Two beats. Finally, he cleared his throat. "May I come in for a few moments?"

I stepped back too fast and nearly tripped over my own feet as I pulled the door back. Real cool. "Of course. Come in. Please." *Pretty please.*

"Thank you." He stepped over the threshold.

"Let's go into the kitchen." It was easier to hide the spread of my thighs under the kitchen table, rather than on the couch in the living room. I looked at myself in the hallway mirror. I was still in my camo-wear and Wolverines. The only thing more sexy would've been my "Creeps Like Me" T-shirt, which he picked up from where I'd left it slung over the kitchen chair and perused.

I braced for a lewd comment. He smiled instead. "Lyle Lovett fan?" I nodded. He nodded back. "Me, too."

My dream man.

He reviewed the array of food. I fiddled nervously with the tiramisu. "I was just sitting down to a late dinner. Would you like something?"

"Egg foo young. Jambalaya. Tiramisu. It sounds perfect. If you can spare some, that would be much appreciated." No snide comments, no cocked eyebrows, like someone else I knew. What a gentleman. I grabbed a plate and a couple of spoons so he could serve himself. "Something to drink?"

"Whatever you have handy, but don't bother yourself. I'll get it, ma'am."

"My mom's a ma'am. Please call me Reyn."

"All women are ma'ams," he said with a wry smile that bespoke some parental brainwashing of his own as he took the glass from me and poured himself some iced tea he found in the fridge. "But I'd be honored to call you Reyn."

Sigh.

"And what can I get for you to drink, Reyn?"

A dose of reality would be nice, because Ranger Clint was definitely too good to be true. "I'll have some tea, too, thanks."

He poured my tea, then sat down in the seat next to mine. I'd been planning on sitting across from him. After all, we'd just met. But I couldn't exactly move now, could I, without hurting his feelings. I tried to ease gracefully into the chair, but caught the back of my knee, which sent me off balance, and my backside thumped into the seat. I offered an apologetic grin. He answered it with an admiring smile that said I was swan-like.

We ate for a moment in silence. Then he cleared his throat. "Reyn, the reason I'm here is . . ."

To ask you to ride off with me on my white horse into the sunset. . . .

". . . to ask you some questions about the Barrister and Roadkill cases."

Darn. "Yes?"

"The Rangers decided to get involved in the case after we heard you on the radio tonight. You see, we usually wait to be asked to help localities investigate cases they can't handle because of a small workforce or lack of investigative experience, or because perhaps internal affairs are involved and they need some impartiality.

"However, in rare cases, we invite ourselves into the investigation when we think it's warranted. Like in this case. Because there are so many departments involved and the case seems so complicated. . . ."

Oh, boy, was I in trouble with Scythe. He had to be catching heat over this.

"Are you all right, Reyn?"

Was Ranger Clint incredibly perceptive, or did I look like I was going to hurl? "Yes—I mean, no. I'm a little worried the local cops are going to be mad at me."

He nodded, his green eyes softening in understanding. "I hear you are involved with Lieutenant Scythe."

"Involved? We aren't involved. We're just, ah . . ." What were we, anyway? "Friends." Contentious ones, but I supposed that was as close as we could get in the English language.

"Friends?" He looked a little dubious for a moment, then brightened. "Good. That will make things less complicated."

Things? What things? *Oh, I get it, Clint, no more worry that our wedding vows will be interrupted.*

"Less complicated." I was beginning to sound like a parrot.

"Yes, we were going to have to remove him from the investigation if there was anything romantic between the two of you."

I barked out a laugh. "Romantic. Scythe? As close as he gets is teaching me how to shoot."

Clint dropped his head and shook it. After another second of mourning, he lifted his head. "If you don't mind, can we go through your involvement with the case from beginning to end and why you think neither the husband nor the daughter is the killer? I apologize if that makes it a late evening for you, but I'd like to get a running start on this in the morning."

"Oh, it's no trouble," I rushed to say.

That Clint Calhoun was a thorough man. Oh, it's not what you're thinking.

I covered most of what had happened over the last couple of days, leaving out the part about clocking the DJ with the dog bone. That was a little embarrassing. I referred to Annette as my confidential source, and all Clint did was encourage me with those clear green eyes into considering revealing her identity. I almost did, but bit my tongue at the last minute. All in all, he asked some perceptive questions and seemed to appreciate my insight, unlike some other cops who will remain nameless.

My home phone kept ringing off and on during his visit, but since my voice mailbox was full, no one could leave a message. At one point, Clint looked at me sorrowfully and said, "I'm so sorry you are being harassed over this."

Ah, dreamy.

After he left, I slipped my "Pony in My Boat" T-shirt over my head, pulled on some ancient boxers, and brushed my teeth, letting Char lick some toothpaste off my fingers. I'd let the girls in while Clint was there because they'd been begging to meet him. They loved him. He loved them. If he passed the coffee-in-the-morning test, he'd be the perfect man.

The doorbell rang. My heart jumped. Had he changed his mind about spending the night at La Quinta? I reviewed my holey shorts. This called for a robe. I threw on my thick emerald terry-cloth robe and ran downstairs with the dogs. I flung the door open, and tried to hide my disappointment.

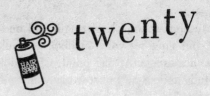 twenty

A FRUMPY WOMAN with frizzy dark hair shot with pre-mature gray pulled back in a tightly hairsprayed bun stood on my doorstep. It took me a good fifteen seconds to place her as the lady I'd admired for her dedication at the Junior League party. It was midnight. What was she doing here?

Why hadn't I looked through the peephole?

Her hand shot out. I jumped, then shook it. She bowed her head. "I'm Mitzi Spagnetti. I don't know if you remember me . . ."

"Of course I do, Mitzi. Come on in."

Here I went again. It was the middle of the night, and I was too polite to turn away a near stranger.

I ushered her into the living room, checking out her outfit—red high-water slacks, kelly green long-sleeved shirt decorated with orange embroidered smiley faces, purple fuzzy socks, and yellow clogs. Hmm. I wondered if she was color-blind—unusual for a woman, but not unheard-of. I excused myself to put the dogs out since

they seemed on edge, probably because they were expecting the luscious Clint or their best bud Scythe, certainly
not Mitzi. Besides, it was past their bedtime. Mine, too.

When I returned, she was hunkered down in my love
seat, wringing her hands, which I noticed were ragged
with bleeding cuticles. Poor dear. She was barely older
than I was, but seemed to have decades on me. I sat
down on the couch across from her. "It's nice to see you
again, Mitzi."

"I am sorry for coming to see you so late, but I've
been calling all night, and I thought that you probably
had your message machine filled up with all the reporters, and I wouldn't be able to get hold of you until
this all died down." She paused, heard what she'd said,
and laughed a lilting little giggle. Odd sense of humor,
but at least she had one.

"It's okay," I reassured her, "I was still awake."

"I wanted you to know I was worried about you, with
all you're going through right now. I think the police
and reporters should just leave you alone. You can come
stay with me if you need to hide from them all. I'm sure
they wouldn't think to look for you at my house." She
gave that weird little giggle again.

"Thank you for the kind offer, Mitzi, but I'm okay. I
have a business to run. It's hard to hide from that."

"Well, can't you just tell the police to go away? You
don't have anything to do with these murders." Her
voice rose, suddenly adamant. It reminded me of the
way she'd talked about her pet projects in the Junior
League. She was caring, if a little off.

I leaned forward and patted her hand. She jumped.
Yikes. "Thank you for your concern, but people I care

about are involved and I'm trying to help them. I don't like to see someone suffer for something she didn't do. The person who's guilty should pay."

She studied me through her thick glasses, her dark eyes bright. "You get as focused as I do about your causes, don't you?"

I shrugged. "Maybe so. And from what I've seen of your dedication, being compared to you would be a compliment. Thank you."

Mitzi bowed her head and blushed. "Dedication can be a blessing or a curse, depending on where it is applied."

"True." The fashion disaster as philospher.

Mitzi wrung her hands again. "Since you are so focused on finding the killer, I guess I should tell you what I know. I really have debated this. But I know it's right to put this information in such capable hands."

I suddenly found it hard to swallow. "What information?"

"It's about another Junior League member. Someone who might have wanted Wilma dead."

"If you suspect someone, why not go directly to the police, Mitzi?"

"I don't have any proof, and if I send the police after her, my career with the League will be over. All those teenagers would be without guidance. Babies would be born into sadness and chaos—"

I put up a hand. "If this woman is involved in Wilma's death, Mitzi, I'll have to tell the police about you and you will have to cooperate."

She brightened. "Oh, I know that. If she really is guilty, then it's a foregone conclusion that I would cooperate. But throwing false suspicion around, that would not be understood within the League."

I sighed. I was losing track of all the people I was supposed to be protecting. "Why don't you just go ahead and tell me what you know?"

"It's Charis Keifer. You met her, at the function at the Harmon home."

I remembered caramel-blond Charis of the flipped-out fashion stooges. I'd sicced Scythe on her because she'd been openly celebrating Wilma's death, sourly proclaiming that Wilma had been practicing Darwinism among the provisional members of the Junior League. Perhaps Charis had decided to practice her own version of Darwinism on Wilma?

I kept my voice neutral. "I remember Charis."

"She is the chairman of the provisionals, the new members of the League. How their probationary year goes reflects on her. Sixty percent of the provisional class from last year quit, some say thanks to the emotional torture Wilma put them through. There was talk that Charis should be removed from her position, that it was her fault the provisionals quit, that the League would dry up and die with such low numbers of actual inductees. Some of her supporters in the organization fought to give her another year to prove herself. Wilma had vowed to be just as tough on the provisionals this year. Charis was livid, and she didn't hide it."

"Why would anyone kill over being removed from a volunteer position?"

Mitzi looked at me like I didn't get it. And I guess I didn't, and never would. "Believe me, it is motive enough."

I shook my head. "I'll take your word for it, Mitzi.

But motive is one thing and opportunity is another."

"She had opportunity. Her husband complained to his buddies while he was golfing at the Dominion yesterday that Charis was late coming home the night Wilma was killed. She told him a moonlight sale at Grove Hill kept her. His friends all groused about similar shopping problems with their wives, but they're all too stupid to know there was no midnight sale anywhere in town that night."

"That could be explained any number of ways, though. Charis could have a boyfriend. She could've been sneaking out for a night with the girls. No telling."

Sighing, Mitzi wrung her hands. "At least I told you. Now my conscience is clear."

Wow, that made me feel guilty. "Okay, Mitzi, I will mention it to the police and keep your name out of it for now."

She smiled. "Thank you." She blew out a breath and patted at her flyaway hair. "Now, if you are dead-set against staying in hiding until the whole case is settled . . ." She paused, waiting. I acknowledged that she was right. "Then I would like to invite you to a fund-raiser I'm hosting to get seed money to restart the Teen Advantage pregnancy prevention program. It's at Fiesta Texas theme park on Friday night. Tickets are one hundred fifty dollars a person, but I'd like you to be my guest."

I hate theme parks, especially roller coasters. "Uh, I couldn't possibly accept such a generous offer."

"Please. I'd love to have a friendly face there. And knowing you'd be handy if I needed you to make sure decorations stay up and everyone gets where they need to be, that's worth the price of a ticket." Her big owl eyes implored. They looked like they were getting moist at the corners. *Please don't cry.*

"Okay, I accept."

Her mouth spread in a wide smile. "Wonderful." She pulled a ticket from the pocket of her Howdy Doody pants and put it on the table even though I'd extended my hand.

I wondered how to repay her. "You know, you have lovely . . ." I paused. "Body in your hair. We could really jazz it up for the party with a little henna job—"

"Oh, no," she gasped as if I'd offered to shave her bald. "I don't need to be attractive. Do you think I need to be attractive?" She bored me with with a fanatical stare. Oops, touched a nerve there, hadn't I?

"Of course not. I was just trying to repay you for your kindness in the only way I know how," I said, standing up and ushering her to the door. "See you at the party."

I'd no sooner shut the door and gotten halfway to the kitchen when the bell rang again. Shoot. What had Mitzi forgotten now? I threw the door open. Annette stood there, wearing a severe black tailored pantsuit and black driving gloves. One day I would learn to look through the peephole. One day too late, probably.

She reached into her pocket. I reached for the umbrella stand. She shoved a piece of paper at me. The umbrella stand crashed to the floor, and she jumped. "What the hell?"

I stared at the paper, which seemed to be a list. "What's this?"

Annette glared at me from six feet up. Even doing that, she was beautiful. I wished I had her perfect skin. Life was not fair. I got the personality. She got the skin. I thought I'd rather have the skin.

"Charlotte called and told me you wanted the names

of Percy's old girlfriends." She looked furtively behind her. "Let me in the damn house, would you?"

I opened the door wider, and she stalked in. "You're the most famous, or infamous, person in three counties. The police, the media, and probably the killer have all got you under surveillance by now."

"Don't forget the Texas Rangers."

She sucked in a breath and revealed the first feminine hint about her. "Oooh, you hit the big time. Don't tell me they sent that hunk Clint Calhoun down here?" She saw the answer in my face. "Lucky, aren't you? I wouldn't mind having the hottie of the Texas Rangers on *my* case."

"You could be lucky, too. Tell him what you know."

She was already shaking that elegant head of hers, any hint of emotion extinguished. "No way. They're awarding that scholarship next week. Plus, they released Percy on bond. I'm keeping my mouth shut."

"Why risk coming here, then?"

"Because the police suspect me."

"Really?" News to me, which was not surprising since Scythe didn't regularly powwow with me over his investigating, just mine. "Is this because you and Shauna were friends at one time?"

Annette paled. I got a shot of gratification at throwing a tilt into the Rock of Gibraltar. She clenched her black-leather–clad hands, which took away a bit of the thrill. "How did you know that?"

"Because there's a photo of the two of you with your arms around each other in Shauna's office. Why did you pretend she was a stranger when you told me about her?"

"Because I didn't want to make it seem like we were conspiring."

"It seems worse now, with Shauna dead. It's too co-incidental that you would work for the man Shauna ended up having an affair with. Maybe the whole thing was a setup and Shauna got too expensive to keep around."

"Stop wasting your time on me and Shauna and spend it on someone on that list." She motioned to the paper in my hand. Sweat had broken out on her upper lip. Hmm.

I looked at the list; no names I recognized except Shauna's. "How do I know you didn't make this up?"

"Why would I do that, when I want you to find who really did this and get the cops off my tail?"

"To waste my time and the cops' while you head off to Bermuda."

Annette drilled me with a hard look. "You know how much I want to make something of myself. To go to law school. I couldn't do that as a fugitive. I'm not going anywhere." Then she held up her gloved hands. "I'm also not going to admit I gave you that list. There won't be any fingerprints, and don't try to identify me because I can lie better than anybody you've ever seen. They'll think you're the one shaking their tree, not me. Plus, I'll poison your dogs."

I nodded. I still believed her.

She let herself out the back door to a chorus of bark-ing. One of the dogs yelped. Char, I think. She's the biggest wuss. The other two went quiet. I walked to the door and let them in. All shuffled in with tails between their legs and scuttled up to bed.

I was getting a pit bull tomorrow.

*   *   *

No telling why, but I slept like the dead. Probably because someone wanted me that way. I just wished I knew who. James Brown woke me with "Aw! I feel good!" and I went through my morning ablutions with a spring in my step. The only thing missing was that guy bringing me coffee in bed, but I could imagine what he looked like doing it and, since I have a superlative imagination, that was pretty close to the real thing.

After selecting a pair of custom-made ocher caiman boots, I slipped on my favorite Levi's 501s and found a little give, which improved my day. This crime-fighting gig was good for weight control. So, with minimal bottom, I filled my coffee cup with Zambian brew and unlocked the door to the salon.

And spit the Zambian across the room.

The hall was full of roses. Orange roses, with petals going pink at the tips, at least six dozen in various vases lining the hall. My heart caught somewhere near my throat. I'd gotten flowers before, but not multiple dozens of flowers at one time.

"You're popular." Bettina, in full womanhood today with water bra and tight-fitting gold sheath, grinned from the other end of the hall. Alejandra stuck her head out of her room and winked. Daisy Dawn put her three-inch nails out of her room and gave a thumbs-up sign.

Enrique jumped out of his room and cocked a hip. "You must be damned good, Reyn."

"Oh, it's nothing like that."

Everyone at once, including the customers already in their chairs, chanted, "Sure it's not."

I snorted and waved them off, marching down the hall officiously to see the appointment book, since I could hardly remember my own name in the face of this surprise, much less who wanted their hair done today.

I glanced at Bettina, who was grinning ear to ear. It was a rare sight, since she tried not to smile for fear of gouging wrinkles into her seamless Asian complexion.

"I'm shocked to see you here. I thought you were going to Hollywood to be discovered."

"Are you kidding? This little salon is more exciting than la-la land ever hoped to be. I'd hate to miss anything."

I grinned. "Thanks for staying."

"Just keep me interested." Bettina swept an arm toward the roses. "Aren't you going to see who they're from?"

"Maybe later." I hated to spoil my fantasy. I wanted them to be from my charming Texas Ranger. They were probably from my grandmother, who watched my antics long-distance with great glee. Or, with my poor luck, the roses were from the killer.

Bettina raised her eyebrows. "I find that very strange for someone as curious and as impatient as you are."

"What did I do with my birthday presents?"

She sulked. "You let them pile up until your exact birthday before you opened them."

I nodded righteously. "Willpower and patience are two different things. I have willpower. I don't have patience."

She sat down at the reception desk and reviewed the phone messages. "You're popular. Mostly among journalists. I'm assuming that you've talked to the one you wanted to talk to, that Roy Gene character. By the way, did you hear he had to be hospitalized last night for a concussion? Speculation is that it was a jealous colleague, angry at him for getting to you first."

"Hmm, I guess everything comes with a price."

Bettina raised her eyebrows again. She glanced at the flowers. "Was this *your* price?"

"No!" I looked at her sneaky face. "And you are not going to get me mad enough to show you the card. Good try, though." I glanced down at her notepad. No call from Trudy. She hadn't called my cell phone either. She'd acted weird last night, not letting me come over. It was one of two things: Either she knew where Lexa was, or she was mad at me for putting her precious Mario in harm's way at Bangers. Forget her. I scanned the message pad again and forced a casual tone. "Scythe didn't call?"

I knew he must be furious that my interview had summoned the Texas Rangers. Cops hated nothing more than having their control taken away. The feds were bad enough. At least they were semi-nerdy in their dark Brooks Brothers suits and wraparound shades. The state cops, dressed up like the law of the Old West, with their requisite Stetsons and all-encompassing power, had to be a worse blow to the Texas law enforcers' machismo.

Bettina shook her head as my nine o'clock pulled up out front. "No call from the lieutenant."

Well, nothing like a little suspense. I tapped my ocher caimans on the hardwood floor and resisted calling him. Like I'd told Bettina, I wasn't patient, but I had willpower. Let him make the next move. Problem was, Scythe *was* patient. No telling how long I'd have to wait for the other boot to drop.

The salon hit its usual midafternoon lull about three or four o'clock. Since I was a night person, my brain usually lulled about then, too, but why the rhythm of the whole world lags, I wasn't really sure. At any rate, I was yawning my way through a perm when a head popped around the edge of my door.

A unibrow troll.

The garlic wafted in as an afterthought.

I yanked a little too hard on Aimee Vokel's roots in surprise. She sucked in air for a scream and I shoved the roller into her mouth, which left her gagging instead.

Apologizing profusely, I led her around Percy Barrister, who looked goofier than normal in a silver and black windsuit I was sure he'd worn to be incognito. It just made him look like an extra in *Star Wars*. I settled Aimee in our customer lounge with a Sprite, pretending not to notice the flask she produced from under her smock. It was a good thing she'd nipped into that a couple of times during her appointment or she might have recognized Percy and been on the phone to every news station in town.

Thank goodness for small favors.

I hurried back into my room. Percy popped out from behind the barber chair. I jumped and almost screamed myself. "Mr. Barrister. What are you doing here?"

"I want my daughter." He leaned into my personal space.

I had to step away as my eyes watered from being garlicked. "I don't have your daughter."

"You know where she is, however."

"No I don't." *Although I have a guess or two.* "Why do you want her, anyway?"

"I want . . ." He paused, his unibrow caterpillared across his forehead, and his face crumpled. "To apologize. To tell her I'm sorry. For everything."

He was sobbing now. I shut the door. "For what everything?"

Sniff, sniff. Wet garlic scent. "For her finding out I cheated on her mother. For using her little scumbag boyfriend to find a conduit for the drugs my associates needed to market in the U.S. so I could pay for the women I was seeing behind Wilma's back. You see, Wilma noticed the odd charges at Tiffany's and the like, and it just got unworkable without the extra cash—"

"You want a tip or two?" I interrupted before I got sick all over the floor. He nodded eagerly, and I continued, "If you want to apologize, I'd recommend not referring to Asphalt as 'little scumbag boyfriend.'"

"Really?"

I nodded. "And I notice you didn't say you were sorry for cheating, just for Lexa finding out about it."

He nodded. Lots of nodding going around.

"Well, I might fudge that a little if I were you and act a little sorry you cheated to begin with, not just sorry you were caught. You could probably imply regret. Hmm?"

"That's satisfactory." He sniffed once more. The tears dried.

"Good. Now, is that the only reason you want to find Lexa?"

"Well, no. She has to help me talk her grandmother out of burning Wilma on a funeral pyre in the middle of the Rockies."

I didn't think that sounded like such a bad idea. It could be a perfect send-off for Wilma the Hun. "So, you didn't kill your wife, Mr. Barrister?"

The unibrow humped grumpily. "You certainly are nosy about all this."

"Since your daughter made me culpable by dragging me into this, I don't think I'm being anything but responsible."

"I suppose you have a point. No, I didn't kill my wife. I loved her."

There were all kinds of love, I was finding out. "That doesn't mean you didn't kill her. You probably loved your girlfriend, Shauna, too."

"Maybe. But I didn't kill her either. In fact, I have an alibi. I was with my associates from south of the border, making distribution plans. I've agreed to testify against them once the police find them, which will probably keep me out of prison. Or at least I'd go into a federal prison, which is more desirable. So there."

I guess Percy was so pleased with himself that he didn't wonder how the cops were going to find the bad guys from Mexico. My guess was that they'd set him loose as bait. Stupid minnow didn't even know it.

"I'd lie low for a couple of days if I were you, Mr. Barrister."

"I think I've taken just about enough advice from you, young lady." He turned his shiny, rotund body toward the door.

I shrugged. Maybe the Indians and Grandma ought to build a double pyre.

"One more thing, Mr. Barrister. Do you think any of your old girlfriends might have gone after Wilma as revenge for you dumping them?"

He narrowed his porcine eyes at me. "What do you know about old girlfriends?"

"No man has ever cheated just once on his wife. Besides you mentioned seeing 'women,' plural."

"Well, I might have had women clients enamored of me over the years. Some of them got a little overzealous and I had to call the IRS to distract them. So you might want to check IRS records. Anyone who was audited might have been fighting mad."

I shook my head. "Not everything is about money."

He opened the door and threw back as he walked out, "Silly girl. Money is everything. Which is why I'd never kill Wilma. Wilma *was* money."

On that happy note, he waddled his silver butt out of Transformations. I leaned against the doorjamb and gazed at my array of roses. I supposed it was time to look at the card. Gran would want a thank-you and an update on the goings-on anyway. If it was the murderer, I was going to have to call the cops. After my fantasies had taken me and the Randy Ranger to a deserted island for eternity, snowed us into a cabin in the mountains for months, and gotten us married with three perfect kids living happily ever after, I was back to reality.

Leaning down, I stroked one of the petals. Orange roses were so unusual. I plucked the envelope off its plastic holder, eased it open, and opened the simple orange card.

Time to pay up.
A deal's a deal.
Tonight's the night.

It was worse than being a note from the killer. It was from Scythe.

twenty-one

I WAS WASHING OUT Mrs. Reinmeyer's foil highlights when I heard the bells at the door tinkle. Bettina had already left for her dance gig at Illusions. So I called down the hall, "Be right with you."

No reporters had shown up all day, thank goodness, now that they had the famous Clint Calhoun to dog. It was probably a walk-in customer whom I'd agree to do just to keep busy. Scythe's note had left me as nervous as a cat in a room full of rocking chairs. The setting sun slanting through the blinds was only making it worse.

Cameron waved as she locked her door. "What's the deal, Reyn?"

Innocent enough slang, but her coincidental choice of words gave me a start. Before I could answer, Enrique walked an armful of towels past to the washing machine. "Yeah, is tonight the night?"

Daisy Dawn waltzed down the hall. "Time to pay up."

"Y'all read my card!" I stormed. Mrs. Reinmeyer started gurgling.

Daisy Dawn grabbed my right arm and redirected

the stream away from the octogenarian's face. Enrique handed her a towel. They all started laughing, except Mrs. Reinmeyer, who was sputtering.

"I consider this a violation of my privacy," I continued, affronted.

"Girl, get real. A violation of your privacy is if we go to Rick and Tessa's with binoculars tonight." Daisy Dawn winked at her coworkers.

"Oh, can I come?" Mrs. Reinmeyer asked.

"Enough, all of you!" I turned to Cameron and said, "Go see who's come in."

I led Mrs. Reinmeyer to my chair and finished her style. Cameron never came back to tell me who'd come in, so I guessed it wasn't too serious. In fact, the whole place had gone quiet. I must've scared them all off, to leave without good-byes. I finished Mrs. Reinmeyer's flip-out style. I'd accidentally given her a Mohawk a while back, and it had changed everything. Once a blue-rinse-only customer, the old gal had gone hip on me. Remember the thing I said about timing? Now Mrs. Reinmeyer got the latest look off the World Wide Web the morning before her appointment. We both smiled in satisfaction at the latest result. She tipped me, advised me to "take the proper precautions," and left with a wink.

Taking out the broom, I began cleaning up the hair on the floor. Then I heard a board in the hallway creak. I plastered myself against the wall and waited, listening. As soon as I saw a shadow cross the room, I spun out, knocking the intruder into the washing chair, straddling him and pinning him down with the broomstick to his throat.

It was Scythe. He had a beribboned bottle of Moët & Chandon in his hand.

"This is a little quick and a little rough for what I had in mind, but I'm sure I could get up for it."

From what I could feel, he was already up for it.

"What are you doing, sneaking around, scaring me?" I demanded, dropping the broomstick and trying to wiggle off his lap. His hands came to my hips to still me.

It just made me want to wiggle more.

"Weren't you expecting me? You called down the hall that you'd be right there. You never came."

"But Cameron, Daisy Dawn . . . Mrs. Reinmeyer?"

"They all tiptoed by with their fingers to their lips. I thought you were taking a nap or had a migraine or something."

"A headache. Yes, that's what I have. Too bad." I tried to get my caiman boots to the ground, but that just put certain parts of my anatomy closer to his. I pushed off the chair handles but my hands slipped off, and I just bounced.

Scythe groaned and grinned. His laser blues burned. I jumped back like I'd been scalded, not caring that I had to ricochet off the wall. He chuckled. "This is going to be fun."

"In your dreams," I countered bravely.

"I've already had those," he admitted wryly.

I threw a glance back as I walked into my styling room. *Him, too?*

I resorted to desperation tactics. "I would've thought you'd be a little mad at me."

He'd crouched down to study his roses, brushing the pad of his finger across the soft petals. "A little mad at you?" he asked carefully. Too carefully.

"Yes, for my interview drawing the Texas Rangers here."

I watched his jaw ripple as he flexed it. Hmm. "I don't know," he finally said quietly. "We probably need all the help we can get at this point."

Sure.

"I did my part to get them off your backs. I told them everything I know."

"Him," Scythe corrected tightly.

"Clint Calhoun," I clarified.

"I wish you hadn't let him in." More jaw flexing. He took a step toward me. "I told you to go home and lock your doors. Then you've got a Texas Ranger and two of your buddies paying midnight visits. At least, I hope they were buddies, otherwise you wouldn't have been dumb enough to let them in. Who were they?"

"You were watching me?" I asked, aghast.

"I didn't say that." He took another step toward me.

"You had someone watching me?" I jammed my hands on my hips.

"I don't now." His hand cupped my chin and brought my lips to his. This kiss was better than his last one, and that one was damned good. The best I'd ever been kissed. His other hand teased the hair at the nape of my neck. It sent pulses of energy places I had no idea were connected to my hair follicles. Somehow my hands ended up around his shoulders.

What was that I said about willpower?

His lips moved across my cheek and he breathed into my ear, "It's time to pay up on your deal, before you have to make another one to get me to keep you out of trouble."

I opened my mouth to argue, to demand whether the only way he could get a girl was with threats. Then I heard the words of Gore of Wretched Roadkill: "You shouldn't argue so much with your copper boyfriend. Guys don't like a chick with a mouth and an attitude." I hated to take advice from a half-stoned member of a headbanger band who sang about squashed armadillos, but heck, maybe he was right. Maybe I was coming across as Katherine in *The Taming of the Shrew*. Of course, I always kind of liked her. I imagined men didn't, though. I couldn't stay celibate forever.

"Okay."

His eyebrows lifted in stunned surprise. He hadn't expected it to be so easy.

"But maybe I'll like it so much that I'll stay in trouble just so we can keep making deals to get me out." I smiled sweetly. I didn't say I'd be a total pushover.

His right eyebrow dropped, leaving the amused left one half-hitched. "Wouldn't that be a nice problem to have?"

"Do I get to spiff up with a shower, or do we go after it right here?"

"How about both?"

"Nope. You have to choose."

"Shower." He sniffed the air as we left my styling room. "Especially since it smells like you had some of that old kimchee in your refrigerator for lunch."

"That wasn't me. Percy came to visit."

Scythe stopped in his tracks. "Why?"

"He said he wanted to find Lexa to apologize for her finding out about him cheating on her mother and for betraying her scumbag boyfriend."

"Thoughtful of him. You tell him where she is?"

I met his penetrating gaze. "I don't know."

He looked away, disappointed. "Your one saving grace is you can't lie."

"My one?" I asked as I locked the salon's front door.

"I might be able to think of another one. Maybe *lots* more, after tonight."

You know, I shouldn't drink champagne. Not four glasses in an hour, anyway. Not expensive champagne either, because it goes down way too smoothly. Of course, I didn't know I was drinking four glasses until much, much later when I realized that Sleazeball Scythe had been slipping into the bathroom, refilling my glass as I steamed myself in the shower, then into the bedroom, refilling the glass again as I searched the closet for the right ensemble. No telling what peeks he snagged while he was at it. Pervert.

Anyhow, I was still ignorant of his deception when I emerged from my bedroom, scented with Ralph Lauren's Glamourous, made up with eyeliner (sienna to highlight the gold in my hazel eyes), and wearing a dress (black denim, but still a dress). Knee-high ostrich boots finished the look. I even had pretty undies on, dragged out of mothballs from three Christmases ago.

I thought Scythe was having a heart attack when he saw me. He started hyperventilating. He grabbed at his chest. It was probably my bare legs. I knew I shouldn't have worn the minidress. I ran to the couch, ready to administer CPR. He pulled me on top of him and started kissing me. Everywhere. My nose, my ear, my neck, my cleavage (I was wearing a push-up bra, so there was a little there). His hands started roving. Everywhere. My waist, my hips, the skin on the backs of my thighs, my . . .

"Whoa." I pushed away and sat up. I don't think the last glass of champagne had hit yet or I'd still be rolling around on the couch with him. "I came over here to give you mouth-to-mouth."

"And you did. I feel much better now."

"So is this the deal? Making out on my couch all night?"

"No. I had a private caterer setting up a gourmet dinner at my house." He looked almost regretful. "With wine, turtle cheesecake, the works."

I might've argued, but the turtle cheesecake convinced me. Plus, I was dying to see his bachelor pad. Maybe Zena's toothbrush was in the bathroom. "Let's go. Grab the champagne."

"Oh." Surprise, surprise. "It looks like I finished it all. Too bad."

I narrowed my eyes at him and hoped I wasn't swaying. He didn't look a bit tipsy for having three glasses to my one. Maybe he was a closet alcoholic, but I didn't think so.

Furthermore, I should've been suspicious when I saw Rick come out of his house and walk toward the Labs, see us just pulling out of the driveway, then turn around and run back in. No, of course not. I was under the influence of Moët and testosterone.

Scythe lived in a log cabin on a ten-acre hill overlooking Cibolo Creek south of town in a little country village called Floresville. It was remote but beautiful, with the moonlight reflecting off the water. Surrounded by rolling hills and lush pastures, it seemed wild and calm at the same time. I could see why a man who dealt with the worst of civilization during the workday might want his home to be away from it at night, and I told him so.

He seemed a bit discomfited by my insight.

"You haven't cornered the market on figuring everyone out, you know," I teased as we picked through the tenderloin dinner.

"Oh, Reyn," he began, then stopped himself. He stood and gathered my wineglass with his, ushering me out the door to the back porch. The moonlight danced off the water below us. He gathered me in his arms. "You don't make it easy to care about you."

Huh? And here I thought I was being easy to get along with tonight. I'd let him cop a feel, kiss me places he'd never kissed me before, even take me to his home, and who knew what else. . . .

Men were hard to figure out, especially on multiple glasses of vino.

Scythe pressed his lips to my temple, and I shifted to face his chest so I could breathe in the mesquitey scent of him. Tipping up my face, I kissed him again, and then the spark that had been there for months ignited. My hands were all over him and his were all over me; we were bumping and grinding and pushing and pulling and . . . panting.

Somehow we ended up in the bedroom. I'd lost my dress somewhere along the way. He'd lost his shirt.

Then a man jumped out from behind the closet door.

He looked familiar.

I opened my mouth to scream, but before the sound could emerge, Scythe had pulled his gun from his ankle holster and aimed.

twenty-two

"DAMN IT, SCYTHE, what the hell are you doing?" the man shouted. "Get your brain out of your pants and drop the piece."

Scythe shook his head like a dog shaking water off his coat. He slid his Glock back into its holster. He rebuckled his belt.

What the hell was going on?

My blood supply was focused in other places, too, which somehow made it impossible for my mouth to work right. Of course, it had worked just fine for the kissing and nipping that had been going on, I noticed as I reviewed the ghost of a hickey above Scythe's collarbone. No telling what war wounds I had. I felt flushed and hot and damp. . . .

I glanced down, and my hands flew to cover myself. I was in bra, panties, and boots. Our interloper was sneaking peeks, but trying not to show it. I pointed at him. "Hey, keep your eyes to yourself."

"Sorry, ma'am." He cleared his throat and turned toward the doorway.

Scythe grunted, reached into his closet, and threw me a set of worn-out warm-ups. My gallant hero. I shrugged into them.

When I saw the guy's profile, I recognized him. "Wait a minute. You're Scythe's bodyguard. I thought you didn't need him anymore since the threat was bogus? And why would you need him in your bedroom anyway?"

"I didn't need Byron to begin with, did I, Reyn? You could've clued me in on that a long time ago." Those laser blues, not so long ago hot with lust, were now razor sharp in anger. "Since you were the one to start the damned rumor."

"It was just a joke. Trudy came to get me at the courthouse and said something off the cuff, and then that started the whole thing and—"

He waved off the story. "Why Zena Zolliope? How did you know about me and her?"

So there *was* something going on. I knew it. My stomach clenched. Good thing Byron had stopped us before we went too far. I guessed her toothbrush was by the sink after all. I felt nauseated. "I know her work. I could tell."

"How do you know her work? You work down there on Broadway, too?"

"Broadway? Her salon is on Leland."

The two men looked at each other, baffled. Scythe turned to me. "What does this have to do with her salon?"

"What else would it have to do with? She cuts your hair, you date her. You think I care?"

Scythe and Byron started laughing. "I don't date her, Reyn." Scythe tried to sober up. "I let her cut my hair so I will have an excuse to be seen with her."

"See!"

"She's an informant. We picked her up doing some extracurricular activities with tourists and turned her in exchange for immunity. We're working a case that has a john beating prostitutes to death. She was getting close until we heard about the death threat against me and we thought she'd been turned by the perp. It really complicated things."

Oops.

"Sorry." I swallowed. "But how was I to know?"

Scythe shook his head. "You couldn't. It's just your uncanny ability to step in the dog-pile no matter what you do."

What an image. Glad he was so enamored that I had him seeing me through these rose-colored glasses.

He reached into his closet and shrugged into a clean, starched shirt. He threw Byron a set of keys he'd taken out of his pocket. "Keep your eye on her at all times. I'll be in touch." On his way out the door, he leaned over and kissed the top of my head. "Be good."

"Hold on a minute! What's going on?" Whatever it was, I didn't like it.

"I tried to put you under house arrest at your own house, but you had midnight tea with how many suspects?" Scythe ran his hand through his bad haircut. I wondered how long this informant hairstyling gig was going to last. "So, I decided the only way to keep you safe, keep you from accidentally starting rumors that bollix up investigations, is to keep you under house arrest at my house, with my bodyguard. When we have it all wrapped up and tied with a bow, I'll be back." He looked me up and down. "And Byron will be excused so we can finish what we started."

"In your dreams."

"We can do all that, too."

With a wink and that promise, Scythe was gone.

I didn't know how those people who were witnesses against the big crime bosses did it. They were kept for months in gross little motel rooms eating pizza and Twinkies, watched by some smelly, scratching cop who pulled the short straw and favored the Sci-Fi Channel. I had a big log cabin with an awesome view for miles, a larder stocked with gourmet fare, and a guard who wasn't half-bad-looking, smelled like Irish Spring, and liked HBO.

And I was still going crazy.

It was only twelve hours into my exile. Scythe had called Byron earlier, asked to talk to me, and said he'd explained to Bettina that I was under the weather and wouldn't be at work for a couple of days. Guess what they were all thinking back at Transformations? Accused of fun I wasn't having. That wasn't fair.

Byron refused to let me watch or listen to any news. I was allowed to answer my cell phone so my absence wouldn't send up a general panic, but only under strict supervision.

"You see her legs?" Byron motioned to the television, where Angelina Jolie was rising from a swimming pool. She did have super legs. "Long but shapely, that's how I like them. None of this stick-leg stuff for me."

I wondered what he thought about my legs, since he'd seen more of them than most of my dates did. Not long, maybe shapely. I didn't think I ought to ask.

I smiled absently as he waxed poetic about his favorite woman's legs. I wished I could show him the best pair of legs I'd ever seen. They belonged to my best friend.

Wait just a minute.

I had an idea.

Trudy and I might be on the outs, but she'd be there for me in a pinch. I was seriously pinched. I dialed, praying that she hadn't lost the ability to read my mind and catch a hint. Byron sat up and turned down the volume on the movie. I felt a little guilty until I realized the legs didn't talk, so he wasn't missing much.

"Reyn." Trudy's voice sank to a conspiratorial level. "I heard you had a big night last night."

What? Was it in the newspaper? It was only ten o'clock in the morning.

"Right."

"So, did you culminate your deal?"

"Not quite. Unless it included a threesome." One day we were going to have to get this cleared up. The whole deal thing was still a little nebulous for me. Scythe knew. Trudy knew. I didn't know.

"There was not supposed to be any threesome! What do you mean, not quite?"

"We got interrupted. He had to leave."

Byron shot me a warning look. I smiled and tried to look subservient. It was an effort.

"Jackson's gone?" Trudy was aghast.

"Yes."

"Where did he go?"

"No telling."

"If he's gone, then why aren't you at work?"

"Some days you just gotta take a break, enjoy some peanuts."

Byron looked around at our array of chips and dip, puzzled. I got up to go to the kitchen. Floresville was the peanut capital of Texas. I held my breath.

"Reyn, are you in Floresville?"

"Yes, I am." I let my breath out slowly.

"What are you doing there?"

"Yep, some days you've just got to enjoy the view, and the water this time of year seems to run so fast."

"You're on a hill and next to a creek."

"Yes, I am."

"You're at Scythe's. He's got you handcuffed to a chair, doesn't he? Bastard. I'm going to find you."

"You know, I was just thinking a little while ago, I'd love to have a pair of those short shorts you just bought—you know, the red leather ones?"

"What does that have to do with—" Trudy paused. "Never mind. I'll wear them."

A leg, tanned and long, bearing bloodred toenails and five-inch gold spike heels appeared in the window next to the television set an hour and a half later. Byron did a double take as it flexed like a stripper's back and forth, forth and back. I thought I saw spittle forming at the corner of his mouth. He licked his lips. The leg disappeared.

"Did you see that?" Byron asked me.

"What?" I looked up from the *Cosmo* I'd found on the

table. I wanted to know if Scythe subscribed to *Cosmo*, a girlfriend had left it, or he was considerate enough to have stocked reading material specifically for me.

"Nothing," Byron mumbled. He rubbed his eyes, took a swig of his coffee, and looked back at the television.

The other leg appeared, in the window on the other side of the television. Same drill. I definitely saw some slobber on Byron's mouth this time. "There!" He pointed.

"Oh, yes." I nodded toward the flexing leg. "Looks like we have company. Should I go answer the door?"

He jumped up. "No! I'll go. Why don't you lie low?"

"Good idea. It's probably one of Scythe's girlfriends. You know, one of the Flavors of the Week, or whatever y'all call them at the cop shop. I'd hate it if she got the wrong idea and ruined his date for the weekend. I'll just hide around the corner here."

His eyebrows drew together like he felt sorry for me. "Okay."

I ducked out and peeked around the corner as Byron opened the door and nearly fell to his knees. Trudy had almost overdone it, in a nearly see-through white halter top and those hip-hugging, butt-cupping red leather shorts. "I'm looking for Jackson," she whined.

"Uh, I'm sorry, ma'am, but he's not here right now. . . ."

Giving Trudy the thumbs-up, I pointed toward the right side of the house. She sent me a half wink as she pointed to her knee and complained of an owee. Byron was in another world. I tiptoed fast to the bathroom, closed the door silently, turned the lock, and climbed into the tub. I yanked at the window and nearly lost hope until I heard a small crack, and it gave way. Hoisting myself up, I shimmied my torso through and then, with an extra shimmy or two, my heinie, and let myself drop headfirst onto the ground, which was a lot harder than it looked.

"Oof."

I wasn't sure where all my body parts were when Trudy came prancing up. All I saw were spike heels and toenails.

"Mangy minxes and conscientious con men, Reyn, get a move on. We've got to split this sundae. He's onto us."

That's when I heard banging at the bathroom door. By the time I got up and started to run, I heard the splitting of wood. Oops. Scythe was not going to be happy about this.

Trudy was flying down the hill. Don't ask me how she did it in spikes, but she did. I, on the other hand, was barefoot and catching every sticker between here and there. Limping, I caught up with her as we reached the oaks next to the creek. "Where are we going? Where's your car?"

"Mario took it. We're taking this." She dragged a six-foot skiff out of the bushes and shoved it into the water. She put one high heel in and let the other sink into the muck on the bank. I bet those were Manolos I was going to have to buy. Trudy was a shoe freak, and no set of heels was too expensive. She probably went out shopping just for this.

I hopped in the boat and nearly tipped it over. With much not-too-graceful throwing around of weight, we got it rebalanced. Trudy shoved off, and we were waterborne.

Now, I know Huck Finn had a bunch of excitement while he was floating on a raft down the river, but let me tell you something. Water moves slowly. I swear he experienced all his adventures along a two-mile stretch of the Mississippi, because what seemed like hours later, even with a paddle, I don't think we were three hundred yards farther than when we started.

"What's your plan, exactly?" I tried to be diplomatic. After all, she had busted me loose successfully.

"We're going to float until we reach someplace recognizable, then I'm going to call Mario, and he'll pick us up." Trudy was very proud of her plan.

We looked around us. Oaks and cypress and more oaks.

"Well, you're free, aren't you? And I don't think they'll think to look for us escaping by the Cibolo."

"True." Scythe just thought he knew me. Wait till he found out about this.

"I say the next house we see, we park this getaway skiff and call Mario."

"But what if Scythe and that leg guy check the neighbors?"

"What are they going to say? 'Hey, I took this girl on a date and decided to hold her hostage. Her friend came over in red leather hot pants and they got away. Seen them lately?' No, I think he might put out an APB for me, put some SAPD uniform at my house, but he won't shake any trees in Floresville. He's in enough trouble with enough police departments as it is."

"Really? Why?"

I grinned like the Cheshire cat. Trudy shook her head. "This is no way to get a man, Reyn."

"I've decided men are overrated anyway. Look what the chump did to me last night. What a tease."

"He did it because he cares about you, Reyn."

"'He's not good, he just has good intentions . . .'" I sang.

"You sound like Lyle Lovett," Trudy groused. She was more of a pop fan, but knew my boy because I played all his CDs until she couldn't help but memorize them.

"Now, there's a perfect man. I want to meet him. I bet he'd bring me coffee in bed. So would Clint Calhoun."

"Are you talking about that dishy Texas Ranger?" Trudy let out a low wolf whistle, then looked at me sharply. "Did you get to talk to him?"

"At midnight, in my house, alone . . ."

"Were you in one of your stupid ugly nightshirts and boxers?" Trudy groaned.

"He wouldn't know. I wore a robe the whole time," I answered with a lift of my chin.

"So Ranger Clint is good, no matter his intentions. How boring."

A house appeared as we rounded the next bend, and we made preparations to land on the right bank. The preparations included me making moves with the paddle on the port side of the boat. Awkward, I know, but this seemed to work for me, although I almost dumped Trude in the drink in the process.

"Tadpoles' tits and fornicating fishes, Reyn. Be careful!"

We got there and Trudy stuck a pump into the bank as an anchor. I jumped out and we went to find out where we were so Mario could come claim us.

No one was home, but we hiked to the mailbox. Fortunately, the residents were the kind who liked country craft fairs and decorating with blue geese. Some artist had painted their whole address on a big goose with little geese numbers and letters. Trudy made a mental note to call them and offer her design services—she liked to do that sometimes to the design-impaired, like me. I pointed out that if they hadn't been so goose crazy, we would've had to hike God only knew how far down the road to find another address. Rural residents weren't famous for advertising their technical position—they had too much real work to do.

Mario was as far away as he could be, assuming, apparently, that we'd hijacked a hydroplane boat and made it to the Gulf of Mexico by now. So we got friendly with a few fire-ant beds while we waited in the bushes. Finally, the bubble-gum-blue Miata came roaring up.

After kissing and cooing over Trudy and her ant bites and barely noticing me, Mario got back behind the wheel and we were off.

"Where to, *mi hermosas?*"

"Your house," I said.

"Her house," she said.

"We can't go to my house," we said to each other simultaneously.

There was a long pause during which we stared in a Mexican standoff. Then I got it.

"Lexa's at your house, isn't she, Trude?"

"Ooh, she's good, no?" Mario whistled. "You could be James Bond. We call you Jamie Bond because you're a girl—"

"No, I'm an idiot. I should've figured that out a long

time ago, with the way you disappeared, the way you've been acting cagey. I don't know why you didn't tell me."

"Lexa asked me not to. She and Asphalt are just scared kids, with absolutely no street smarts. She's upset she dragged you into this. We knew we couldn't have you come over to the house in case you were being followed. She didn't want you culpable for their disappearance."

"Did she tell you the whole story?"

Trudy nodded. "She says about a year ago, she brought Asphalt over to her parents' for dinner. Wilma, as could be expected, hated him. Behind Wilma's back, Percy pretended to like him and acted interested in the band, and he offered to come watch the Roadkill one night.

"Well, Lexa now knows that Percy just wanted a conduit for the drugs his associates were peddling, but then, she just thought Dad was being supportive. Asphalt is clueless. He's a lower-middle-class kid from a nice family who played in the school orchestra. He's working his way through UT by dressing the part and playing in the band. He wants to be a band teacher when he gets out."

"So they don't know any more than we do about who killed Wilma?"

"No. And that's what scares them."

"Okay, we'll give them a couple more days while Clint and the gang sort this all out." I still thought the link was Shauna. She had to have done the clown makeup, but for whom and why?

"We could go to my mama's house," Mario offered.

I shook my head. Mama Tru lived catty-corner to my house. "Too close."

"Daffy's?"

"No!" Being in that museum-perfect mausoleum gave me the heebie-jeebies. I knew all those antiques were beautiful and expensive, but it was too much combined history in one place. Besides, it hurt me to watch Daffy blink for extended periods of time.

"I have an idea," I said on impulse. "Take the next exit."

twenty-three

"COME IN, COME IN," Charlotte whispered, brandishing a big black sheet and wrapping it around us as we got out of the Miata. I knew she was just trying to protect us, but I imagined any neighbors looking out an upstairs window at her backyard would be more alarmed by a trio under a black sheet than three unfettered folks walking into the house. It wasn't like we were on the FBI's Ten Most Wanted list.

Not yet, anyway.

"Thanks for having us," Trudy said.

"Are you kidding? This is my next assignment. Didn't Reyn tell you? I'm the Holmes to her Sherlock!" She giggled. "Get it? Even the name is right. It was meant to be. Isn't this fun?"

Trudy raised her eyebrows. I shrugged. Charlotte gasped, "Oh no." We all jumped. "I didn't mean to hurt your feelings, Trudy. I know you're a big help to Reyn, too. You're her best friend, but it's just that I'm her assistant. We just work together, you understand."

Trudy put her hand on Charlotte's arm. "I'm glad she has such a wonderful assistant."

"When do your parents get home, Charlotte?" I asked. I doubted that Mr. and Mrs. Holmes would consider her associating with me any safer than her driving to the corner store. They were probably right.

"They both get home from work at about seven."

"Okay, I have another assignment for you." She nodded, looking an overeager puppy. "Get Bettina to let you into my house through the salon. Next to the telephone is a ticket. Grab that and something for me to wear tonight. Footwear included."

I had decided that I needed to find out more about Shauna's business. I needed to talk to the people who worked and lived around her, the '09ers. Then I'd remembered that Mitzi had invited me to that fund-raiser. Who went to fund-raisers? People with money. Where did most people with money live in San Antonio? 78209.

I was going to the damn fund-raiser after all.

Charlotte gave me the thumbs-up, grabbed a brand-new trench coat off the coat stand next to the door, and left to talk to the chauffeur. Having a driver take her on her various detective assignments probably compromised her effect, but oh, well. Mario went back to work. Somebody had to make some money, since amateur sleuthing didn't pay so great.

"What are you up to?" Trudy demanded.

I explained about going to Fiesta Texas.

"You're not going alone."

"I only have one ticket."

"I can get in."

I didn't doubt it. Trudy was one of those women who

managed to get in anywhere she had a mind to. Good gams did their part, but her exceeding beauty and dazzling charm probably had something to do with it, too. She'd probably gotten into bars when she was twelve just by winking at the bouncer. She was a handy friend to have around. For that and lots of other reasons.

As per Charlotte's invitation, we took showers in a bathroom with an Arabian theme that reminded me of Omar the Tent Maker. It was gussied up with her array of overpriced cosmetics. I'd never worn Lancôme before, and frankly it felt the same as Revlon, but what did I know? I bet if you had better than peasant skin, it did make a difference. It still didn't cover up my freckles.

Charlotte did own some cool colored eye shadows, which forced me to resist going overboard. I stuck with golds and browns since I didn't know what I was doing when it came to makeup. Where was Shauna when you needed her? Trudy helped a little, but I didn't trust her to improve me much because she started with perfection every day, so she couldn't be very adept at transforming ordinary.

After an hour went by, we started getting nervous. I wondered if Charlotte had gotten lost, was undergoing fingernail torture at the hands of the feds, or had been kidnapped by the killer. After we'd speculated enough to put my stomach in knots, the alarm system informed us of an opening door. Still in our towels, we rushed downstairs.

"What took you so long?"

"I'm sorry." Charlotte blushed. "I got a little sidetracked. It was so much fun, this sneaking around!"

"You did get the ticket?"

She nodded, holding it out to me along with a grocery

sack of clothes. "Oh, yes. Bettina said things were under control at the salon, and Rick is taking care of your dogs. There was a guy parked in front of your house." She described Byron. "He didn't look very happy."

I bet not. I bet he was in big trouble. Punished for a leg fetish.

"When I was upstairs, I thought I noticed a scary-looking pair of men in a car parked in the alley behind your house. But when I looked again, they were gone."

Percy's drug-dealing "associates" maybe? I felt guilty for putting Charlotte in potential danger.

"But then, as I was returning to my car, a man walking his toy fox terrier stopped me. He was bald, but really handsome, and a little . . ." She paused to giggle. ". . . sexy. Anyway, he wanted to know if you were going to keep messing around in the Barrister murder, and if so, he was going to put his Porsche in a guarded garage for a couple of days for safekeeping. What did he mean?"

Humph.

"Anyway, he gave me some vitamin samples, and we talked for a while—"

"About what?"

"Oh, this and that. Not the case, of course. I am your Holmes, I know better than that."

Uh-uh.

She started blushing again. "Before he took Kisses—"

"Kisses?"

"That's his dog's name. Isn't that cute?"

I made a noncommittal sound. Maybe I was looking for less testosterone, but I wasn't sure I could fantasize anymore about a man who named his dog Kisses.

"He said he thought my coat was handsome, then he asked me on a date."

"What?!" Trudy and I exclaimed simultaneously.

"Yes," Charlotte said, blushing madly. "We're going out tonight. Unless you need me for the case, that is."

"No, go ahead, have a good time."

I peeked into the bag of clothes and groaned.

Trudy looked like she was headed for a *Vogue* cover shoot, and I looked like someone's idea of a bad joke. I was a checkerboard come to life on a really bad high. Huge black and white blocks made up the peg-leg pants. Smaller black and white checks made up the spaghetti-string blouse. It was a rayon blend, which made it a little clingy. I didn't wear patterns below my waist for a reason. I didn't wear clingy for the same reason. And I didn't wear peg-legs—well, you get the idea. I didn't like to draw any extra attention to my booty. The whole thing made me look like a big target. So much for blending into the crowd at the fund-raiser. I knew Charlotte meant well, thinking I'd just bought the damned outfit because it still had its tags on. But the truth was, Aunt Big gave it to me for my twenty-fifth birthday (probably so I'd be the only one who looked bigger than she did), and in five years I hadn't had the heart to throw it out or the guts to wear it.

The worst part was the shoes. I didn't wear shoes unless they were running shoes to walk the dogs or flip-flops on the rare occasions I was feeling brave and wore shorts. All other times, I wore boots. Mostly cowboy boots. I was up to about a hundred pairs of boots by now. I knew it was a fetish. And, as the youngest of five kids who lived a childhood wearing holey, worn-out hand-me-down boots, I knew where this psychological baggage came from.

And I definitely didn't want to do anything about it.

Anyhow, these shoes were pointy-toed patent leather with cutouts that showed parts of my foot, mirroring, I suppose, the checkerboard pattern. They had three-inch heels. I'd probably kill myself.

"You really didn't have any shoes to go with this outfit. I don't know what you were thinking. So I bought those for you, Reyn. I saw them in the window as I drove by Carr's on North New Braunfels. I thought they looked like so much fun!"

I'd rather have had a trench coat. "They don't look much like Sherlock's shoes."

Charlotte's face fell.

"But they're perfect for a disguise. Who'd guess I was investigating anything in these?"

She brightened. I glanced down at the shoes again, trying not to pull a face. Being considerate was certainly painful to one's pride.

The doorbell rang. The plan we'd come up with was that Mario would be our chauffeur, taking us to and picking us up from the fund-raiser. He came in, and Charlotte and I had to withstand the minute or so of cooing and kissing and nuzzling that always went on with these two. They'd been married more than ten years, you'd think they'd get over it, but I swear it was getting worse.

Finally, we were on our way, wishing Charlotte well on her date.

"Isn't that funny, Reyn? You've lived there all that time and never talked to the vitamin salesman. Charlotte is there five minutes and he asks her out."

"Hilarious."

"It just means you and Scythe are meant to be." She paused thoughtfully. "Or that you just have really bad luck."

I was voting for that one, since I never wanted to speak to Sneaky Scythe again after what he'd done, luring me to his house, acting like he wanted to be romantic. And I'd bought it! And what's more, I'd been so thrown by the Zena revelation that I hadn't let him have it then and there. Just wait until I saw him again!

"I'd vote for the bad luck," Mario said.

"Thanks."

"It's a compliment, Reyn. You are one pretty hot mamá, but still there is no man like me to *besate*—kiss you, love you—every day. Why? It's *mala suerte.*"

I looked at poor, lumpy, dim-witted, sweet Mario, and thought how *bueno* my *suerte* was. If some guy hung all over me like that, it would make me crazy.

Well, maybe not if the guy was Clint Calhoun. . . .

We turned into the immense parking lot of Fiesta Texas. Set in the middle of an old limestone quarry, it was prettier than most theme parks, with its jutting white cliffs. The sun had just set behind one of them, throwing ocher light over the scene scattered with neon lights and streaming flags. People were streaming through the gates. Mario pulled up in front.

"Oh, I almost forgot. Lexa's been at home searching the Net to help you with the investigation. She asked me to tell you three things she's found. One was an article in a law journal that quotes her mother as saying all men should have male assistants, that females are too distracting in the workplace. The second thing is that Annette, her dad's paralegal, and Shauna went to high school together, and Shauna beat out Annette for homecoming queen. And, third, Shauna was a member of the Junior League before she dropped out a couple of years ago. Oh, and Asphalt got a call on his cell phone from Blood from jail. Blood told him to hightail it because DD's got something to implicate them all in the murder."

"What would that be?"

Mario shook his head. "I don't know. The poor kid is scared to death and clueless about the whole drug deal. Percy just used them."

Trudy and I got out. I paused to warn Mario to watch out in case he was followed on his way home. When I turned around, Trudy was already inside the gates, waving at me. The woman was a magician.

Of course, when I gave my ticket to the gate guard who was dressed up like an eagle, it had a little corner torn off where Char had chewed it. She almost wouldn't take it and was ready to refuse me entrance. Trudy called out to me to hurry.

The guard looked at me. "You're with her?"

This was probably the kiss of doom. I nodded.

She waved me through. "Go ahead, then."

Humph.

"How did you get in?" I demanded when I reached Trudy.

She just smiled enigmatically and kept walking through the crowd. Couples were milling through the courtyard, which was decorated to look like a Mexican marketplace. The mayor and his wife were in attendance, as were several city council representatives and a half dozen former and current San Antonio Spurs. This must be a big deal. Waiters in various animal costumes passed out margaritas and hors d'oeuvres.

I was just trying to place a familiar caramel-blond flip do I'd glimpsed through the crowd when I felt a hand clamp on my upper arm. "I'm so glad you made it."

I turned to recognize Mitzi's face poking out from under the big ears of a burro costume, complete with a rainbow stitched shawl, obviously not looking any more fashionable for her big event. Of course, I, currently the human checkerboard, was one to talk.

"Thank you for inviting me," I answered, trying to shake loose of her viselike grip.

A waiter in an iguana suit appeared at Mitzi's elbow with a request that—answer to my prayers—drew her away about ten feet. She'd started back toward us when she was intercepted by a woman dressed like a gopher, complete with the buckteeth, who motioned frantically with a walkie-talkie. Mitzi shook her head, bouncing her burro ears, then grabbed the walkie-talkie and hollered into it. In my peripheral vision, I recognized a toy-soldier walk. I turned to see Annette on the arm of a handsome man I knew to be the most famous criminal defense lawyer in town. Her ambition knew no bounds. Trudy got my attention with that best-friend telepathy we had, and we began inching away.

"Where are you going?" Mitzi dismissed the gopher by showing the bucktoothed critter her back. Nice. She had to be really stressed.

"You're busy. We hate to keep you."

"You're not keeping me at all."

"What's with all the animal costumes?" Trudy asked.

"We allowed the girls in the program to choose the theme of the party, 'Beasts for Teens.'" Mitzi narrowed her eyes at Trudy. "What are you doing here?" I wrote off her unfriendliness as nerves from her party.

Trudy smiled expansively. "I'm here to support your wonderful charity."

Discomfited but unable to argue that point, Mitzi turned back to me, dismissing Trudy entirely. I wondered why she seemed to not like Trudy. Everybody liked Trudy. Perhaps her low self-esteem made her uncomfortable in the presence of beauties, which was why she felt completely comfortable with me.

"How are things with the investigation?" Mitzi asked me, half an eye on a waitress balancing perhaps one too many glasses of champagne on her tilting tray. "Are the police and the media leaving you alone?"

"I haven't seen a cop or reporter in a while," I assured her. She nodded, satisfied either with me or with the waitress's safe arrival at a table haven for her tray. I continued, "But I did just discover something interesting perhaps you could help me with."

"Yes?"

"Shauna, the makeup artist who was killed in Alamo Heights, was a member of the Junior League, too. Did you know her?"

Mitzi went stiff. A guest was ranting loudly just south of us. Mitzi made a hand signal to a park attendant to tone him down. She spared me a glance. "Know her? I don't think so. Or maybe. I can't be sure."

Something envious in Mitzi's face made me think she did remember her. Shauna was another beauty making her uncomfortable.

"I just wondered if she and Wilma had any dealings you knew of."

She relaxed a little. The man to the south had been reined in. "This girl, she might have worked on one of Wilma's projects at one time. That's why her name would sound familiar to me. I'd have to check the records for you. Perhaps tomorrow?"

"That would be great, Mitzi. I really appreciate it."

"No problem. Now, Reyn, if you don't mind, I need a little help myself." She pointed to the roller coaster against the back wall of the man-made canyon. It glittered with a kaleidoscope of pulsing lights. "That's the WonderWoman coaster. The wonderful management agreed to debut it tonight for my fund-raiser, which is why we have such a great crowd. I want to make sure all the decorations are in place before the end of the evening, when folks are going to get the chance to ride it. Can you do a quick check for me?"

"Uh, sure." I couldn't say no, even though I wanted to work the crowd to find out more about Shauna, especially having realized that the caramel flip I'd seen earlier belonged to Charis. I scanned the crowd and found her again, in the middle of her circle of like-do friends.

"It won't take a minute," Mitzi promised, gripping my forearm with one hoof-covered hand. "I have to find the park director for a quick question, then I'll meet you over there."

I nodded.

"Maybe we'll even get a chance to try the ride before everyone else!" Mitzi whispered excitedly.

I nodded again, trying not to look nauseated. I hated roller coasters more than I hated plucking my eyebrows.

twenty-four

"THAT WOMAN IS WEIRD," Trudy said.

"It's not her fault she has to dress like a donkey," I threw back.

Trudy raised her eyebrows. "You don't think as head of this shindig, she got to pick her costume first? Would you have chosen a pack animal commonly referred to as an ass?"

"Maybe it is synonymous with her life—she feels like she carries a load for others."

I got the Trudy eye roll. "You know, Reyn, you need to give up hairstyling and go back to school to be a psychologist. You do enough pop psych in daily life to make a living at it."

"Come on, Trude, I feel sorry for Mitzi. You just don't like her because she doesn't like you, and you aren't used to that."

Trudy didn't comment beyond an additional eye roll. We rounded the corner into the part of the park set up like a little German town and nearly ran into a swarthy man in a suit. I jumped and squealed. Was this one of the Mexican henchman? He reached to his back pocket and unsheathed a . . . walkie-talkie. "I'm sorry I frightened you," he said without a trace of an accent. "Are you ladies lost?"

What I'd lost was the use of my voice, since I'd thought we were going to be filleted by a drug dealer on a mission. Trudy spoke for us. "Mitzi Spagnetti sent us to check the decorations on the new roller coaster."

He nodded. His walkie-talkie squawked, calling all officials to the front for a problem. He talked into it and excused himself, giving us directions to the coaster before he left.

The WonderWoman coaster rose up around the next bend like an electrified monolith, a neon-charged snake, an oversize labyrinth of disaster. I knew other people thought of these sources of amusement with a charge of excitement. I preferred to get my charges from a caffeine buzz or a chocolate high. I'd much rather leave my fate in the hands of Mother Nature. Maybe I didn't trust man to make something unflawed. Maybe I knew that, with my sorry luck, I'd be the one person stuck in the loose car. Maybe I had a genetic fear of heights.

Maybe I was just a wuss.

Trudy smiled. "This looks like a blast."

The cars were floorless; riders were strapped into seats that left their feet dangling. The coaster's signs advertised loop-the-loops three hundred feet in the air and speeds up to eighty miles an hour. Shouldn't one have a windshield at that speed? I'd worry about catching flies, bees, and stray birds in my teeth.

"Let's check the decorations and get out of here before Mitzi comes and wants to ride this damn thing."

"Spoilsport," Trudy groused.

The metallic streamers blew in the gentle breeze. One of the poles guiding people to the coaster had fallen down, and I righted it. Signs thanking people for supporting the Teen Advantage program and information about teen pregnancy and Bexar County's record for having one of the highest teen pregnancy rates in the country lined the walk leading to the ride. I paused to read some of the facts, which were news to me. I saw the need for such a program, and wondered why Wilma had been so dead set against it.

I thought I heard something behind the control room. "Mitzi?"

No answer.

"It was probably the wind." Trudy waved it off as she stared, transfixed, at the highest loop.

The errant pole went down again, and I left Trudy by the coaster as I returned to right it. Mitzi walked up the way we'd come, smiling with pleasure at the decorations.

"Did Trudy decide to stay where all the fun was?"

"No, she's here." I nodded back. "Gaga over the coaster."

Mitzi's face clouded for a moment. She checked her watch in that disconcerting, jerky way she sometimes moved. "Oh. Okay. Well, everything looks in order. Since Trudy's so eager, why don't you two take a twirl? You can be the first two in San Antonio to debut the WonderWoman."

"Oh, no, I couldn't ask you to do that. You are way too busy—"

"We'd love to!" Trudy effused as she walked up behind me. Dirty dog.

Mitzi's face spread in a long, slow smile. "Wonderful."

The canned music that had been playing softly over the loudspeakers paused, and a voice came on to ask everyone to enter the theater for the flamenco show. I'd noticed the theater just to the left as we'd walked into the park. Saved by the bell.

"Oh, too bad. We have to go watch the show. No time for the coaster."

"Nonsense," Mitzi said. "This is San Antonio, you can see a flamenco show anytime. This is probably the only time in your life you'll ever be the first to debut a roller coaster."

I could live a long life never having done that and never regret it. She was so eager, though, so insistent, that I felt like I had to capitulate. Here we went again with that politeness brainwashing. I didn't want to do something, yet didn't want to be rude.

Besides, I was afraid Trudy was going to hurt me if I said no. Her nails were long enough to scare me.

I made one last-ditch effort. "Why don't I watch while you two ride it? I can report how it looks from the ground."

Mitzi shook her head, holding up a walkie-talkie. "I wish I could, but I have to keep in constant contact with the crew, in case we have a problem with the event."

That settled that. Trudy nudged me, and I walked the plank to the first car in the coaster. We passed a sign that promised to take us upside down sixteen stories in the air. My dream come true. I tried to turn around, but

Trudy put her hands on my shoulders and pushed. A stuffed armadillo was standing at the controls. Great. I had such confidence in roller coasters already, now I had to be a guinea pig in one run by an armadillo.

"You have to take off your shoes, or you'll never see them again," Mitzi said with a giggle.

I looked down at my patent pointy-toes. Sounded good to me. Maybe one would fly up and bean Trudy in the head for making me do this. I kept them on, but the stuffed critter snatched them off before he put our seat bars down on our laps.

It sounded to me like the barred doors shutting in prison.

He returned to the controls and glanced at us. His eyes looked familiar to me somehow. The motor powered up with an ominous hum.

"Hang on," Mitzi warned. "Zero to eighty in two-point-two seconds." Another giggle. I didn't feel as sorry for her anymore.

Trudy was breathing so fast in excitement it sounded like she was having an orgasm. Could this get any worse?

I shouldn't have asked.

With a jerk sure to leave us with whiplash, we were off. My legs felt like they were being stretched an extra foot by the g-force. Maybe I would end up with legs like Trudy's before it was all over. The skin was pulling back from my face. Maybe this would wipe out my laugh lines. Of course, as we did the first loop-the-loop I realized my intestines were also undergoing a renovation, probably not a positive one. And my hair, well, it was sure to look like Wilma's.

Flipping over the highest loop took us higher than the canyon wall. I could see for miles at eighty miles an hour. It wasn't that good for me.

Finally, we were approaching the end. I had survived with only lengthened legs, a lineless face, reorganized insides, and bad hair. I began to relax as the car slowed as it entered the departure area. But for some reason, we kept going. Past the armadillo at the controls. Ahead to the track once more. Zero to eighty in two-point-two seconds. It had happened so quickly that I hadn't even called out.

I looked at Trudy. Grinning ear to ear, she looked like my dogs do when they have their heads stuck out the window of my truck. "Did you see Mitzi back there?"

She shook her head. "No. Isn't this just awesome?"

"It's something all right," I hollered back.

The second time around, my terror morphed into irritation. I looked down at the park and saw hundreds of people filing into the theater for the flamenco show. That could've been me, I thought. Had I not been so polite.

As we approached the end of the line again, I was braced to call out and protest. No Mitzi. No armadillo at the controls. Uh-oh. We were off.

Trudy's eyes were looking a little glazed, like the dogs stoned on too much fresh air. My irritation had turned now to resignation. I wondered if victims of torture experienced these phases. If so, it defeated the purpose to drag it on too long, because we were begging to be put out of our misery by the end of it.

Be careful what you wish for.

We reached the sixteen-story point on the highest

loop-the-loop, and stopped. Dead in our tracks. Upside down. Trudy and I looked at each other. This moment was too much for words. We screamed.

That didn't do any good, but it made us feel better.

"Frogs' fannies and birds' bustiers, what are we going to do?" Trudy asked.

"Why don't you think of something, smarty-pants, since you're the reason we're on this damn ride to begin with."

"It wasn't my idea to come to the theme park, so it's your fault we're stuck up here."

"No, it's the dumb operator's fault for sending us around so many turns that he burned out the contols."

"You think it's going to burn? I don't want to die like some oversize shish kebab."

I smiled. She gulped nervously. Being the sicko that I am, I waited for a few seconds before I answered, "Don't worry. I don't think metal burns real well, Trude."

I started yelling Mitzi's name. Trudy joined me for a minute or so. We listened. Nothing but a few high-altitude crickets on the canyon rim below us. I finally got the nerve to crane my neck to look down. The angle left me with not much of a view, but I could see that the skinny maintenance stairway reached the bottom of our loop.

"Look, if we get our car to the bottom of the loop, and we can figure out how to shimmy out of our bindings, we might be able to crawl down the stairway."

"How do we do that?"

"We have to shift our weight to set it moving. It shouldn't take much." I began rocking back and forth, wiggling to and fro. Trudy had closed her eyes and wasn't doing much backing and forthing or toing and froing. Go figure. The g-force ride was a thrill, but stopping scared her into paralysis.

Our seats began to drift forward, building momentum quickly as we slid down the backside of the loop. Trudy screamed again. We were going so fast I was worried we'd end up at the top of the next damned loop, but instead we just slid up, paused, then slid back, and up and back, for long enough to make me nauseated. Finally, we were still. I looked over at the stairway and there stood Mitzi.

"You heard us!" Trudy exclaimed. "You're a dear for climbing up here to save us."

Mitzi's lips stretched in what might be described as a smile only by the criminally insane.

That's when I noticed the gun in her hand. Pointed at me.

My hair wasn't the only thing about to look like Wilma's.

twenty-five

"WHAT ARE YOU DOING, MITZI?" I said evenly. "I think shooting out the bolts in our seats probably isn't the best way to free us."

"The only thing you're getting free of tonight is this mortal world, Reyn," Mitizi clarified. She glanced down at her Colt .45. That gun lesson had really come in handier than I'd realized. Everyone should know what is going to send them into the next world.

"I'm sorry to have to do this, Reyn," she said. "I really like you. You're a hard worker and you have a heart, unlike a lot of women I'm stuck with in these charities. Unfortunately, your heart and your work have been focused on the wrong place these last couple of days. If you'd just left well enough alone, everything would have worked out for the best for everyone."

"Except Wilma and Shauna and whoever got railroaded for their murders."

"Reyn," Trudy whispered with a whimper. "Don't make her mad."

"Trude," I whispered back, "I think she's already over the top of the mad scale. Has been for a long time."

Mitzi was waxing on: "I do feel bad about what I had to do to Shauna. But Wilma, she deserved everything she got and more. And your pal here, Fashion-Maven Beauty-Boss Trudy Trujillo, I'm doing the world a favor by getting rid of her, too. No one should be that beautiful and that fashionable all the time, it's not realistic and makes the rest of us look bad. She makes me feel like the frump Wilma Barrister always told me I was."

So much for "Don't make her mad." Trudy had stopped whimpering, narrowed her eyes, and opened her mouth to argue. I elbowed her to shut up.

Spittle formed at the corner of Mitzi's mouth as she went on in a mocking queen voice, not unlike Wilma's actually: "Why couldn't I dress better? Why did I always look like an unmade bed? A cheap, bad-taste, unmade bed. I was a poor representative of the Junior League." She lapsed into her normal voice. "Other women her age, other sustainers, thanked me for the hard work I did, never mentioning my dress. They knew what was important, but they didn't have the power Wilma did. She killed my programs that supported teen mothers, that prevented teen pregnancies, saying the Junior League was to enrich children's lives, not teenagers' lives. Like teenagers aren't people, too. I finally told Wilma what I'd never told anyone else in the League—the reason I had to buy clothes at the thrift store was that I am a single mother raising a teenager. The reason I had a baby at fourteen was that my parents didn't tell me about sex, didn't give me the information to be defensive."

Trudy and I shared a look. The kid in the armadillo

costume—could that be her son? No wonder his eyes had looked familiar.

"I finally told her that the teenage pregnancy prevention programs would make sure no one else ended up like me. And you know what she did?"

By this time, Trudy and I were transfixed. I felt sorry for Mitzi, even as she held a gun pointed at my heart.

"She laughed. She said all teenagers who got pregnant were stupid hussies who couldn't be helped anyway. She told me that she'd overlook the fact that I was a whore, keep it our dirty little secret. But only if I learned to dress the right way, have the right friends, eat at the right restaurants, live in the right neighborhood, and talk the right way would I maybe get what I wanted out of her organization." She paused, shook her head, and, with her free hand, reached under her glasses to wipe angry tears from her eyes. "The Junior League is a positive force, and Wilma was endangering it with her out-of-control power trip. She had to be stopped." Her face transformed into a mask of steely fanaticism, her eyes far, far away.

Whoops and hollers drifted up to us from the theater. Calling for help wouldn't help. Trudy screamed anyway. Mitzi's eyes snapped back to the present. "It won't do any good. I called all the security guards to the office for a pseudo-problem. Everyone else is in the theater. Even if someone is out, you are too far up for them to hear."

I caught a glimpse of a group running through the maze of walkways, but I lost them because I didn't want to move my head and alert Mitzi to her need to kill me quicker. I hoped the guards had figured out their problem was on the WonderWoman and not wherever Mitzi had sent them.

I needed to stall her long enough for someone to gallop up on a white horse, or fly up on a unicorn, rather. I eyed the stairs. A mountain goat would work, too. I wasn't picky, I'd take anything. "But why Shauna, Mitzi? Was she part of Wilma's power trip?"

"No." Mitzi looked almost regretful for an instant. "I met Shauna doing my required hours working the rummage sale in the Coliseum. She was sweet, pretty, and stupid. I knew I had to get rid of Wilma, but it seemed to me that killing her was just too good an ending. It didn't really make her understand what she'd done. So when Shauna mentioned that she was an expert in clown makeup and that she liked older men, I figured out a plan to properly torture Wilma. I started writing Percy Barrister notes signed by Shauna. Percy was easy. He was a longtime philanderer. When he started sending her flowers and expensive jewelry and taking her to romantic getaways, they really did fall for each other. I think they would have made a good couple after we got Wilma out of the way, if only Shauna had kept her mouth shut about the murder."

"So Shauna was in on the murder?"

"As an unwilling accessory, if you will. I got her there by saying Wilma was going to a masquerade party and needed clown makeup. That girl was obsessed with clown makeup. She was uncomfortable coming to her lover's house to do his wife's face, but in the end she couldn't resist. When she saw I had the gun on Wilma, she balked. But then I threatened to kill her, too. She did the makeup, and I made sure Wilma knew Shauna was her husband's hussy. But the best part was the look on Wilma's face when she saw her own face in the mirror. Good thing I always carry my only luxury with me at all times—my Main Mane hairspray put the finishing touch on Wilma's demise." Damn, that's why her tight little bun smelled familiar to me. Mitzi had a look on her face like she'd seen heaven. Trudy and I shivered simultaneously.

"Then I shot her. Shauna started crying, and I almost shot her, too. I should have. I should have put the gun in her hand and made it look like a murder-suicide. But I'm a softie. A stupid softie. I thought Shauna was so empty-headed that she had no conscience. I thought she and Percy could live happily ever after.

"And she might have, except you had to pay her a visit. And then send that cop. It's all your fault. The next thing I know, Shauna tells me she can't live with herself unless she tells the truth. I went over to make sure she couldn't live with herself anymore. Now, Reyn Marten Sawyer, I'll do the same to you."

Her finger began to squeeze the trigger.

At least I was going to be spared the clown makeup. Although being shot dangling from the WonderWoman roller coaster wasn't terribly dignified.

"Freeze!" yelled a voice from below, but not too far below. It was pretty close. But the familiar baritone was also shaky. I looked down and saw Scythe only two flights away, holding his Glock on Mitzi. "Police! Drop your weapon and put your hands up."

Even from my vantage point through my bare toes, I could see his face was glazed with sweat. His shirt was marked with huge wet patches. His hand might have been shaking slightly, but his eyes were hard and focused. I didn't think he'd miss. So why didn't he shoot already?

"I thought Jackson was in better shape than that," Trudy whispered. "A sixteen-story jog up the escape stairs shouldn't make him look like a couch potato in a marathon."

We heard sirens in the distance.

"I think that's EMS for your boyfriend," Trudy added in a stage whisper.

At least my friend's sense of humor would send me laughing into the next life.

"Shut up," Mitzi ordered. "There's nothing you can do to help yourselves except say your prayers."

"Throw down your gun," Scythe yelled. I noticed his free hand gripping the handrail so hard it was bloodless. Hmm. Was macho man afraid of heights? His shirt was completely saturated now. His hand left the rail and went to the gun. "This is your last warning."

Mitzi jerked, and I instinctively braced for the bullet. I heard a ping over my head and saw Mitzi slump like a rag doll over the handrail. Suddenly the ride jerked forward. We picked up speed, racing past Scythe, whose face looked an odd shade of green. Mitzi passed us in the air, falling faster than we were going. Trudy screamed. Don't ask me what I did. I don't remember. I just hope it didn't involve regurgitation.

The WonderWoman transported us into the belly of a welcoming committee at the base of the ride. Lexa and Asphalt were there amid a milling mass of uniforms and familiar faces. Trudy started telling the story a mile a minute before the ride even came to a halt.

I just smiled.

Terrell Hills police chief Ferguson waved and winked, flipping me a thumbs-up sign. Manning looked disgruntled that I'd come out unscathed. Harland looked relieved. I saw Mama Tru with her arm around Mitzi's crying son, who had his armadillo head under his arm and was talking to a plainclothes detective. Someone I hadn't seen in a long time helped me out of my seat. Detective Fred Crandall, Scythe's old partner, slapped me on the back, got all choked up as he tried to say something, and wrapped me in a mushy two-hundred-and-fifty-pound bear hug instead.

"Fred, what are you doing here?" I asked.

"You messed around in every jurisdiction except San Antonio proper with this craziness. You were beginning to hurt my feelings. Thanks for having the grand finale on my watch, little girl, although you had us fu—effing scared down here." He gave me a noogie on my head. Aw, shucks.

"Course, next time you go on a death mission, you probably don't want to wear a getup that makes you a good target at twenty miles. Gee, I could have picked you off from the ground."

"I'll remember that, Fred," I said as I gave his balding head a noogie back.

Trudy'd gone through the story in four different versions by now. She had the uniforms transfixed. Mario had reached her and was nuzzling her as she told the story. It didn't seem to put off her admirers.

Lexa came from behind to give me a hug. I noticed a uniform sticking close to her and Asphalt, who stood just to her right. I guessed they still had some explaining to do. "I'm glad to see you're okay," I told her. "I wish you'd let me know you weren't dead in a ditch somewhere."

"I was attempting to keep you out of danger," she

said, shaking her head. "I guess I was a little late in that."

"They called us, though," the uniform said, "when they got worried about where you'd gone. Otherwise, you might not be alive right now."

I hugged Lexa again. She explained, "I finally got hold of the work records from the Junior League. I noticed that Shauna and Mitzi had worked side by side in November. After that was when my father started taking weekends away and acting secretive. I remembered Mitzi had been pretty combative a few times with Mother. I knew she despised Wilma. I merely acted on a hunch with the advantage of hindsight."

"Good hunch."

"Thank you for everything you did for me, and for my mother." She gave me one last hug. Asphalt took my hand, kissed it, and bowed.

"Thank you, Asphalt."

"It's Phillip Pallister, actually," he corrected.

"Good name for a high school band teacher."

He bowed with a grin. The patrolman ushered them to a waiting police car.

"Miss Sawyer." Another patrolman approached, talking intermittently into his two-way radio. "There is a Charlotte Holmes in the parking lot, asking for you. She says she's your associate."

"What does she want?"

"Apparently, the car she was riding in was accidentally totaled on the access road by one of our cars that was rushing to the scene."

Charlotte! I'd made it this far, and now her *parents* were going to kill me. "Is she okay?"

"Yes, ma'am, she and the gentleman with her."

"The car the police hit . . . it wasn't a brand-new Porsche, was it?"

"Yes, ma'am. I'm afraid it was." Emphasis on "was," I noticed.

I groaned. "Tell her I'm incapacitated. Unable to talk. Unable to see her. Or her date."

The uniform gave me an odd look and wandered off. I watched a Stetson work its way through the madding crowd. I met clear green eyes that chastised as they welcomed. Boy, was he dreamy. I was suddenly embarrassed again by my outfit. Did I have my priorities in order or what? "Ranger Calhoun."

"Clint to you."

"Clint." Wow, would that be considered intimate or just friendly? Why did I feel like a cheating wife? Just saying his first name made me feel guilty for never calling Scythe by his.

"You are certainly a hero. Again. We might have to sign you up with the Rangers."

"Nah, I don't look very good in cowboy hats."

"I don't know about that." He took his off and tried it on me. *Where have you been all my life?*

"I have a few questions, Reyn. But first, the most important one." Clint put his hand on my elbow and guided me to a quiet corner. A quiet, dark corner.

Something felt off. Wrong. Missing. What was nagging me?

Scythe! Where was he? I looked around Clint's fine form at the crowd. No Scythe.

Uh-oh. With his fear of heights, was my daring detective still stuck fifteen stories in the air?

Clint was talking, but I hadn't heard a word he'd said.

He looked questioningly at me, waiting. "So, what do you think?"

"Sure," I said. *Whatever you said.* "Have you seen Detective Scythe?"

Ranger Calhoun drew his black eyebrows together in a frown. "No. Why?"

"Excuse me for just a minute. I have to check something." I darted around him and ran out into the open, looking up at the top of the WonderWoman. Sure enough, there was a lone figure on the escape stairs, hanging on to the railing for dear life, looking at the sky probably so he wouldn't look down. I was pretty sure Scythe's fear of heights was not common knowledge around Testosteroneville, and that he wanted to keep it that way. He had saved my life. The least I could do was try to get him down. But how? When does a man forget everything around him, from common sense to phobic fear? I had an idea.

A young patrolman stationed nearby watched me curiously. "Can I use your two-way radio?"

"No. I'm sorry, ma'am."

"Look, can you keep a secret?"

He looked interested, so I went on: "Detective Scythe saved my life up there, and now he's having a bit of a problem coming down." I cocked my head skyward.

He looked up, his eyes widening. "I better call for help."

"No! Sometimes if you go after guys with vertigo, it magnifies the fear. I want to try to talk him down." I held out my hand. "May I?"

"Only if I can listen in."

What choice did I have? I nodded and asked him to

get us a private channel. He held the radio close to my mouth but kept hold of it himself. Cozy. Not very conducive to what I had planned, but I'd have to wing it for Scythe's sake.

"Scythe, this is Reyn. Please talk to me."

We waited and watched. Nothing. He was a statue.

"Uh . . ." What could get his attention? I threw some throat in my alto. "Jackson, please, I need you to come down."

I saw him reach carefully for the radio on his belt. Slowly, he lifted it up. His voice sounded hoarse. "Did you say you want me to *come?*"

He caught on quick. "You know that deal that we didn't get quite to its *climax* the other night?"

"I know that deal."

"Well, maybe we should talk it through in detail, right now."

"In detail? Sounds good to me." I could see him relaxing against the handrail, starting to bring his gaze down.

"Let's go through one stage of the deal for every flight down you take. You must correct me if something is not what you *desire.*"

Scythe sucked in some air that whooshed in our ears. The patrolman was blushing madly. "First, let's talk about where you want to put that whipped cream . . ."

By the time we got through stage fourteen, I thought the patrolman with me was going to pass out from embarrassment. I was squirming with sexual frustration. I blew out a breath as Scythe told me he'd see me at the bottom. I looked at the patrolman. "At least you switched to a private channel, right?"

Oops. The look on his face said it all.

Crandall came out of WonderWoman central, his body shaking so hard with laughter he couldn't walk straight. "Good job, Reyn. You caught the bad guy—or gal, as the case may be—saved your savior, and even earned some extra money along the way." He held up a handful of twenties.

I watched Lieutenant Jackson Scythe make it down the last flight of stairs, worn out but back to his sexy self. I shot Crandall a look. "What is the money for, Fred?"

Jackson and I met halfway. He drew me into a sweaty hug and whispered his thanks. "You called me Jackson." His laser blues glowed and added some silent promises to that deal.

Crandall slapped Scythe on the back. "These are payments for the phone sex you two just had. Better than any such call, is what those with that experience are reporting. You've got enough to pay for all those little details you two described. So that means you and Scythe better get busy tonight. We expect part two tomorrow." He winked. Mario peeked around the corner with a go-for-it sign. Trudy popped up next to him and gave me an odd look, then cocked her head toward a space beyond me. Was she trying to tell me something?

Jackson looked at me and raised his eyebrows. "Are you free?"

"No, Reyn's got plans with me this evening for the Lyle Lovett concert."

We turned to see Clint Calhoun holding up two tickets.

Somehow, "uh-oh" didn't quite cover it. . . .